PRAISE FOR BE

"Magically delicious! Darynda Jones knocks it out of the park with Betwixt. If you love Charley, you're going to be be obsessed with Defiance. Hilarious, heartwarming and oh so addictive."

-ROBYN PETERMAN ~ NYT AND USA
TODAY BESTSELLING AUTHOR

"Darynda Jones brings her original style to paranormal women's fiction, and I for one couldn't be happier. Also, maybe be wary of inheriting from strangers...or not. Go get this book!"

-MICHELLE M. PILLOW, NEW YORK TIMES
AND USA TODAY BESTSELLING AUTHOR
OF THE WARLOCKS MACGREGOR SERIES

"Betwixt takes readers on a heartwarming, spellbinding journey packed full of intrigue. Ms. Jones has outdone herself with this gem."

-MANDY M. ROTH, NY TIMES & USA
TODAY BESTSELLING AUTHOR

BEWITCHED

BETWIXT & BETWEEN BOOK TWO

DARYNDA JONES

BEWITCHED: A PARANORMAL WOMEN'S FICTION NOVEL

(BETWIXT & BETWEEN BOOK TWO)

©2020 by Darynda Jones

Cover design by TheCoverCollection

EBook

ISBN 10: 1-7343852-2-7

ISBN 13: 978-1-7343852-2-9

Print

ISBN 10: 1-7343852-5-1

ISBN 13: 978-1-7343852-5-0

"I'M NOT THAT TYPO GIRL"

Sadly, all books have typos. Including this one. If you see any and would like to let us know, please email us at writerlyd-books@yahoo.com. No pressure! THANKS SO MUCH!

www.DaryndaJones.com

Available in ebook and print editions

For my Netterly and all her Netterly lurve.

ONE

Time flies over us but leaves its shadow behind.
—Sign in The House of the Seven Gables, Salem, MA

Again with the knocking.

A persistent pounding forced me out of a fitful slumber. I tried to pry open my lids, but my bed was far too comfy. Or I was sleeping on air.

I couldn't seem to separate my lashes, as though they were superglued together. I swore the last time my BFF did that to me, she would rue the day. Clearly, Annette didn't rue it enough.

After an eternity of struggles, I finally managed to create a narrow slit in one eye. I looked around, despite the lack of depth perception, only to find I really *was* sleeping on air. Hovering, actually, about a foot off a beautiful ebony four-poster bed. A soft white gown floated around me, along with a silky mass of long black hair. Thankfully, it was mine.

Either Earth's gravity had called it quits and moved to Mars or I'd met my maker via a watery grave. I drew in a breath, testing my surroundings. Definitely not in water. Then it hit me. No wonder I couldn't open my eyes. I was still asleep.

Asleep or not, however, the knocking continued. Seemed even in my dream world, I'd have to answer the door if I wanted any peace. I gritted my teeth and fought with the other lid, rehearsing in my head the firm talking-to I was going to give the transgressor. I might even throw in a stern glare for good measure.

After managing to coax it open, I had to figure out how to get down. I was working through that conundrum when I noticed the vines. They cloaked the entire room, as black as velvet at night, with roses to match. Only a slight blush of crimson colored the base of each blossom, the edges so dark they looked burned.

Best. Dream. Ever.

Much better than the dreams I'd been having. The dark ones that slithered through me and left me coldly unsettled. I shuddered, glad to shove those puppies into the recycle bin so I could get back to enjoying the nice, floaty one.

And... cue the knock again.

For the love of the Sanderson Sisters. I could either wait for my prince—and who knew how long that would take—or I could answer the dang door and get back to sleep. Still, if I was dreaming, wasn't I already asleep? I must've been exhausted to crave sleep while asleep. This was like a fairy tale gone horridly wrong.

I floated—like, literally—down to the bed, my landing pillow soft. As far as dreams went, this one rocked. When I swung my legs over the side and stood, the vines there parted for my bare feet. A good thing, since they boasted thorns the size of my palm, as though Mother Nature had decorated the room with her own version of razor wire.

The moment I flattened my feet onto the wood floor, a soft vibration hummed through me. I took a few seconds to gain my bearings, then stepped forward, trusting the dream not to shred my feet.

Sure enough, the vines parted with every step I took. I scanned the room again. The vines had crawled up the walls and over the ceiling, but I could still tell I was in my grandmother's bedroom. The grandmother, who preferred to be called Gigi, I'd very recently inherited.

The vibration must've been Percival, the house, for all intents and purposes, that came with the grandmother who preferred to be called Gigi. Only now that I knew what she'd done, now that I knew her deep dark secret, I didn't know if I could call her that anymore.

I opened the bedroom door, amazed as the vines parted with the billowing grace of a fine mist, soundless and fluid. When I looked out onto the mezzanine, I realized they'd covered the entire house.

Every floor.

Every wall.

Every stair.

I placed my hand on the banister and started down one set of those stairs. The matching set of stairs rose along the wall on the other side of the immense foyer. Together, they led up to the mezzanine lined with rooms and down to a marble-floored entryway.

Again, the vines did its Red Sea thing as I slid my hand down the polished dark wood, each strand curling into itself and moving aside. One would think black on black—the black foliage covering the black walls of the mansion—would've made the house lifeless and bleak.

One would be wrong.

Natural light streamed in from the huge plate-glass window in the parlor and the bay windows on either side of the front door, reflecting the deep touch of red on each rose. The effect was nothing short of magical.

Then again, the house was named after the witch who haunted it, my grandfather, Percival Goode. It was a very magical place.

I made it to the door just as the interloper intruding into my lush dream knocked for the umpteenth time. As I turned the knob and pulled, the vines withdrew from the door. I cracked open the heavy wooden portal. Light spilled in.

A man stood on the other side of the threshold, aiming a broom at me. Surprise registered on his face to a comical degree as he watched the vines retreat to the border of the doorframe. Stumbling back, he held the broom like an assault rifle.

"Mr. Shoemaker?" I remembered him, just barely, from when I'd arrived in the infamous town of Salem, Massachusetts, only a few days ago.

My fair-haired neighbor lived down the street and was part of several beautification committees with more letters in their acronyms than should be legal. Committees that wanted Percy torn down. Or, at the very least, vastly renovated.

"Ms.... Ms. Dayne?" Mr. Shoemaker seemed shocked that I'd answered my own door.

Had he been expecting a butler? 'Cause we didn't have one of those. And though I hadn't been in town long, I'd made it clear the last time he'd knocked on my door that I wasn't going anywhere. "Call me Defiance."

He straightened his shoulders, repositioned the broom

at his side like an infantryman standing at attention with his rifle, and thrust out an envelope.

I deflated. This again? For realsies?

"Defiance." He had to clear his throat like my name got stuck in it. "This is a petition for you to vacate the premises immediately."

On second thought... "Call me Ms. Dayne." I took the envelope but didn't bother opening it.

I'd always had a sixth sense about people, and I didn't feel hatred from Mr. Shoemaker. I didn't feel dislike from him either. I felt concern? And definitely fear. The vines *were* a lot to take in. But at the moment, I liked them. And I finally understood the broom. He'd been using it to get past the razor-tipped foliage so he could knock on the front door. Dreams were cray-cray.

He pushed up his square-framed glasses with an index finger. "Please, Ms. Dayne, go back to Arizona."

"How did you know I was from Arizona?" I'd only been here a few days, and it wasn't like we'd had tea and biscuits.

"What?" he asked, stumped. "I just... That's not the point."

"It may not be *the* point, but it's definitely *a* point."

"I don't know what to tell you." He glanced around, his gaze landing on my vintage mint-green Volkswagen Beetle.

My pride and joy. I looked at it like a loving parent.

"Your license plate." A proud grin widened across Mr. Shoemaker's boyish face. "Yes. That's how. Arizona tags."

"Ah."

He pointed to the papers in my hands. "This is your final warning, Ms. Dayne. Leave, or else."

"Okay, then." I saluted with the envelope. "Thanks for the heads-up. No one wants *else*. It's so vague and open-ended."

He jammed his free hand on his hip. "Ms. Dayne, I feel like you're not taking this seriously. The state of this"—he looked around as though unable to come up with an acceptable euphemism—"crumbling monstrosity was bad enough a few months ago, but now?" He gestured to Percy.

"Now?"

"Well, look at it."

I did. I leaned out and marveled at the black vines that had covered the entire house. It looked like a Victorian lover's paradise, which would explain my fascination. "Wow."

"Wow, indeed. Something must be done."

"And that something is my eviction?"

"Yes." He raised his chin a visible notch. "I'm sorry, but if you aren't going to do anything about this... this eyesore, then the town of Salem will be forced to tear it down."

"Tear down Percy?" I glared at him. "Are you even human?" Giggling like a maniacal serial killer, I slammed the door before he could answer, then glanced around at the subject of Mr. Shoemaker's worst nightmare. "Don't you dare listen to him, Percy. You are stunning."

He hummed beneath my feet again.

Smiling, I turned to see three people standing behind me, all with mouths slightly open in shock. Or awe.

I preferred awe. "Hey, guys."

Annette, my spunky sidekick, blinked at me. Her mop of curly chestnut hair had seen better days, including the large lock that covered one teardrop of her turquoise cat-eye glasses.

Next to her stood the tall glass of water known around these parts as Houston Metcalf, the city's chief of police, and the tasty love interest of my deceased grandmother. Not that she let her state of deadness interfere with their relationship. The fact that he was graying at the temples did nothing to detract from his sweltering good looks.

But the pièce de résistance was the stunning specimen of drop-dead male beauty next to the chief. Standing just as tall, Roane was lean, muscular, and right off the cover of *Men's Health*. His dark-red hair, streaked with gold, brushed wide shoulders that tapered down to washboard abs. Not that I could see them now, but I had a fantastic memory when it came to all things Roane Wildes. A close-cropped beard, only a shade lighter than his hair and tinted silvery gray, framed his perfectly formed face.

And then there was, of course, the kilt.

As always, he wore a dark leather kilt and work boots like they'd been created just for him. I'd never been more grateful that this dream chose not to deviate from reality. Normally, my dreams would've had him wearing something ridiculous like polka-dot pajamas and bunny slippers. Not that he wouldn't still be spectacular. Especially with all the ink. But I liked reality much, much better.

I walked over to him and brushed my fingertips along his ribs, his thin T-shirt doing little to disguise the reflex of his stomach hardening under my touch. "Now this is my kind of dream."

"Dream." One corner of his seductively sculpted mouth rose.

But I didn't know if he was questioning or confirming. "Dream," I verified, just in case.

"Defiance," Annette said. She covered her mouth with both hands and said from behind them, "Oh my god. You're... you're here. You're alive. You're awake."

"I am." I moved in for a quick hug, and she stiffened. Even in my dreams, she wasn't a hugger. I gave her a quickie, then pulled back and smiled up at the chief. "Hey,

Chief." When I gave him a quick hug as well, he leaned into it but didn't reciprocate.

Odd. He was a total hugger. "Daffodil." He seemed just as surprised as Nette to see me. Also odd. A warm smile softened his face. "Are you okay?"

"Never better, Chief." Turning to Roane, I grabbed a handful of his T-shirt and pulled him toward the stairs. "Come with me, mister." Our hugging needed to be a little more... private. "Since I'm dreaming anyway, I may as well make it a wet one."

The surprise on the chief's face was precious, the wicked grin on Roane's priceless.

"Deph." Annette shifted her weight like she was suddenly uncomfortable. "We should probably talk."

I turned to her. "Yeah, I don't think so." She wasn't about to ruin what came next. "See this man right here?" I leaned in and bopped Roane softly on his perfectly shaped nose.

His grin widened, and he shook his head.

"This just happens to be the man of my dreams. And since I'm dreaming, there's simply no better time to have sex with him." I gave Roane a saucy once-over. "We might should hurry before I wake up. Talk about coitus interruptus."

He disguised a laugh as a cough behind a very large closed fist.

I almost drooled. "I can't even imagine what those hands are capable of."

He sobered and pulled his lower lip between teeth, eyes glistening with interest.

"Defiance." Annette stepped closer. "You don't understand. You're not dreaming."

"No, you don't understand. Things like this don't

happen in real life." I demonstrated by putting my hand on the banister.

The vines parted soundlessly, their movements graceful and hypnotic. "Therefore, this is a dream." I practically melted against Roane. "Therefore again, you and I are going all the way. Twice." I took his hand and led him up the stairs. Speaking over my shoulder, I elaborated, just in case he needed clarification. "We're getting it on."

"Defiance!" That time Annette seemed more appalled than hesitant.

The chief only chuckled.

"We're taking a trip to pound town."

"Stop," she begged.

"We're burying the bone."

"Oh my god, Deph, please."

"We're buttering the biscuit."

"I'm not kidding."

"We're parking the Plymouth in the garage of love." I lifted his hand over my shoulder and led him up the thick wooden steps. "I haven't had a cookie dipped in this cream in far too long." Then I turned and speared him with my best come-hither. "Can you tie a knot in a cherry stem with your tongue?"

"Wait!" Annette ran up the stairs. "Look." She pointed to the boots she wore and, more specifically, to the vines crushed underneath them. "They don't move for anyone but you."

"Because it's my dream, silly goose." I looked up at the landing above me. Two gorgeous men stood there, insanely handsome despite the state of their unhinged jaws. "See? Even my dads are here. Now I know it's a dream. They wouldn't be caught dead in matching shirts."

The eldest of my adoptive fathers frowned. "What's wrong with our shirts?"

"Told you," Papi said.

I'd called him *Papi* since I was a kid. Even though, unlike the dad I called *Dad*, he didn't have an ounce of Latino in him. What could I say? I was a confused child.

"It's a great color on me," Dad said, his soft accent soothing and welcome. "And I put mine on first."

My dads were always perfectly groomed, and today was no exception. Dad with his olive skin and thick gray hair and Papi, the Viking, the silver-streaked blond fox who still worked out every day and had the biceps to prove it.

Their love had always been an inspiration to me. I wanted what they had more than anything, which probably explained my rush to marry my ex. Not the biggest mistake of my life, but damned close.

I ran to them and threw my arms around both their necks at the same time. Like the others, they leaned into my hug but didn't hug me back.

"Cariña." Dad turned and kissed my cheek almost cautiously. "*Dios mio*, are you okay?"

Leaning back to get a good look at them, I nodded. "I am so much more than okay."

"How did you... when did you wake up?" Papi asked.

"I haven't. Have you seen the vines?"

He frowned. "I don't understand."

"Exactly. This all feels so real."

"Cariña." Dad's silver brows slid together. "I think we should talk."

"Totally. But right now"—I gestured to Roane—"I'm going to tear this man's clothes off. With my teeth. Then we'll do breakfast. How's that?"

My younger and only slightly more fit Papi cast a withering glare in Roane's direction.

He held up his hands in surrender. "You know I wouldn't."

"What?" I turned to him with a pout. "You won't dip your cookie in my cream?"

Roane pinched the bridge of his nose, but there was a distinct smile behind his hand.

Annette ran up to the landing, crunching the poor vines on her way. She started to put a hand on my arm but stopped herself. "Deph, think about it. You live in a magic house haunted by your dead grandparents."

A sickly kind of horror threatened to blossom in my chest. I tamped it down. No way. "You don't get it. I was floating on air when I woke up. Floating. On air. My hair was swirling around me like a leviathan. And then there's the vine thing. They move when I move." I held out my hand and willed a vine into my palm.

One rose off the banister and curled around my fingers, as soft as silk.

"See?" Although I was starting to doubt the dream theory despite all the evidence supporting it.

"Magic," she said, as though she was sorry she had to. But even she was impressed. I could tell. Her gaze held as much fascination as understanding. "Watch." She lifted a hand to my arm.

A vine rose up and curled around it, tucking its tip underneath her hand.

She jerked back and held her hand open for me to see. A line of blood plumped along her palm.

I grabbed her hand. "What happened?"

"He's protecting you. He's been protecting you this whole time."

A quick glance at my dads told me she was right. They waited, giving me a moment to let it sink in. The horror I'd tamped down ricocheted with a vengeance. It exploded in my chest and set fire to my skin. I dared a quick glance at Roane. Heat burst through me, and I could practically see the blush sliding up my neck and over my cheeks. I worried it would be permanent.

"He wouldn't let us near you while you were... resting." The fact that she spoke softly, as though I were a child, didn't help.

"Resting? I was floating, for fuck's sake."

"You were in some kind of suspended state," Papi said. "Like stasis."

"For how long?" Wary to hear the answer, I asked anyway.

"We can talk about that later," Annette said. "The important thing right now is—"

"How long?" I pushed.

She pursed her lips, glancing at the others as if she didn't quite know what to do, then said softly, "Almost six months."

What the ever-loving fuck?

My fingers tightened around the banister, and vines curled around them as if they were comforting me. If not for the support of the railing, my knees would surely have buckled.

"After you brought your grandmother out of the veil, you passed out," Annette added.

"For six months?" I looked at her through blurred vision. I'd come to the witch game late in life. At forty-four, I'd learned about powers I never knew I had. I'd learned I was a *source*, a *charmling*, one of only three in the entire world, and that others wanted to kill me to steal the immense power I had lying just beneath the surface.

When we'd finally coaxed the dormant powers forward, they'd almost killed me. And ever since, whenever I did a spell that required a lot of energy, I passed out. It'd happened more than once in those first few days, but I'd only been out a couple of hours at most.

Then I'd accidentally pulled my deceased grandmother out of the veil and back onto this plane. That took a lot more energy than I was ready to expel. But holy hell, six months? How could anyone sleep for six months? Especially without medical supervision? I had terrific bladder control, but damn.

"Ruthie said it must've been too much on your system." The chief's voice carried up the stairs. "You needed time to recuperate."

Dad reached out to me, then pulled back.

I took his hand, and the vines that had been holding mine retreated to allow room for his.

"It was too much on your body, cariña." He squeezed my fingers lightly. "Your grandmother didn't even know a witch could pull someone out of the veil. That it was even possible."

Speaking of grandmothers, where *was* Ruthie?

Before I could ask, Papi said, "You are remarkable."

"You are," Annette agreed, looking around. "Percy, may I?"

The vines retreated instantly, and then Annette did something that would've proven this a dream if it weren't— she rushed forward and hugged me.

Still in shock, I hugged her back. "You've embraced the darkness?"

"Darkness?" A few inches shorter than my five-five, she pulled back and looked up.

"Hugging."

She laughed through a soft sob and hugged me again. My dads joined her, and we stood in each other's embrace for a solid minute. Partly because it felt wonderful and nourishing and reassuring, and partly because I was too humiliated to ever face Roane Wildes again. Mostly because I was too humiliated to ever face Roane Wildes again.

"Let's get you dressed," Annette said after we disentangled ourselves.

It was only then that I realized the gauze gown I wore was a tad see-through. Great. My face caught fire as I looked back at Roane, whose expression was full of sympathy. Humiliation stung the backs of my eyes.

"The answer is yes." His voice, smooth and deep, sent a ripple of heat straight to my core.

"Yes?"

He graced me with a lopsided grin. "The cherry stem."

And my mortification was complete.

"I'll demonstrate whenever you're ready." To the warning glares he received from my dads in response, he added, "On an actual cherry stem. Naturally."

TWO

Q: How many witches does it take to change a lightbulb?
A: Into what?

I sat on my bed with Annette, our legs tucked under us as we discussed my recent sabbatical. "How is this even possible?"

"Deph, it was like you were trapped in a fairy tale." Excitement brimmed not just in her face but across her whole body, turning her into the proverbial kid in a candy store. "I tried to convince Roane to kiss you to wake you up, but he didn't want his throat slit."

I gasped. "Percy would really do that?" He'd make a killing as a bodyguard. If he could leave the house.

She lifted a noncommittal shoulder. "He wouldn't let us near you. I don't know what he would've done."

I dropped my face in my hands and mumbled into my palms. "How am I ever going to face him again?"

"Percy?"

Shaking my head, I lowered my hands to my knees.

Nette grinned like she'd just eaten every morsel in said candy store. "Do you honestly think Roane wasn't flattered?"

"Which time?" The words dripped with sarcasm. "When I suggested he bury his bone or when I proposed he butter his biscuit?"

"Well, I'm no Roane—"

"Thank God."

"But I rather liked the cookies and cream thing."

I dropped my face into my hands again, and she hesitantly patted my head just in time for me to realize I hadn't washed my hair in six months. I winced.

"Oh," she said, oblivious. "One other thing. You turned forty-five a few days ago." She threw in a quick "Happy birthday" as if that would soften the blow.

"What?" Lifting my head, I screeched at the unfairness of it all, figuring theatrics might help. "I missed the one day I gave myself permission to hide under the blankets and eat copious amounts of popcorn and chocolate while watching old Humphry Bogart movies?"

"Sorry."

"I was just getting used to forty-four."

"Well, now you don't have to."

She had a point. "Okay, take me back. What happened? How did I end up in here? And what the bloody hell am I wearing?"

With a wiggle of her butt, she settled further into the blankets and leaned forward, her expression full of adventure. "It's crazy. The whole thing is crazy."

"Which is why I'm asking," I said, feeling a tad less adventurous than my cohort.

"When you, I don't know, pulled Ruthie out of the veil... is that what you did?"

I lifted my shoulders, just as clueless.

"We'll go with that. Afterward, you were like, 'Is it true?' And she was like, 'How did you do that?' And you were like, 'Is it true?' And she was like, 'I don't know what you mean.'" Annette's hands moved as fast as her mouth. "And you were like, 'How many people have you killed?' And she was like, 'I told you. I've killed three men.' And you were like, 'Not men. People. How many people have you killed?' And she got all ashamed and was like, 'Four.' And, stunned off your rocker, you were like, 'Ruthie, did you kill my mother?' And she kind of freaked out, went white as a ghost—which, since she is one, looked really good on her—and then, soft as silk, she said, 'Yes.'" My bestie feverishly took a breath.

I opened my mouth to interrupt—

—but she wasn't finished yet. "And then, Deph... I don't know. It was like it hit you. The spell or something. Or maybe her words. Either way, you stumbled back, tried to grab the cabinet for balance, then you just crumpled to the ground. You would've face-planted if not for a certain startlingly handsome, kilt-wearing journeyman."

Who I'd just propositioned *publicly* about twenty-seven times.

But back to Ruthie. In my grandmother's defense, she'd had a really good reason to kill all three of those men. The jury was still out, however, when it came to her killing my mother.

I'd read about the mother I'd never gotten to know in Ruthie's diary—after using my energy to reveal the black words hidden on what had seemed a blank page. *She's gone. I had no choice. May the great Goddess embrace her soul.*

I let the emotions wash over me again, just as I had six months ago, only this time I kept them under some semblance of control. At least outwardly.

There had to be a reason for what Ruthie had done. But at the time, I couldn't think straight. Maybe I still couldn't. I was running on pure instinct. Or pure magic. Was that even a thing? I was so new to all of this.

Apparently, as a kid, I'd been so powerful that my grandmother had sent me into hiding. She'd suppressed the magics inside me to keep me concealed from those who would steal them—as the only way to steal my magics was to kill me.

But what else had happened then, when I was three years old, that caused not only my banishment but also my mother's death? Why would my grandmother kill her own daughter? I needed those answers PDQ, but right now, I had to get my head wrapped around more recent events. Like the floating thing. "And then?" I asked Annette.

"And then what?" She was staring at me intensely.

It was my hair. It had to be my hair. I fluffed the flatness as best as I could. "How did I get here? Into these clothes? Onto this bed in my room?" Well, really Ruthie's room. And where was she sleeping?

"Oh, right." Annette snapped out of it. "At first, we had Roane bring you upstairs."

Roane. I groaned.

"Since the longest you'd been out up to that point was only a couple of hours, we just waited. And waited. And waited. And waited."

I gestured for her to get to the point.

"We took turns watching over you, but nothing changed. Your dads wanted you comfortable, so Ruthie and I put you into one of her gowns."

I looked down at the gown I'd been wearing for six months. It smelled like wet grass and roses. I took a handful of the gauze and pressed it against my face, breathing deep.

"You smell good," Annette said. "You do not want to know what I smell like when I haven't showered for six months."

"And you'd know that how?"

"Based purely on what I smell like when I don't shower for a day."

A smile tugged at my mouth then gave up. "And the floating thing?"

"Oh." She waved a dismissive hand. "That happened when your dads wanted to take you to the hospital. Ruthie argued that you weren't in a normal sleep but a magical one, even though it was new for her too. She reminded them that you were special. A charmling. And that the rules simply didn't apply to you."

"But they were insistent." Did I know my dads, or did I *know* my dads.

"They were insistent. They came upstairs to gather you up, and there you were, floating a foot off the bed."

"And no one thought to summon a priest?"

"Well, your head was on straight, and you weren't spewing pea soup."

"Small blessings."

"But that's not all."

"Of course not." It wasn't anything close to all. A sudden tightness gripped my chest. There were things I wanted to tell her—things I'd seen while I'd been sleeping, things that scared the shitake right out of me—but I couldn't. I just... couldn't. So, I shoved them away.

"There were the vines. Percy wanted to protect you. I

think he was mad at your dads for even considering taking you to a mundane hospital."

"Mundane?" I asked. "*Et tu*, Annettus?"

"Hey." She lifted a shoulder. "I embraced the life long before you did. I just don't have any magic in me like you do."

I took her hand. "That's where you're wrong."

She squeezed. "The roses were incredible. Every time someone tried to get near you, vines with thorns sprung up." She splayed her hands in the air to demonstrate. "We tried to keep them under control. But eventually, they covered the whole house. They moved aside for no one until you woke up."

I reached out, and a vine sprang from the side of the bed, curled over the bedspread, and wrapped around my fingers. "Thanks for keeping me safe, Percy."

The house hummed around us.

"That is the coolest thing I've ever seen." Her expression turned dreamy.

"So, you had to leave me here all these months?"

"Yes. We couldn't get in the door. And here's the strange part."

"Like all of this isn't strange?"

"True." She laughed. "But get this. Percy can't get into the secret passageways."

Okay, that really was strange. "I forgot all about those." One of those doors was in the bathroom connected to this very room. Surprisingly well lit, the passages were narrow halls with walls painted lighter than the rest of the house. But we'd never gotten around to exploring where they led. "What do you mean he can't get in?"

"The vines. They can't go past the threshold of any of the doors to the passageways. Roane told your dads about them, and they were able to drill through a wall and set up a camera so we could at least keep an eye on you."

Now we were coasting past odd and sliding right into disturbing.

"I think Percy knew," Annette said. "He never covered up the lens. He didn't seem to mind we were keeping an eye on you, as long as we didn't get too close. And that's what we've been doing. Taking turns watching over you for the last six months."

"Even my dads?" They had vineyards in Arizona, an entire hillside of paradise with a series of gorgeous Spanish casitas around a pool. They'd been looking at land near Salem in Ipswich before I'd pulled a Rip Van Winkle.

"They bought that farm in Ipswich, but they've hardly left your side." She thought about it. "Well, the monitor's side. It's set up in the adjoining room."

I left the bed and walked to one of the floor-to-ceiling windows that lined a wall of the massive bedroom. "And here I thought my first few days in Salem were surreal. All of this is just so much." Too much. I couldn't seem to let go of the aftertaste those horrible dreams had left. It lingered like a foul breath that hung in stale air.

Suspended   animation?   One   star.   Would   not recommend.

Annette came up behind me. "I've had time to absorb it all. I've read a ton of stuff about the craft and the religion. And I've practiced every day. But I can't find a thing written about the charmlings. They really are a well-kept secret, even in the witch world. Also, I don't mean to rush you, but we need to get this thing going."

I turned to her. "What thing?"

"The biz. Our business. Our livelihood. Oh! And I've come up with the perfect name." Before I could stop her, because the biz wouldn't be happening, she grabbed a stack of index cards off the nightstand and resettled herself on the bed. After working to cross her legs like a pretzel, she shuffled like we were practicing for Vegas. "Are you ready?"

Absolutely not. Wondering if she'd be able to unpretzel her legs when the time came, I set my hands on my hips. "I'm not sure." How could I tell her about what was coming? What might be coming? Hell, who knew how real those dreams had been or what they'd meant? Certainly not me.

Oblivious to the thoughts churning in my head—some psychic she was—she giggled. "Imagine this on our business cards." She turned over a card. *Bibbidi Bobbidi Sleuths* was written in thick black Sharpie.

"No." I fought a grin because it did fit her to a tee.

"Okay, no worries. There's more where that came from."

"I can hardly wait."

She rummaged through the stack and held up another. *DefiNette Investigations*.

"Absolutely not."

"Hmm." She pulled one from the middle. "This is the one. I know it." She flipped it over. *ESPI Investigations*.

I pinched the bridge of my nose.

"Get it? ESP and PI together? No? Okay, hold on." She searched the deck frantically, brought out another card and held it to her chest. "Ready?"

"I'm breathless with anticipation."

She flipped it over. *Charmed Investigations*.

"No."

"No?" Her grin fell away.

"No, but closer," I encouraged, fighting a grin.

"Wait! One more!" Fanning out the deck across the bed,

fingers dancing, she searched for just the right card. She plucked one up and held it to her chest again. "Okay, I really like this one, but I'll understand if you don't—"

"Annette—"

"I was just warming you up with the others." She turned the card over and read slowly. "Breadcrumbs, Inc." She waited. Let it sink in. "What do you think?"

I thought it was perfect. A sad smile played across my lips as a garden of infinite possibilities blossomed inside me. Unfortunately, it would never happen. Yet, I couldn't stop myself from admitting, "I kind of love it." I also couldn't stop disappointment from lacing my voice.

But she didn't seem to pick up on it. "I knew it!"

"But why?"

"Because it's catchy. And it's like we follow the trail of—"

"No, why the business? Why now?"

"Because, unlike you, I am not a bazillionaire."

I'd supposedly inherited a fortune from Ruthie. A lot of good it did me. "Are you broke?"

"Monetarily or emotionally?" Nette asked.

Alarmed, I walked back to the bed. "I can give—"

"No!" She held up her hand. "I would never just take money from you. I want to earn it. I want our business to work. And I don't want any handouts. Although, I wouldn't say no to a Brazilian. It's been, like, six months."

"Annette, you quit your job out of the blue and moved from Arizona to Massachusetts. You've done tons of research that will come in handy if we ever do open a business."

"If?"

"You've helped watch over me for six months. My

giving you money would be payment for services rendered, not charity."

"There can't be an if. There is nothing iffy about our futures."

"Annette—"

"So, when do we start? My pizzazz. Your powers."

My powers. The ones I couldn't—no, wouldn't—use. Not anymore. I turned back to the window.

Outside, brilliant fall colors covered Salem in bright oranges and golds. Green was still the dominant hue, but it wouldn't be long before Salem looked afire.

"Dephne," Annette prompted.

I had to be honest with her. Or make her believe I was being honest. She hadn't seen what I saw. Felt the fear. She didn't know what was waiting for me in the dark. What could sense my powers every time I used them. Feeling bad, but not bad enough to share the truth, I sighed softly and turned to face her. There was only one way out of this. "Annette, I don't know how to tell you this, but I lost my powers."

Blinking at me in disbelief, she got off the bed. Well, tried anyway. For, like, ten minutes. Groaning, she fought with her legs. When she finally uncrossed them, she glared at me. "Why did you let me sit like that?" Then she scooted across the mattress. But it was a really soft mattress and a really tall bed. In the end, she had to roll to the edge and throw her legs over the side. After a short adjustment period, she slid off the bed and straightened with another groan, using the bedpost for support.

I could've showered by now.

"Defiance, are you serious?" Taking on her best mom stance, she faced me down. "Your powers are gone?"

I nodded.

"You just lost them?"

I nodded again. The guilt over the lie caused a tiny stabbing pain in my heart.

"No." She shook her head in denial. "No, that can't be. You can't just lose your powers. You're a charmling. In order for you to lose your powers, you'd have to die. That's what Ruthie said. So, there's just no way." She started pacing.

Percy matched her rhythm, parting the vines for her the way he had for me.

I crossed my arms over my chest. "Is there another reason you want to get this business going that you're not telling me about?"

"No." Pausing halfway between the bed and the dresser, she lied through her teeth. "Not at all. Other than trying to get you back in the saddle after your stay-cay. Or is it back on the horse?" She looked up at the ceiling, lost in thought. "I know so little about equestrian idioms."

"I'm not sure I want back in the saddle or back on the horse."

Her head snapped toward me. "We have to get them back. Where did you see your powers last?"

"I didn't take them off to do the dishes, if that's what you mean."

"Right. No. Of course not."

"Okay, I'll ask again: Is there another reason you want to get this business up and going so soon?"

"What? No." When I deadpanned her, she caved. "Well, yes. Lots, actually." She went to her bag, brought out a pocket folder, and crawled back onto the bed where she sat cross-legged exactly like before. The girl never learned. "These are from all the people who've called or come by in the last six months wanting your help." She opened the folder, and handfuls of messages fell onto the bed.

Handfuls! "Are you kidding?"

They'd been written on everything from store receipts to restaurant napkins. One was scrawled across a coaster from Notch Brewery and Biergarten. In Annette's defense, some were torn out of a preprinted message pad. Those looked very professional.

"Admittedly, some were just tourists wanting to get a look at you. Or your grandmother. Or Percy. It was hard to tell. But most of these are legit."

"What about Ruthie? Where is she, anyway?" I looked around like she might beam in from the *Enterprise* or something. "She can do this stuff with her eyes closed." She'd been helping people long before I came along.

"She won't." Annette shook her head. "She's locked herself in her room and won't come out. The chief is really upset. She won't even see him."

"What?" I sat back down. "Why?"

"Well, right before you slipped into a mystical coma, you brought her out of the veil and onto this plane and then asked her if she killed your mother."

"We've already covered that part."

"And she said yes."

"We covered that too."

"And then you flatlined. Metaphorically speaking."

"Nette."

"I think it took a toll on her. I think..." She bit her bottom lip. "I think she's heartbroken." She hedged a bit. "She could use a friend."

When I'd come to Salem, at the request of a lawyer who'd told me I'd inherited this house, I'd met my dead grandmother, Ruthie Goode, on the internet. She'd somehow managed to communicate from beyond through Wi-Fi. She'd helped me get my powers up and running so I could then use them to create a kind of shield around myself. For protection.

After that, I went to work on other powers, including how to reveal things that were hidden. That was how I'd revealed the writing in her Book of Shadows, her journal, and found out she'd killed my mother. "I'm not sure I'd be much of a friend to her right now."

"Deph, come on." That she had sympathy for what I was going through showed in her voice. "Your grandmother would never hurt her own daughter without a very good reason. Even if we don't know what that reason is just yet. Surely you know that."

I did. But I still needed a moment to process and get my bearings and plan my next move. Stalling, I went back to what Nette said earlier. "You said Ruthie locked herself in her room. This is her room." I gestured toward the massive bedroom we were hanging in.

"Her arts and crafts room in the basement. There's more, but I'll let her tell you. Or, well, show you."

Since I wasn't quite ready for more, I rerouted Nette's train of thought. "Hey, how did you get all these messages? Exactly whose phone is ringing?"

"Oh my god. You are not going to believe this." She paused for dramatic effect. "Ruthie has a landline."

Huh. I was expecting more. "You realize we all had landlines too, until a few years ago."

"Yes, but actual people use this one. Not just telemarketers. It gets better reception due to all the paranormal activity pumping through the walls. I gotta warn you, though, I think the phone is older than your grandmother, and it rings loud enough to drown out the screams of your enemies. Should you ever need to make them scream."

"Good to know." I glanced down.

One of the messages on the bed had started to glow. Actually, it was the ink that glowed.

I pointed at it. "What is that?"

Annette picked it up. "Oh, this one was so sweet." She put a hand over her heart. "A little girl lost her dog. She wants you to find him."

"No."

"Okaaaay...?"

"No, I mean, that's not what this is about." I took it from her. Hot energy burned my fingertips, proving just how much I still did have my powers. I dropped the paper and wiped my hand on my gown like a toddler after eating spaghetti.

Thankfully, Annette was rummaging through some other messages and didn't notice.

"What else did she say?" I asked.

"She said her mother told her about you. Said if she ever needed help to call you." She reached over and picked it up again. "She was so worried, she forgot to leave a number. I barely managed to get her name." She looked over at me, her gaze questioning. "Why?"

"It's nothing. Just tear it up. Tear them all up."

She didn't. She put them back into the pocket folder and wrapped the elastic band around it.

The light from the message seeped out the corners.

"Some of these people are in a real crisis. We have a chance to help them."

"For a small processing fee."

"Well, there is that. But is a doctor taking advantage of a patient when she sends him a bill?"

Couldn't argue with that one. "I think your idea is great. I just... until I get my powers back, there's nothing I can do."

"Of course." She gathered her things. "I have to get to

work."

"Work?" I asked, surprised.

"Yes. Like I said, I didn't inherit a bazillion dollars. Some of us have to work for a living." She started out the door. I almost ran after her, but she turned back to me before I had to lift a foot. "Just so you know, we weren't the only ones watching over you."

"Oh?" Each of her revelations were more disturbing than the last. I could only hope my hair had behaved during all of this.

"Ruthie's coven. They're all dying for an introduction. They're so nice, Deph. Meeting you would be like me meeting Buddha. Or Jesus. Or Kurt Cobain."

Wow. "Okay, well, maybe in a few days." By then, I'd be outta here. So, so outta here. No way was I sticking around for what was to come. And neither was Nette. Or my dads. They just didn't know it yet.

"Great, so—I almost forgot!" She put her bag back down and combed through it. "I bought you something." She brought out a wooden box and ran it over to me.

"Really?"

"Yes. For when we open our business. It's okay. I can take it back."

I cradled it to me. "Let me see what it is first."

She smiled in relief. "Okay."

I lifted the dark wooden lid. Inside lay a perfectly shaped crystal ball tucked into a blue satin lining with an iron pedestal. "Oh my goodness. This is beautiful. I don't think these really work, though."

"I figured, but it'll make a great prop. You know, if we start Breadcrumbs, Inc." She started to leave again, then turned back. "Then again, how do you know it won't work if you don't give it a shot?"

"Maybe, you know, if my powers come back."

She nodded. "I got lots of stuff like that—a bible box, a spinning wheel, some tarot cards. And, according to the ads, they're all authentic. They were really owned by witches."

"Mm-hmm," I said dubiously.

"'Kay, off to make coffee."

"You make coffee for a living?" I was suddenly jealous.

"I do. I can't wait to make you my famous pumpkin-spiced cinnamon macchiato with vanilla-bean whipped cream."

A dam burst in my mouth at the thought. "Hey. Before you go, what did you tell Kyle, about me being... unavailable for so long?" My ex was a weasel. The marriage had lasted five years. The scars threatened to stay forever. No telling what he'd do if he found out I'd been a goner for six months. He and his mother had tried to snatch Percy from me after they'd already stolen everything else in the divorce. Stupid me for letting Kyle put everything, including *my* restaurant, in her name.

"Please." Nette wrinkled her nose. "Why would I tell him anything?"

"I was just worried he'd snoop around. Maybe wonder where I was." Panic over losing Percy welled up and overflowed.

"I wouldn't stress about that. I think he and your monster-in-law—"

"Ex monster-in-law." Thank God.

"Right. I think they got the message loud and clear when the chief ran them out of town the first time." Satisfied that she'd calmed my concern—or maybe she was just late for my dream job—she took off.

On my way to the bathroom to clean up, I took the scenic route through the kitchen and did a drive-by past the coffee maker for a scalding cup of brew that definitely wasn't a pumpkin-spiced cinnamon macchiato with vanilla-bean whipped cream. Then I ran upstairs before anyone—and by anyone, I pretty much meant Roane—could see me.

There was nothing like a hot shower and a cup of coffee after a six-month nap. Feeling much refreshed with cleaner hair, I took the stairs to the basement and stopped in a small foyer-like area at the bottom.

I had my choice of three closed doors, one on each wall. It was like the game Cups, except I knew what was underneath two of them already.

The one on the right led to Roane's immaculate apartment. The one on the left led to Ruthie's arts and crafts room, though I hadn't known she'd called it that until now. And her kind of *arts and crafts* involved anything but construction paper and glue sticks. Though the more I thought about it, witchcraft *was* more of an art than a science.

The door in front of me had been locked the last time I'd visited the dungeons. I had no idea what lay in wait behind it. I tested the antique lever handle again. Still locked. I felt a presence behind the door. Though I recognized it—its scent and texture—I couldn't tell if it was friendly or malevolent, so I decided to leave it alone for now.

While I did need to apologize to the hottie next door, facing my murderous grandmother seemed like the more appealing option. Turning left, I stood in front of the portal to her humble abode. Could she even answer the door, with her being dead and all? And more important, did I want her to?

It took some heavy lifting, a little Lamaze breathing, and a lot of repressing, but I finally raised my hand and knocked.

THREE

Not to brag or anything,
but I got the high score on my scale today.
—True Fact

Ruthie did answer the door, and she stood there as beautiful and ethereal as ever.

Judging by her expression, she was only a little surprised to see me. "Defiance," she said, her voice hesitant. "You woke up."

"That's the story."

"They told me, of course, but I didn't... I wasn't sure you'd want to see me."

She read me like a tabloid. Could this be any more awkward? What did one say to the woman who had killed her mother? *Hey, Gigi, how's it hanging? Want to grab a latte?* Although a latte sounded fab at the moment. With extra, extra whip. Damn Annette and her new job.

Ruthie touched her hair—a silver bob, perfectly coiffed

—that didn't quite reach her shoulders. That and her general disposition were the same as when I'd pulled her from the veil. But her dress was different. It wasn't the cream-colored one she'd been wearing the whole time she'd been "stuck" in my laptop.

This dress was more like the gown I'd woken up in. Layers of soft ivory gauze with lettuce edges gave her a shabby-chic appearance any witch would be proud of. Even wrapped in faux tattered clothes, she had the bearing and grace of royalty.

Then again, it could've been the soft luminescence that encompassed her.

After opening the door farther, she waved me inside and stepped back almost nervously, as if she expected me to decline the invitation.

Part of me wanted to. The other part walked in.

A huge variety of dried flowers and herbs hung from a low ceiling. Vintage jars of every shape and size sat atop dozens of shelves that lined the walls. But the thing that drew me in the most, that had drawn me in the first time I'd seen the room, was the lighting. Gas lamps hung every few feet, burning with a soft hiss that was hardly audible, unless you listened for it specifically.

"I've been doing research." Ruthie walked over to a table scattered with books. She moved a cup of tea to the side and thumbed through one of the many ancient texts. "Contacting friends from all over. We've held circles and cast spells of protection and summoned your sisters." Her hands shook. "I knew you'd be okay. I knew it." She drew in a deep breath and turned away, hiding her face.

The cavity around my heart tightened. Not wanting to deal with that just yet, I stared at her for another reason. "You're solid," I said in confusion. She was definitely solid.

Flesh and blood and those little capillary things. "But you kind of glow." The glow was soft. Ethereal. Almost angelic. But just barely there. Not enough so anyone would notice outright.

She whirled back to me, her ivory dress floating around her. "I knew you'd be powerful, Defiance, but I had no idea you'd be capable of something like this." She looked down, gesturing to herself. "You brought me out of the veil."

"Yes, but you're solid," I repeated.

A sad smile spread across her face. "As the day I died." She held out her hand to show me.

I pretended not to see it and stepped to her potter's bench to examine a bottle of seeds.

An adorable brown mouse peeked out from behind it.

Surprise wrenched a yelp from my throat. Retreating, I bumped into one of her shelves.

Glass jars wobbled and clinked together in a crystalline chime before settling back down.

Annoyed with myself, I clenched my teeth. I needed to get a grip. To focus. I was here for a reason, and it was not to kiss and make up with my formerly dead, and maybe still dead, but solid grandmother.

A single vine slid up the shelves beside me and eased into my palm. The calm that followed was both welcome and reassuring.

Ruthie's expression morphed from dejection to irritation. She entered a staredown with the vine. "I'm only letting you stay for our granddaughter, Percy." Then she broke her glare and glanced up at me. "He's not normally allowed in my arts and crafts room." Her ire didn't last long. Wrapped in a silver glow that matched her hair, translucent and luminous, Ruthie smiled at me. "You did this, Defiance. Never in all of my years on this Earth have I even heard of someone being lifted out of the afterlife. It's a miracle." She spun in a circle like a princess whirling around a dance floor.

I smiled despite myself. She was delightful. For a mass murderer.

"You did this," she repeated.

"Yes, and then I fell asleep for six months. Some witch I turned out to be."

"No." She started forward but held herself back. "It's only because it's all so new, sweetheart."

"I did stuff as a kid and was fine. Look at Roane." I'd been asked to find a missing boy—who'd turned out to be Roane. Kind of. The real boy had already been killed by his father and buried, so when I'd sent out my magics to find him, I'd accidentally transformed a trapped and injured wolf pup into the boy. And the rest, as they say…

"And then you slept for three days."

Surprised, I gave her my full attention. "I did?"

"I've had a lot of time to think about all of this. I remembered you being exhausted after a spell, but you were a child. It was expected. Then I remembered on three separate occasions, after particularly taxing spells, you fell asleep for days."

"Days is a lot shorter than months. How was I stronger as a kid than I am as an adult?"

"That's not the case at all." She sat on a stool at the table and opened another book. "For one thing, your magics are even more powerful now. You should've grown with them. Into them. Not have them thrust upon you out of the blue. I didn't realize what that would do to you."

"It's not your fault, Ruthie." And that wasn't. It was the other stuff…

She stilled for a moment, the slightest wince crossing

her face as though I'd hurt her. It had meant a lot to her, before, when I'd called her Grandma and then finally Gigi. But either way, she was simply Ruthie at the moment. Delightful and elegant and strong but still Ruthie.

Like maybe she understood that, she recovered with a quick shake of her silver bob. "I think thrusting this upon you was like putting a bomb into a steel box to let it explode safely."

Not quite following, I frowned at her.

"If the metal isn't properly conditioned, the bomb will destroy the box regardless. The steel has to be heated, forged in fire, to be able to withstand the immense pressure of the explosion. I think that's what happened to you. You haven't been properly conditioned, and we just tossed all that power into you with no fortification and no release valve."

"Maybe that explains why I've never done well under pressure." My joke fell flat.

She stood and rounded the table. "But you didn't explode. The magics didn't destroy you. They nourished you. They shaped you. Just like the fires of a blacksmith, they made you stronger."

Percy squeezed my hand with the vines as though he agreed.

Ruthie studied me. "I can feel it emanating out of you. You're like a huge ball of energy seeking an outlet, and—"

"You're wrong."

Her gaze returned to mine. "I'm wrong?"

"Yes. You're wrong." I pulled my hand away from Percy's embrace. Lying to her would be harder than lying to Annette. "They're gone."

Her forehead creased. "What are gone, sweetheart?"

I bit down, then lifted my chin and charged forward. "My powers. I don't have them anymore."

She laughed in disbelief. "Defiance, I can feel them from here."

Of course she could. She saw things Nette didn't. "I don't know what you're feeling, but it's not my powers. They're gone." Was there a way to hide them from her? I'd have to look into that.

"No." She shook her head, confused. "No, they can't be gone. You'd be dead."

"I don't know what to tell you." I lifted a hapless shoulder. "They took the midnight train going anywhere. Thus, there's no reason for me to stay." And so many for me to go. I saw what my words did to her, the distress they caused, yet still I pressed forward, like the cold-hearted bitch I'd never been. But it had to be done. "I'm moving back to Arizona as soon as I can."

She gaped at me. "But... but your dads are here." Her expression almost broke my resolve. "And Annette. And... and Roane."

"I'll tell them tonight," I said.

"You just need to practice. To get stronger." She lowered her voice. "They will come for you."

"Oh, right. The big bad wolf."

"No, he's next door," she said, only half teasing.

"Let them."

"Defiance, you must take this seriously. The most we did by dispersing your aura was buy you some time. You must be ready." Her voice cracked, and she turned away again.

I fought the sting at the backs of my eyes. "I'll be gone by the end of the week. But first, I would like an explanation."

She settled back onto the stool and kept her gaze down-cast. "I suppose you'd like the whole story."

My stomach flip-flopped. I reached down, let a vine wrap around my wrist and tangle into my fingers, and braced myself. "I would like the whys and wherefores, yes."

Ruthie nodded. "Do you remember the video I showed you of you finding Roane when you were three?"

I nodded. Now we were getting somewhere. "And I was three when my mother died."

She nodded in turn. "That night, we had no idea you'd performed more than a simple *reveal* spell. We didn't know, and quite frankly wouldn't find out for years, that you'd actually transformed a wolf into a boy."

"Who's now a shapeshifter." If we were being honest, I was still in awe over the whole thing.

"Exactly. But you fell asleep that night. We knew instantly you were in a suspended animation. It was the third time it had happened to you, so when a couple of days passed, we weren't terribly worried. Still, someone always stayed with you." Ruthie's eyes glistened in the gaslight. "Your mother insisted she would watch over you when I went to sabbath." She fidgeted with the neckline of her dress, her gaze sliding into the past. "While there, I felt a prickling."

"A prickling?" Like the one niggling at the back of my neck, standing up all the hairs there?

"Percival's essence had never gone beyond the walls of this house, but I... I felt him. Like pinpricks on my skin."

Percy's hold tightened, and I swallowed hard, dreading where this was going.

"I hurried home and..." She took a sip of what now must be stone-cold tea.

When she didn't continue, I encouraged her with a firm, "Ruthie."

"I caught your mother trying to siphon your powers."

As I absorbed what she was trying to tell me, her cup clinked against the saucer.

"But that would mean..." My voice was a mere whisper, so quiet I wondered if she could hear me. "She was trying to kill me."

Her fingers tightened around the cup. "I'm sorry, Defiance. That's why I felt I had no choice."

"You killed her to save me." Her revelation left me stunned and heartbroken. All these years, I'd dreamt of a mother who'd given me up for adoption because she'd had no choice. She'd wanted me to have a better life. She'd sacrificed everything to let me go.

As far as lies I liked to tell myself over the years, that one was a doozy. The woman who bore me had no love for me at all. Probably never did. I was forty-four—nope, forty-five—and I stood there, chin quivering, like a child mourning the loss of a love that never existed. "I'll be gone by the end of the week."

I disentangled the vines again and swung open the door, only to come face-to-face with Roane's closed door across the foyer. I needed to apologize to him. To explain my horrid behavior. But I just didn't have it in me at that moment. I had a murderous, soul-sucking mother to mourn.

"He isn't there." Ruthie stood behind me. "I believe he's making you dinner."

The scent drifting down the stairs almost dropped me and made me suddenly ravenous. Too bad sorrow and humiliation would prevent me from partaking.

"Before you leave..." Ruthie's voice filled with sadness. "The coven would love to meet you."

I pivoted to face her. "Why? I have no powers."

"They know what you did. How you saved not one but two women's lives. How you extracted me from the veil. They've helped watch over you for months. They'd love to meet you, even for just a few minutes."

I nodded, then took the stairs and hurried to my room. Only my door was blocked by a plant. I stepped forward, but this time the vines didn't move. "Percy?" I asked warily. "What's going on?"

"Dinner." My dads appeared on the mezzanine behind me. "You haven't eaten in six months, cariña."

I turned to gape at Percy—well, the part of him covering the door—then turned back to my dads. "You guys are in cahoots?"

"We are cahooting," Dad said.

The vines flourished behind me, pushing me toward my dads.

"Hey," I said, pretending to be offended.

Papi joined in. "We have decided to cahoot. It's for your own good." Each dad took an arm and led me back down the stairs, Percy still nudging me from behind.

"Is this like an intervention or something?"

"More of a cahoot-uh-vention," Papi said, ever the wordsmith.

By the time I'd been cahooted all the way into the formal dining room, I was livid. Or I could've been if I'd given it my all. "I am not a cow, Percy. You don't need to herd me."

He backed off at last while Dad pulled out a chair for me, waiting behind it, his expression insistent.

I sat, and he smiled.

The scent of whatever Roane had been cooking reminded me of every meal I'd missed over the last six months. I could only hope no one noticed the drool. I focused on the spread, recognizing Dad's handiwork in the carnitas. And Papi's baking with the homemade Hawaiian rolls and the pineapple upside-down cake he knew I loved. Even Annette had pitched in with her turkey and green chile pinwheels. There was no order to the meal. It was a hodgepodge of all my favorite foods, including macaroni and cheese, lobster bisque, and shepherd's pie.

"This looks amazing." I grabbed a plate. "Who made the shepherd's pie?"

"I did." A smooth, deep voice drifted toward me.

I didn't want to look. But his voice had the power of a giant magnet that picked up old cars, and it pulled me in like I was a wrecked Malibu in dire need of an oil change and some minor body repair.

Holding a drink loosely in his hand, he took a seat at one end of the table, leaning back in his chair with an elbow on one elaborately carved arm.

My insides melted. Then I remembered the accosting I'd given him. And my cheeks melted too. "It looks delicious." I decided to feign amnesia.

He decided to give me a simmering once-over with a side of hot flash.

I sat at the opposite end of the table, facing the wolf head-on.

Annette and the chief joined my dads, sinking into chairs they'd obviously claimed a while ago. The only one missing was Ruthie. The world had changed so much while I was out. It was like they'd become a family, and I was the awkward cousin who'd come to visit.

Platters of food were passed around, and I took a little of everything. Not to be nice, but because it all looked so good, and there was something voracious about breaking a six-month fast.

Halfway through the meal, my grandmother was still a no-show. "What about Ruthie?"

The chief dropped his gaze. "She won't come up."

"Because she doesn't eat?" Maybe she didn't. Although, she had been drinking tea.

"We really aren't sure," Annette answered.

"All we know for certain," Papi chimed in, "is that she can't leave the house."

"What do you mean?" That was a tad alarming. "She's stuck here too? Like Percy?"

He nodded. "As far as we know."

"Well, that sucks." I pointed my fork at Annette. "I thought you were supposed to be at work."

"I got fired."

"Again?" Papi wiped his face with a napkin and poured himself some water from the pitcher in the middle of the table.

"It's the tourists. They're rude. They get in my face, I'm gettin' in theirs." She added some flavor to that last part with a mediocre *Godfather* impersonation.

Papi laughed. "You realize we're only one step up from being tourists ourselves."

"We're worse," Dad said. "We've seized the land and taken up arms. We're interlopers. Trespassers. Invaders."

"Have you been studying that thesaurus again?" I grinned at him. "Quick, what's the opposite of a carpetbagger?"

"Scalawag," he shot back.

It was a good word. I'd have to remember to use it later. I took turns eating small bites of all the different food I'd crammed onto my plate while everyone else talked and laughed. Watching them interact warmed me to my toes.

Roane, quiet as always, kept his gaze focused in my direction. It was both unsettling and exhilarating.

Several things needed to be said, but I didn't dare apologize in front of everyone. I'd embarrassed him—and me—enough for one day. Maybe for tomorrow's daily dose of humiliation, I could talk about the female reproductive system or hunt down some pics of wolf pups and pass them around as Roane's baby pics. Do the job right.

Under the table, something brushed my ankle, curling around it as soft as a cat's tail.

It wasn't Ink. He'd jumped into Roane's lap. And Roane was making him a small plate, holding it while the ragged beast joined us in the festivities.

Smiling at the cat's loud purr—that I heard all the way across the table—I looked down at my ankle to see Percy's vines.

Percy had scaled back the vines dramatically. For the most part, they were no longer on the floors or the walls. They'd latticed up the corners and along the black-lacquered crown molding to create a gorgeous frame. The roses seemed a deeper red now, but they were still framed in a dusky black, every petal a work of art.

A stunning Murano chandelier, made from black hand-blown glass—that probably took a huge chunk out of what would've become my inheritance—hung low over the table. It twirled and corkscrewed, forming the general shape of a spikey teardrop. The décor, all heavy wood, thick and black, finished the room with a morbid kind of elegance. Ruthie was nothing if not avant-garde.

After swallowing yet another spoonful of a lobster bisque I wanted to get drunk on, I looked at the vine gliding across the table. Rather than dropping the bomb that I was leaving, I picked a safer subject. "Why can't Percy go into the secret passageways?" Since the only person in the room who might have an answer sat directly across from me, I glanced at him.

"You'd have to ask him." Evasive as ever, Roane stroked Ink's patchwork fur but kept his gaze locked on me. The fact that he didn't mind an animal at the table made me worship him all the more. Then again, he was an animal. It would've been rather bigoted of him to banish the furball.

"Percy doesn't talk much," I countered. "So, I thought you might know."

The vine brushed the back of my hand lovingly.

"The house was built in the early 1800s." The chief stopped eating long enough to speak up. "There isn't much information about the original owner, your ancestor, except that he was a shipping magnate. And that the whole family, save one, died of fever. Not even Ruthie knows more than that."

A heaviness pushed against my chest. "That's sad." The overwhelming majority of a family lost in one fell swoop. "I wish I could ask you," I whispered to the vine.

It coiled, almost into a smile, and urged my hand up, encouraging me to eat. Having a pet plant was the best thing that had ever happened to me. It so beat a pet rock.

The meal was quickly coming to a close. Not that I was going anywhere without a slice—or seven—of pineapple upside-down cake. I had lost meals to make up for. But when it came to that bomb, it was now or never. Mustering all the courage I could, I cleared my throat. "I have to tell you guys something."

Everyone stopped talking and gave me their undivided attention. Well, everyone except Roane. I already had his.

Even divided, his attention was a heady thing, though it did make breathing difficult.

I swallowed hard. "I've lost my powers."

My dads stared at me, blinking occasionally to let me know they were still alive. The chief seemed shocked as well.

"I already told you," Annette said. "You just have to pick yourself up, dust yourself off, and slip back into the saddle."

"The saddle has nothing to do with it. My powers are gone. There's nothing I can do about it." I winced, hoping my dads wouldn't kill me over this next part. "And I've decided to move back to Phoenix for a while."

"You what?" Papi was the first to speak.

"Cariña," Dad said, "maybe you should give this some time."

"Exactly." Annette's face lit with hope. "You can't just leave. What about Percy?"

"Percy has survived decades without my help. I think he'll be fine." I looked down at the vine near my wrist, but it was gone.

"Defiance." Dad's soft accent hardened like it did when I was about to get a lecture.

Except I was forty-four—forty-five—and plenty old enough to decide for myself where I would live.

"What is this really about?" he asked.

"Right?" Annette pointed her knife at him as though he'd nailed it. "There's something else going on here. She can't just lose her powers. To do that, she has to die."

"*She*," I said, growing annoyed at being spoken about like I wasn't here, "never wanted the powers in the first place. Therefore, *she* says good riddance."

Unlike the rest of the group, who gave new meaning to

the term *up in arms*, Roane hadn't moved a muscle, his hawklike gaze missing nothing.

She stood, placed her napkin on the table, and headed out of the kitchen before the grilling could commence. And, sadly, before *she* got a piece of cake.

As I left, the group sat there, talking over the odds of me losing my powers. "Maybe they're just dormant." "Maybe Dephne's just scared after what happened." "What does it all mean in the grand scheme of things?" "What will happen when she leaves Percy's protection to go back to the A-Z?"

But *she* was nowhere near that selfish. They had to know I would never abandon them. Annette and my dads had moved a thousand miles from home to be with me. To be here for me. To help me through this time of transition. I just needed time to breathe. Time to think about what to do. Time to research and figure out how to get rid of my powers for real, because no way could I face what was coming. And if they knew what was coming, they wouldn't want me to.

They could call me a coward when the time came, but they were clueless about what was out there. They didn't realize that true evil existed. And I wasn't talking about serial-killer evil. Or total-disdain-for-human-life evil. But an evil that could rock the foundation of the world as we knew it.

An evil that was coming for me.

Everyone I'd left sitting at the table thought Percy had been protecting me—even from them. And he may have been. But if my dreams were to be believed, he'd done so much more than that. The vines were as much of a supernatural barrier as a physical one. And with them, Percy had kept things at bay that would terrify most humans.

And he'd done it over and over and over while I'd slept.

FOUR

In my defense,
I was left unsupervised.
—Meme

Since the thought of being stalked by that dark nightmare filled me with a crushing fear that rivaled the time I thought I'd killed Annette with a cheese grater, I decided not to purposely seek it out. My beauty rest could wait. Instead, there were a series of secret passageways calling my name.

Not literally, thank God. It was enough that Percy was alive and had a mind of his own.

Flashlight at the ready, I entered through the movable shelves in my bathroom. A light came on the minute I stepped through. I turned back to Percy. "For real? You can't come in here?"

A multitude of black vines snaked across the bathroom wall, twisting and curling over the surface, stopping at some invisible barrier between the privy and the narrow hallway.

I reached across the threshold and wrapped one around my finger. "It's okay. I'll be right back."

He let me go. A good sign in my book. If the passageways were dangerous, he would've tried to stop me. At least, that was what I told myself. A false sense of security was better than no sense of security—especially when it came to watering down my fear.

The only thing in the hallway besides the wall sconces was the camera my dads had installed to keep an eye on me while I slept. The walls were lined with whitewashed shiplap that smelled of sea and salt and brine, making me wonder if the wood really came from a boat.

The maze behind the walls seemed to access every room in the house. One set of narrow stairs traveled over rooms and halls to get to the next. Trailing up and down throughout the entire manor, some walkways were no more than four feet high.

One even took me all the way to the basement. Or at least I thought I was in the basement. The musty scent of earth hit me as I descended a thousand steps farther than should be possible. Somehow, I'd gone deeper even than the rooms downstairs. I was underneath them. And there were no lights down here.

Turning on the flashlight, I tugged on a thin wooden door. The rusted hinges squeaked in protest, then opened into a cave.

An explorer's wet dream, rock walls lined a massive cavern. Water pooled in several places, as though the sea was somehow getting in. The floor to the house above me had been braced with massive smoothly finished columns.

Cool air brushed over my skin. It flowed from one side of the cavern to the other, and I swore I heard waves lapping against rocks nearby. Turning, I felt the wall beside me. It was damp and smelled like salt. But we were over half a mile from the ocean. So, where were the waves coming from?

I couldn't see without going deeper inside. I bit back the urge to call out "Is anyone there?" I'd seen more than one movie about people who explored creepy, dark rooms alone at night. Visions of entrails had me backing away. No matter how brightly my curiosity burned, it would have to wait. I could come down tomorrow during the day to see if any sunlight filtered through.

I was just about to hightail it out of there when an apparition walked out of the darkness—a woman shrouded in silver—and I almost ruined a perfectly good pair of underwear. As it was, I suffered a small arrest of my left ventricle. But that was less humiliating. A story I could actually tell at parties. I clicked off the flashlight as quietly as I could.

But the apparition heard it and turned. She didn't need the light. She came with her own luminescence.

Dropping the flashlight, I stumbled back in horror, a scream about to rip from my throat—

"Defiance?"

"Ruthie?" Retrieving the light, I beamed it at her.

She blinked. "What are you doing down here?"

"What am I doing down here?" I put a hand over my heart attack. "What are you doing down here?" Foregoing the safety of the last stair, I stepped into the cave but held on to the doorframe for dear life, my nails digging into the wood.

"I'm just... I was thinking." Her glow softened.

"Thinking about what? How this place is creepy AF?" Though, with the right designer, it would make a fantastic mass grave. Or a dungeon for a serial killer. Or even a summer lair for Shelob. Moving the light off Ruthie, I bounced it around the cave. "Does this lead somewhere?"

Her slippers silent on the dirt floor, she drifted toward me.

"Have you ever been down this deep?"

She scanned the cavern. "Defiance, until a few days ago, those stairs ended at the basement."

I stilled. Considered how my day was going. Backed up and planted my foot on the last step. The vines, the six-month stint in suspended animation, the fact that my dead grandmother was alive again I could handle. But stairs that magically appeared overnight and led to a cave underneath a house I'd just inherited from a witch? Nope.

"This was not here," she continued, oblivious to my mental breakdown that would be talked about for generations to come. "At least not that I know of."

I backed up another step. It creaked beneath my foot.

"I think it leads all the way to the waterfront. Do you hear the waves?"

And one more for good measure.

Like Ruthie had suddenly caught some of the fear I'd been projecting, she turned toward me. "Defiance, yes, go back upstairs. Hurry."

She did not have to tell me twice. I turned and flew up the stairs, stumbling and scraping my shins more than once, until I got to the very top. Only then did I realize I was lost. And dying. I hadn't done cardio in months, and that was before my sabbatical snooze.

My breath wheezed in and out as I tried several of the doors, pushing as hard as I could to get in. None of them would open. Probably a good thing. Knowing someone could sneak into my room at night was disturbing as Dante's hell.

At the end of a very long hall, I came to yet another set of stairs that led up, but I was already on the top floor. The second floor was as high as Percy went. So where did these stairs lead?

I reconstructed Percy from memory. The main section was round with six black gables that formed a circle. The front door, and the bay windows on either side, faced the street. Another section, square but just as stunning, was attached on the right, shorter when one considered the gables. Did Percy have an attic above to even out the dungeon below?

I turned on my flashlight and took the stairs slowly—because of that cardio thing—as the steps shrunk and narrowed more than the rest. They groaned and squeaked under my weight, ripping up my self-esteem and handing it back in the form of one huge-ass complex. Twenty stairs later, I emerged inside a round windowless room with the same salty shiplap and wood floor.

Gazing up, I turned full circle. A high, pointed ceiling topped the room, which coned down to meet six doors. They were evenly spaced, creating a perfect ring around the common area. The distressed wood had seen better days, and the floor creaked when I walked across it, but it was solid like the rest of Percy.

The doors were rather small, as though meant for a child. I tried each one of the vintage doorknobs, all of them locked. The keyholes proved it would take a skeleton key to open them, which I did not have. "I feel like Alice in Wonderland," I said to absolutely no one.

I tried again, this time using a different technique. After checking over my shoulder to make sure no one was looking, I lifted a hand and drew a symbol on the door closest to me.

Light burst out of the lines I'd drawn, radiating bright and hot.

Pressing my hand to the door, I pushed that light past it and into the room and scanned the area with a searching energy. At first, all it found was a vast nothingness. Far too vast to simply be a room.

Then something scratched. Scratched my energy. Scratched me.

I pulled the energy back, but the thing's claws sank in. It buried its teeth and wouldn't let go. My eyes flew open as I tried to pry my hand off the door. It wouldn't let me. Keeping me glued to the spot, it catapulted toward me. A darkness, cold and angry. I felt it rocket through space like a cannon. I struggled to free my hand, and it let go without warning a microsecond before it slammed into the door.

I stumbled back, tripping on my own feet, and covered my face with my arms, expecting to be blasted with shards of splintered wood. But the only thing that fell on me was dust from the rafters above.

Amazed I was still alive, I patted myself down then scrambled to the stairs, half running, half falling. I tried to find my way out.

All the steps down and all the steps up formed a zigzag of mazes that Jareth would be proud to install in his goblin castle.

After a short eternity, where I got lost several more times—honestly, the house wasn't *that* big—I emerged from a panel strategically placed behind a potted plant on the mezzanine. My room was only a few doors down. But if my calculations were correct, this two-story house—or three if one counted the attic—was actually thirty stories high. And a million feet deep.

Gawd, I was bad at math. Next time, I'd bring Annette.

Still, either this house sat directly on top of a hellmouth or my ancestors were into way more than just shipping.

Chest heaving, mostly because of the cardio thing, I closed the panel and pressed against the wall. Having Percy around calmed my nerves. I drew in several deep breaths, wondering how no one was awake. How no one had heard the crash of the house almost falling down around us. How that small door stayed on its hinges.

A clock ticking downstairs was the only sound coming from the belly of the beast, also known as the first floor. I crept down the stairs, careful not to awaken anything that might be lurking in the dark, and headed for the kitchen. A place of nourishment and respite. A place where both friends and memories were made. A place where pineapple upside-down cake lived, waiting in the shadows, beckoning me closer.

I needed sustenance. And sugar. Mostly sugar. And I deserved it, damn it. I was living in some bizarre interdimensional hellhole, no offense to Percy. And cake would help. Cake always helped.

With hands still shaking from the evening's events, I felt around until I found the light above the industrial stove and turned it on, ready to begin a new quest that did not involve hidden passageways or secret dungeons or creepy rooms that linked directly to the seventh circle of hell.

If I were a pineapple upside-down cake...

"It's over here."

I jumped 12.2 feet into the air and whirled around with a hand over my heart to find a highlander sitting on the counter like he'd been raised in the wild. Then again, he had.

He held a fork and a small plate and was taking bites out of a piece of the very cake that had been calling to me.

In between said bites, a grin as sinful as my deepest desires lifted one corner of his exquisite mouth.

Obviously, we'd had the same idea.

With zero confirmation, he reached around, took another dessert plate out of the cabinet, and held it out to me.

I walked forward and took it.

He cut me a piece of cake, lifting it carefully onto my plate.

"Maybe I'm here for the carnitas," I said.

"The way you were making love to this cake with your eyes? I don't think so."

Heat infused my face. Why was I constantly going red around him? Thankfully, the room was still dark enough to cover for me even with the stove light on. Unless... "Can you see in the dark?" He could come in handy.

He grinned. "Worried?"

"No. Maybe. A little." I put the plate down and hopped onto the counter—not an easy feat—putting the cake pan between us. "Did you know this house lives on top of a cave?"

"No, but that explains a lot."

"And there are six doors at the top of the stairs in the secret passageways."

"Yeah. I tried opening them. They won't budge."

"It's a good thing. I think they lead to hell or something. Or at the very least, one of its outer offices. This house is getting more disturbing by the minute."

The countertop quaked beneath me.

"Sorry, Percy. I didn't mean it that way." I decided to shut up and eat my cake. It melted in my mouth. No matter how much I despised the word, *moist* was the best way to describe it. And rich. And delicious. I may have moaned.

Roane laughed softly and handed me a cup of coffee he poured from the pot sitting on his other side.

I swallowed, the bitter taste blending with the sweetness from the cake almost orgasmic. I took another drink, then said, "And you didn't answer my first question."

"I can't be certain, but I do think I see better in the dark than humans."

"Okay, that's the coolest thing I've heard all day."

"The coolest thing I've heard was that you woke up."

I thwarted an exhilarated grin by taking another bite. "I'm sorry," I said, my mouth half full.

He stopped and looked over at me. "For what?"

"Making everyone worry."

"Yeah, because that was your fault."

"You know what I mean."

He hopped off the counter and put his plate in the sink. "Since we're both very aware you did not lose your powers, what's up with that?"

"Are you calling me a liar?" I asked, pretending to be appalled, right before I shoveled in another bite.

He put the plastic cover on the cake and turned to me. "Big, fat, and bald-faced." Coming from any other man, I would've taken that as an insult. But Roane could've mistaken me for ET, and I still would've ovulated.

He studied me, his gaze full of challenge. And humor. Mostly humor.

A warmth spread low in my abdomen. "That last spell must've been too much for my system." I shrugged. "The powers just vanished."

In all honesty, I had no idea what lying about my powers was going to accomplish. That would take introspection I didn't want to introspect at the moment. I mean, obviously, the big bad dark coming after me had something to do with it. Sure, I'd been unconscious when I'd seen it, so one could argue that I'd imagined it. But it felt real enough to have me scurrying into a corner for six months.

Ruthie had said there were other witches, warlocks even, who would stop at nothing to get a charmling's powers. Was that what I'd seen? What I still felt? What Percy fought against for me? Was it as simple as a warlock seeking the ultimate power high? Perhaps. Except somehow it felt more personal.

"Fine," Roane acquiesced. "Then we need to get them back."

His nearness caused my breaths to quicken. "My powers?"

A dimple appeared on one side of his mouth. "Your powers."

"I don't think that's a good idea." I dropped my gaze and bit the bullet while changing the subject at the same time. Two birds. One stone. "I owe you an apology first, anyway."

"Yeah?" He walked to another cabinet on the other side of the massive kitchen and took down a box.

"About earlier." I put the last bites of cake on the counter and closed my eyes. "I... I can't believe I did that. Said that." I could believe I'd thought it. "I'm so sorry. I thought I was dreaming, but that's no excuse. Especially since, you know, I wasn't."

He was beside me again. I felt him. His essence. His aura. Also, he'd slid the cakepan over and put the box next to me. That was a big clue.

"I'm so sorry, Roane. I practically assaulted you and—"

"Is that why?"

I lifted my lids. "Is what why?"

"Why you're lying about your powers."

I released a long breath to let him know the depths of

my annoyance. It had layers. And texture. And made a weird grating sound. "I'm not lying."

"Mm." He took out a candle and set it on the counter. Then another. And another. Soon there were a dozen candles scattered over varying surfaces throughout the kitchen. He placed the last candle on the stove and turned toward me. "Okay, light these with your mind."

My expression flatlined. "For real? You've clearly seen too many movies."

He lifted a shoulder. "It'll be a test."

"I think we should test you instead." I crossed my arms over my chest. "Test if you can see in the dark. Do you have wolf vision when you're not a wolf?"

He walked back and stood in front of me nose-to-nose. Then he pressed his hands to the counter on either side of my hips. "How about we take turns." His hair hung to his shoulders. He raked a hand through it, pulling it back from his face, then put his hand back on the counter, his sinuous arms trapping me.

"Deal," I said, trying to ignore the fact that a tenacious lock of auburn hair fell forward again. "You first."

He shook his head. "Uh-uh. You first, gorgeous."

A tingle raced up my spine.

He eased closer, speeding up my pulse exponentially. "What good is testing my powers if I don't have any powers to test? You first, then I swear I'll try."

"Are you sure you want me to leave? I'd have to walk all the way over to the stove to turn off the light."

The light flickered and shut off, drenching us in total darkness.

My eyes rounded to the size of my dessert plate. I was certain of it. "Did you do that?"

He laughed, the sound low and husky, and my nether

regions flooded with molten lava. "That was all you and your nonexistent powers."

"Maybe it was Percy."

"Right." Tilting his head, he moved closer.

I parted my knees to make room for him, and his lean hips slid between my legs, the fit perfect. With me sitting on the counter, I was a couple of inches taller than him. I liked it.

He leaned in, brushed his lips along my jaw, stopping at my ear.

I marveled at the fact even the softest touch from him caused a trembling in my core. And that he smelled like soap and soft, earthy aftershave.

"If you light one candle"—his warm breath fanned across my cheek—"I'll make you breakfast in the morning. Anything you want."

What if I wanted him for breakfast? "You got it. Do you have a match?"

A humorous sigh escaped him. "With your gift."

"Oh, it's a gift now?" His face was a gift. "I'm not so sure I agree."

He nibbled on my earlobe, and my girl parts clenched in reflex, which was odd considering they were nowhere near my ears. "You're five seconds away from losing out on French toast and a seafood omelet."

"It's sad how appealing that sentence is."

"Four."

I closed my eyes and reveled in the feel of him. "Wait. I'm concentrating."

"Three."

"Maybe if you did the ear thing again."

"Two," he said, then nipped.

I sucked in a soft breath.

"One."

"Can I call a timeout?"

He released a deep, throaty laugh that washed over me like cool water as he stood back and said, "I win."

The lids I didn't remember closing fluttered open, and I wanted to cry when a cool rush of air hit me in his absence. Then his words sank in. I looked around, scrambled off the counter, and almost fell to the ground. Every candle was lit. Every. Single. One. They bathed Roane in a soft glow, and as alluring as that was, I didn't do it.

"That wasn't me," I said, backing away.

"You're the only witch here."

"No." I took another step back, shaking my head. "This wasn't me."

He nodded, crossed his arms over his chest, and perched his lean frame against the counter I'd just deserted. "Whatever helps you sleep at night, gorgeous."

I ran like the coward I was. I hurried up the stairs and hid under the covers, boots and all. Ruthie would kill me if she knew.

"That wasn't me, right, Percy?" I put my hand outside the blanket I'd pulled up to my chin.

A vine curled up the side of the bed and around my wrist and palm.

I brought it to my cheek, closed my eyes, and fell asleep, wondering if I'd ever actually woken up at all.

FIVE

Four out of five dentists agree:
lying through your teeth does NOT count as flossing.
—Meme

What seemed like five seconds later, I jerked awake to find a curly-haired, cat-eyed bibliophile reading on the bed beside me and an actual cat, albeit a tattered one, curled up in her lap.

Annette sat against my headboard in an old T-shirt and a pair of sweats so holey they could be nominated for sainthood. "Percy let me in," she said without looking up from her book.

I tried to wiggle to a sitting position, but my butt still weighed too much, as it often did before coffee. Also, I was wearing boots. In bed. And the sheets had clearly fused with them. "How long was I out this time?"

"I don't know. What time did you go to bed?"

"No clue." I reached over and gave Ink's ears a scrubbing. "I thought you two didn't get along."

She looked over her book, a vampire story she'd read at least a dozen times. "We didn't. But we've had six months to rethink our relationship."

I tried once again to ease into a sitting position. The sheets were simply not having it. "I totally should've taken off my boots first."

"There's a reason most people do. I have an idea."

"Uh-oh."

"Unless you're going to be too busy packing, what with the big move and all."

She'd evidently blown past denial and slid solidly into anger with seconds to spare. I ignored her mini-rant. "Does it involve baby dills or glitter paint?"

"Not this time." She flattened the book against her chest. "I know what you need."

"A lobotomy?"

"A manicure."

"So close."

"There's nothing like a mani-pedi to ease tension. Your powers will be back in no time."

"Ah. I'm not sure I want to trust powers that hinge on the state of my cuticles."

"And you never really got to see Salem."

"Of course." Make me fall in love with the town so I'd stay. Clever.

"I've seen it all since moving here. I've also worked at like half the stores and restaurants in the city proper."

"How many jobs have you had?" I asked, appalled.

"A lot. I was hoping our business would take off sooner."

"I was in a mystical coma."

"I know." She pouted. "I don't blame you, per se."

I laughed. "Thanks. Can I shower first?"

"Yes, but hurry. I want to get there before Parris does."

"Our neighbor?"

"There's something about that woman. She's icky. And she's a menace. It's Saturday, and she always steals Fiona from me. Fiona is the best technician there. I kind of love her."

"You've really settled in."

"I had no choice. It was kill or be killed."

I frowned at her.

"No, that's not right." She bit her lip in thought. "Survival of the fittest? Yeah, that's it. I had to survive somehow."

"Maybe you shouldn't have gotten fired from every place you've worked."

"Who says I got fired?"

"Papi. Last night."

"He was referring to the one time I did get fired. I kept quitting. I only wanted to work at each place long enough to get to know the owners and the clientele. If we're going to start our own business, we need to know the locals. We need to blend in. We need them to like us."

"Then maybe you shouldn't have quit every business in town."

"Yeah." She bit the inside of her cheek. "I didn't really think it through."

"I'll be ready in forty-five. You should probably change into something less devout."

She sulked. "But these are my favorite sweats."

"They have more holes than a can of Spaghetti-O's."

"And?"

Two hours later, we walked out of the nail salon with hands and feet we could proudly display in public. Thank

God. The state of my toes had really been weighing on me.

"Feel better?" Nette asked, hope shimmering in her gray irises.

"My toes do." I did a perfunctory search for Roane. I could've sworn I saw him while the technician was doing her own kind of magic. But when I'd looked back, he was gone.

"A step in the right direction. I'll take it. So, what was it?" she asked for the tenth time.

We hadn't been able to talk about... well, *anything*... in front of the technicians, so she'd been digesting what I'd told her about my underbelly tour of the house before we went in and had to hold her questions the entire time we were being pampered. She'd kept squirming, like it was her bladder I'd asked her to hold, until I was worried her head would explode having to keep all that angst inside.

"I don't know. But it was very dark and very powerful."

"But it couldn't get past the door?"

"No." I chewed on a freshly manicured nail that tasted like battery acid thanks to all the chemicals they'd used while Annette led me through the beautiful city of Salem.

We dodged tourists and stopped at various kiosks to check their wares. But my mind was too occupied to pay much attention.

"You're sure?" she asked. "It can't, like, escape and kill us all in our sleep?"

"Salt," I said as a thought emerged. It happened.

"Salt as in yes you're sure? Or salt as in no you aren't?"

"The shiplap." I turned to her as she held a pair of earrings up to my ear. "It smelled like salt all through the passageway and in the attic. Even in the dungeon, the walls were drenched in it."

"Which we need to discuss in much greater detail." She put the earrings back, thanked the vendor, and continued down the path. "I mean, seriously. A dungeon? Are we talking *The Princess Bride* or *Fifty Shades*?"

I thought about last night with Roane, heating up all over again. "It could go either way. What if salt really does keep spirits out?"

Annette stopped so abruptly, I almost ran into her. "Or in." She turned and pointed an index finger at me. "Percy has never been able to leave the house. Now Ruthie can't. Do you think it's the salt in the wood?"

I looked around. She'd had led us farther down Essex. "I thought the restaurant was the other way?"

"Um, it is." She started walking again, dragging me behind her by my hand. "We just have some time to kill."

I'd known her far too long to mistake her hedging for anything other than hedging. "Why would we have time to kill?" I asked, feeling suspicion furrow my face. I wished I were less suspicious in general. Furrowing caused wrinkles. And I was already forty-four. Forty-five. I forced my face to relax.

"What?" she asked, hedging again. "Oh, because I-I made a reservation."

We hurried past shops and cafés and an incredible statue of Elizabeth Montgomery in *Bewitched*. I wanted a picture, but apparently we couldn't kill *that* much time. "I thought they didn't take reservations. That was why you wanted to get there early." Tired of being dragged, I moved so we were walking side by side.

"They do now."

"They've changed their policy since ten this morning?"

"'Parently. Hey, your hair is longer." She picked up a heavy black lock, trying to change the subject.

"I couldn't really get out to get it cut during my hiatus, now could I?" I said through gritted teeth. "Why do we have time to kill?"

She drew in a deep breath. "I kind of told the coven they could join us for lunch, but a couple can't be there until eleven thirty."

"You what?" I yanked her to a stop.

"Hey, you told Ruthie you'd meet them before you bolted."

"I'm not bolting," I said, even though that was exactly what I was doing. "I'm taking a vacation."

"You're absolutely bolting."

I hadn't told Nette about Roane or the light or the candles. What if it *had* all been me? What if my powers were not only still here—which, they were—but they were taking over? I hadn't drawn a symbol on the air. I hadn't used my magics. What if there was something else inside me? Something with a will of its own? I didn't want her to know any of that, though I did want to tell her about Roane's nibbling. I got goosebumps just thinking about it. I tugged at my earlobe absently.

"Bolting, not bolting, either way," she said, "we need to check out the competition. You know, in case you unbolt and come back to us." She took my hand again and dragged me toward a psychic's lair—the exterior black with gold lettering that read *The Witchery*.

"The competition?" I asked. "Nette, there's no competition. I'm not a psychic."

"Her name is Liliana Lovett, but she goes by Love. She's a little... off center, but she's super nice even though I'm certain she's hiding something." She speared me with an all-knowing glower and tapped a finger against her temple. "I see a darkness in her past."

"Like last night? It was pitch black."

"She's running away from something. I can feel it."

"Are you sure you're not checking her out because she's *your* competition? You're the fake psychic, after all."

"That hurt." She feigned being put out. "But you could be right. A little. I just want your impression because she's really good. Damn it. Better than I am. She's also a witch, but she's not part of your grandmother's coven." Turning to me with the most damning evidence of all, she added, "And she's new in town."

"She isn't," I said, disgusted.

"She is."

"Where's a pillory when you need one? Amirite?"

Nodding, she tugged me all the way inside the gorgeous little shop of horrors, decorated with witch-themed paraphernalia new and old, and I kind of fell in love.

We'd walked in during a session. A girl was having her palm read in a small raised area with a three-foot iron rail and a swing gate. She leaned forward, toward someone I assumed was Love, her attention rapt, eager to hear everything the psychic had to say. Two other girls looked up at us from the waiting area, where they were browsing through a plethora of trinkets and bobbles that were for sale. All three were in their early twenties and dressed in costumes, even though Halloween wasn't for weeks.

Love looked only a little younger than me, with an elegant jaw and nose and long blonde hair that she'd lowlighted with black and purple streaks. Her profile painted her as a young Lauren Bacall.

I kind of fell in love again. The last time I'd felt such an instant kinship with someone was when I'd first laid eyes on Annette in ninth grade. This was very similar. There was a pull. A gravitational force.

"Oh," Annette whispered, leaning close. "I forgot to mention that Love doesn't like me."

I snapped out of it. "I'm sure that's not true." Who wouldn't like the adorable creature standing next to me?

"Oh, no, trust me on this one."

I pursed my lips. "How do you know?"

"She told me."

"Oh." I glanced over my shoulder at the beauty. "Did she give you a reason?"

"Not in so many words. She just kind of kicked me out and told me not to come back."

"And yet here we are." I took Nette by the shoulders and turned her toward the door. "And now we should go."

"I'm so sorry," Love said, breaking off her reading. She scooted back from the table and looked around. Her gaze landed on me and Annette. Mostly Annette. "I'm getting interference from the peanut gallery."

"Sorry." Annette waved an apologetic hand. "We'll shut up."

Our talking had broken her concentration? How much concentration did it take to rob people blind?

The other women in the store gaped at us. One brought out her phone, grasping for her fifteen minutes of viral fame.

Love's fiery gaze turned livid. "I thought I told you not to come back."

"Yeah, but you didn't say for how long. And I needed"— Annette's gaze darted about wildly before landing on—"a refrigerator magnet in the shape of a cauldron." She grabbed it and held it up like a trophy. "Found one!"

"What in the fiery hell did you do to her?" I asked, my voice low.

She pasted a smile on her face and spoke without moving her lips, like a ventriloquist. "I'll tell you later."

Love walked from behind the rail and strode toward Annette. It was a small store, so it didn't take long. Only before she reached us, she stopped short. Or something stopped her short. Her mouth formed an O. She looked at me and took a step back, as though astounded by what she saw.

I wanted to be flattered, but I knew better. "Crap," I said under my breath. "Do I have a praying mantis in my hair again?" That was such a horrible experience.

Annette seemed mesmerized by Love's reaction. She reached over and patted me absently, unable to take her eyes off the blonde. But she kept patting, her hand eventually finding its way to my face.

I slapped it away and told Love, "We'll just be going."

It was as though she couldn't catch her breath. Her face turned a soft pink, and her amazing eyes, a stormy emerald green, shimmered with wetness.

I grabbed Annette's hand and hauled her out of the shop and through the mass of tourists, anywhere that was away.

"Did you see that?" she asked.

"Seriously?"

"That was crazy." Her enthusiasm, like champagne, came with lots of bubbles.

"I'm going to go out on a limb and say she's the real thing."

"Ya think? This proves it. You still have your powers."

Crap on a cracker. "This proves nothing of the kind."

"Please. Why else would she react that way to you?"

"A history of mental illness comes to mind."

"Clearly your powers are still there. Like they were

before Ruthie taught you how to access them. We just have to work on getting them back." She looked at her hands. "Also, I shoplifted, but it's kind of your fault." She showed me the stolen item in the shape of a cauldron as proof.

I took it from her. "It's so cute."

"Right?"

I flipped it over. "Twenty-five dollars!" That was an expensive refrigerator magnet. "We have to go back and pay for it."

"Not in this lifetime. I'll mail her a check."

"That works."

We headed back toward the restaurant, Annette rambling about my powers and Love's reaction and how hard it was to be a psychic in a skeptic's world. It did make one question a few of life's certainties. Like the fact that psychics were fake. That belief had been so firmly ingrained that even knowing what I knew now about witches and magics and the preternatural, it still made any evidence to the contrary seem trivial.

Something in my periphery dragged me out of my thoughts. I turned to see Roane among a group of tourists. He was leaning against a house one minute, watching me with that dark gaze of his, but gone the next. Then I saw the house.

"Wait." I stopped before Annette could adjust.

She ran into me from behind, then followed my gaze.

I read the sign. "The Witch House," I said, my voice full of awe.

Like with Love, I felt a pull. A gravitational tug. But unlike with Love, the energy wasn't positive. Not totally. It was a mixture of light and darkness. I knew enough about the house to know that it had belonged to one of the judges in the Salem Witch Trials.

"It's so cool," Annette said. "It belonged to Judge Jonathan Corwin. They believe that many cases were initially investigated here. You have to buy tickets in advance, but I know a guy."

"You know a guy?"

She grinned. "Wait here," she said before heading inside.

I frowned and studied the ground around the house as a man tried to get me to sign a petition to stop the demolition of an old print factory. I signed it, because why not, then studied the manor. Made of thick black timber, it towered above the tourists posing for selfies. I looked for Roane again, but like before, he was gone.

When Annette came back with two passes, I said, "It's been moved." Either that or my bearings were off.

"Yes," she said, impressed. "They had to move it thirty-five feet to keep it from being torn down when they widened North Street. How did you know?"

I lifted a shoulder. "I must've read it somewhere."

Annette studied the spot I'd been staring at. "I don't think so. What did you see?"

"Nothing. It's just, I don't know, off center."

"Let's go in. You'll love it."

Normally, I would agree with her. I loved history. But the closer we got to the entrance, the more uncomfortable I became. Dark energies swirled around me. Light as well, but the dark was disorienting. Dizzying. Nauseating.

I pulled up my bootstraps and soldiered on. We ducked inside and traveled four hundred years into the past. Wood floors creaked beneath our feet as we perused the entryway. Glass cases displayed items from the era, including a woman's boot and a witch bottle. I found the bottle particularly interesting.

"This is the only structure still standing with direct ties to the Witch Trials of 1692," Nette said.

I wiped all expression from my face. "You just read that in the brochure."

She brought a brochure out of her back pocket and waved it. "True. Doesn't make it any less cool. Or sad. Depending." She tapped it on my arm and led the way into the parlor. "Many would say Judge Corwin paid dearly for his part in the trials."

"How so?"

"The Corwin Curse. Eight Corwins died in this house."

"That's awful."

The former magistrate's parlor was appointed with primitive furnishings and household items like candles and quills and some gorgeous silver platters. A huge brick fireplace took up an entire wall. A table, where the judge had likely heard the accusations of the residents, sat along another.

The kitchen was no less impressive, only the fireplace was even bigger with a beehive oven on the back wall and a cast iron pot hanging inside. An ornate carpet lay across a thick wooden dining table, and a butter churn sat in one corner along with thick milk bottles and tin cups.

We took a set of narrow wooden stairs up to the second floor to the master bedroom. The energy hit me hardest there. A wave of dizziness washed over me as we examined the contents of the room. A cradle sat near another huge fireplace with a bedpan hanging from it. A silk dress was on display in one corner, and a bible box sat on a nightstand beside a canopied bed. Inside it, the Corwins would've kept their Bible and important documents.

But the most interesting thing about the bedroom had to

be the little blond boy dressed in period clothing dangling his feet over the side of a small writing desk.

"He's adorable," I whispered, not wanting him to break from his role. "A little boy in period clothes. He's dressed so authentically."

He looked up at me and waved.

I put a hand over my heart. "I want to take him home."

Annette turned to me. "Okay, but don't get us arrested again like last time. Most children are accompanied by at least one parent."

Several other people were perusing the room at the same time, but none of them paid the least bit of attention to the boy. "Where do you think they are?"

"Who?" she asked, checking out a picture of a woman.

"The boy's parents."

He smiled again, hopped down from the desk, and darted out of the room. Only he didn't go through a door. He went through a wall.

I froze as a wave of terror gripped me like nothing I'd ever felt before. No idea why. It wasn't like he was scary. I'd thought I'd seen a ghost once as a kid. Turned out to be Papi wearing an avocado mask.

"What boy?" Annette asked, looking around.

I felt a tug on my jacket but didn't move. I knew it was him. It had to be. No one else in the room was that short.

"Deph?" Annette snapped her fingers in front of my face. It was super helpful. "You in there?"

I snuck my left hand up and pointed nonchalantly to my right side.

She looked and shrugged.

I gritted my teeth and tilted my head.

She looked again and tilted her head back.

I had no choice but to risk a quick glance to clue her in.

Blond boy. Big blue eyes. Period clothing.

After offering her my best deer-in-the-headlights look, she shook her head. "I don't get it."

He tugged again, and my lungs seized. Why? It was just a boy. A gorgeous, playful little boy who couldn't have been more than two or three. The gravity of what was happening began to sink in.

Annette froze too, but only for a moment before she whirled around, her gaze darting about wildly.

The boy lifted his hand as though he wanted me to take it, but I was still in the throes of terror and couldn't move.

Annette whirled around again like a drunk ballerina, gaining the attention of everyone in the room. They cast glances over their shoulders that were both curious and irritated. "Where is it?" she asked, flapping her jacket as though trying to shake him off.

It was the little boy's actions that snapped me out of my stupor. He wilted, the hope in his eyes vanishing as he lowered his hand and began to walk away.

"Wait," I whispered to him. He stopped but didn't look back, and I had to wonder how many times he'd tried to get someone's attention over the years. Hell, over the centuries. How many times had he tried to connect? I closed my eyes a moment, then knelt. "Wait," I said again.

Annette stopped her Elaine dance, her expression equal parts interest and horror.

He turned toward me, his face the loveliest thing I'd ever seen.

"I'm sorry," I said. "You just startled me."

Two dimples appeared on his cheeks, and I melted, almost falling through the floorboards to the kitchen below. He walked up to me and put his hand on my face. I could barely feel it, like a brush of cool air.

By that point, we'd gained the attention of the others in the room. There were only five, but they were very interested in what we were doing. One of them, a woman in her early thirties, brought out a phone to record the crazy lady talking to air.

I was pretty much done with others seeking their fifteen minutes at my expense. As calmly as I could, I leveled my best glare on her and explained, "I am a witch. If you even think about recording me, I'll fry your phone and the 4,738 pictures on it."

Slowly, as though I were a snake about to strike, she lowered the device and tucked it into her pocket.

I turned back to the boy. "How old are you?"

He struggled to raise the proper number of fingers, using his other hand to help, then held up three. "Free."

Three? If he was three, he'd only recently seen that birthday when he'd passed. He looked younger.

I crossed my arms over a knee and buried a smile behind them. "What's your name?"

"Samwell."

"Samuel?" I asked.

He nodded, then turned and pointed to the open doorway. "Open."

"Deph?" Annette asked. "I need some verbal cues here."

A man came rumbling up the stairs and skidded to a halt. We'd been ratted out.

"Hey, Karl," Annette said. He had to be her guy. "We're just looking around like everybody else. Nothing to see here."

His face was bright with wonder. "Is it the little blond boy or a man?"

"A man?" I asked him, afraid to take my eyes off Samuel

for very long. Considering my crouched position, I had to wonder why he would think it was a man. Or what he thought I was doing to a man in said position.

"Sir," Samuel said. Then he pointed again.

"Yes." Karl chanced a step closer. "There've been several accounts over the years, but all of them report seeing either a blond boy or an older gentleman. They believe the man is Jonathan Corwin himself, but pictures of him don't match their description. The boy could be one of his children. He lost five. But we just don't know."

Annette had taken out her phone and was already looking something up. She shook her head. "He's not one of the judge's children. Jonathan Corwin didn't have a son named Samuel."

"His name is Samuel?" Karl asked, astonished.

It amazed me how he didn't even question the authenticity of my sighting.

"Can I take a picture?" he asked. "I might get an orb. Or even an outline."

I finally acquiesced. "Just a picture. No video."

He took out his phone, and everyone else in the room followed suit. In fact, our audience had grown by about six more people, all wanting to see what the hubbub was about.

I held out my hand. "Is Sir here?" I asked the boy.

He nodded and pointed again. "Open."

"Okay, I'll try, but you'll have to show me." Before I could follow, he vanished through the wall again. "Excuse me," I said, squeezing through the crush at the door.

Annette and Karl followed, everyone else trailing behind them.

I thought I'd lost him until I went down a few of the steps and spotted him in the entryway.

He stood by a glass display case and pointed at the top shelf. "Open."

I hurried to him. "The case? You want the case open?"

We had a couple of new people join the group. The crowd behind me was taking pictures like crazy. Wonderful.

Samuel shook his head and pointed again.

I scanned the case. The only thing that high that I could open was the witch bottle. I stilled. Witch bottles were historically filled with urine or hair or fingernails, and they always had pins or nails in them, supposedly to trap a witch inside. Fine. Whatever. But this sweet boy was no more a witch than I was a warlock. Had the bottle somehow trapped him? Anchored him to the house?

I turned to Karl. He was good-looking and rather nerdy. A dark-haired, college-aged kid with a clear affinity for all things supernatural. "Could a witch bottle somehow trap a small boy?"

He blinked in thought. "I don't know. I mean, maybe. It's all so speculative. I never believed a witch bottle could trap a witch, but if it can, why not a boy?"

I got to my knees, and Samuel put his hand on my face again. He had perfect pale skin and a soft, ethereal glow, rather like Ruthie. I had to try.

People were whispering all around us, the newbies trying to ascertain what was going on. The more experienced in the group, those who'd been with us since the beginning five minutes ago, were explaining. They jostled and volleyed for a better view.

There was nothing I could do about that now. "Karl, can I open the bottle?"

"Sure." He put on a pair of gloves, brought out a set of keys, and opened the case. "But I have to say, it's been opened before."

"Really? I don't know what to tell you. He wants it open," I said with a shrug.

He shrugged back at me.

Annette knelt beside me. "Deph, maybe we should think about this."

"What do you mean?"

"I mean, maybe he only looks like a kid. Maybe he's, I don't know, a demon seed who's going to open the gates of hell and suck us all in."

The corners of the boy's little mouth turned down.

I almost laughed. "One thing I've learned—quite recently, in fact—is that I can feel the difference between a malevolent spirit and a friendly one." I looked back at him. "There is not a mean bone in this baby's body."

"Because he has no bones!" she whispered through clenched teeth, making a valid argument.

Someone nearby chuckled softly, a deep, exhilarating sound. Roane.

I glanced around in surprise but didn't see him. But I'd recognize that laugh anywhere.

"I mean, who's to say what you'll release?" Annette asked.

"Karl said the bottle has already been opened."

"They even had to replace the cork a few years back," he added.

"See? What harm will my opening it do?"

"Have you not been paying attention for the last six months?" Nette asked.

"Not really, no."

Karl gave me a pair of gloves.

I put them on, and he handed me the bottle, a small ceramic cask in the shape of a gourd vase. I took it, gave my BFF one final challenging glare, and popped the cork. So to speak. And... nothing happened. Unless you counted the room filling with a foul stench that reminded me of old urine and vinegar.

The onlookers groaned. A few of them left.

"Wow." I quickly pressed the cork back on and waved a hand in front of my face.

"That didn't happen last time." Karl held a sleeve over his nose as he took the bottle back and replaced it.

I looked around for Samuel. But he'd vanished. "He's gone!" I stood and turned in a circle before whimpering.

"Serves you right," Annette said. Then she gagged. "I threw up a little in my mouth."

"Serves you right back, missy."

Before we left for lunch, I searched for Samuel again. I even checked under tables and called his name. Nothing.

"I just hope you didn't just unleash a deadly plague upon the people of the land," Annette said as we hurried to the restaurant.

"Fingers crossed." Bummed about losing Samuel, I vowed to come back every day for the rest of my life if I had to. Then a thought hit me. "Hey, maybe I really did set him free. Maybe he, you know, crossed to the other side."

"That would be amazing."

"No, it wouldn't. I'll never see him again."

"Defiance," she said, clearly appalled.

"I know." I was appalled too. "But I still want to see him again. He's so beautiful, Nette."

She put her arm in mine and pulled me closer. "Like me?"

"Exactly like you."

SIX

*If overthinking situations burned calories
I'd be dead.*
—Meme

The Ugly Mug Diner, a restaurant on Essex, was known for its mimosas, homemade sodas, and mimosas. Mostly its mimosas.

Before we stepped inside the restaurant, I felt a sense of serenity, like a cool breeze on a hot summer day. After we stepped inside, that serenity was bolstered by a surge of relief as I spotted a certain blond-haired boy grinning at me from behind a patron wearing a *Hocus Pocus* sweater. He waved and then took off, disappearing into the madding crowd.

Smiling, I let Nette lead me toward a table of ten women and two men.

Ruthie's coven stood, all of them, and waited for us to make our way over.

"Hey, guys." Annette gestured toward me, putting me on display like Vanna White turning over the next letter. "This is Defiance. Defiance, this is the Salem Arc of the Coven-ant."

"We are not called the Arc of the Coven-ant," an older woman said.

Annette looked at me. "Only because I haven't convinced them yet."

I smiled and offered a sheepish wave, especially since they all stood there, half with their mouths slightly ajar and half with them open to the floor.

"You'll have to forgive my coven mates," the woman said. She had red hair and a wisdom about her. "They've never met a charmling." She held out her hand. "I'm Serinda."

"Defiance," I said when I took it.

"Yes, I know." She chuckled.

"Right. You've met a charmling before?"

"Goddess, no." She shook her head. "I've never even... well, I never dreamed I'd meet one. Or that we would have one right here in Salem." A telltale wetness suddenly shimmered between her lashes. "You can't imagine what this means to us. We are blessed and honored."

"Thank you," I said, a little overwhelmed. "I'm the one who's honored."

"Oh, posh." She waved a dismissive hand. "Let me introduce you." She went around the table and shared the names of each member of the coven.

I didn't even try to retain them. That was a skill I'd never possessed, even on my best days, and it didn't look like that was something my magics were interested in changing. I'd already forgotten woman number three.

After Serinda introduced the last member, an early

twenty-something bundle of nerves named Minerva with long dark hair and a nail-biting habit, I waved an overall greeting. "Thank you all so much for watching over me while I... napped."

They laughed softly, completely reverent if not a little starstruck.

It was a new feeling—I'd never struck anyone with a star in my life.

We sat and chatted, and I quickly caught onto the routine. They took turns. One sat beside me for a few minutes for a more intimate introduction and then another took their place. On and on through ordering and lunch and coffee.

Serinda stayed by my side, and I got the feeling she was the leader of this here gang-o-witches. I liked her, and she kept me grounded through all the polite conversation.

"Is Salem always this crowded?" I asked Serinda and my newest acquaintance, an older woman whose name began with an *L*. At least, I thought it was an *L*.

Serinda scanned the area. "Goddess, no. It gets much worse." When I wilted over that news, she chuckled. "Our biggest tourist season is in September and October. The closer to Halloween, the thicker the crowds. The locals know to steer clear of downtown for a couple of months. The rest of the year, it's a pretty constant flow of visitors but not nearly like now."

I looked out onto the street, at the leaves that were just beginning to change. "I like it here."

She smiled. "We like that you like it here."

I studied my coffee, then lowered my voice. "I don't think I'm staying."

My words didn't faze her, as though she'd already known what was in my heart before I did. "You do what you need to do, Defiance Dayne. None of us can know what you're going through. What having something like this thrust upon you must feel like. Even your grandmother, as much as she likes to think she knows everything, can't imagine."

A gracious smile spread across my face. "Thank you for understanding."

"Of course, dear. Also, chocolate helps." She nudged the last brownie my way.

I couldn't help but break off a bite.

There was only one coven member left to talk with. The nervous one named Minerva. I worried I was all out of small talk.

Annette, however, was doing more than her fair share with one of the male witches, a handsome kid in his very early twenties, if that, with thick muddy curls and shimmering eyes that made him look like he was about to cry all the time. The effect was rather mesmerizing.

About three seconds before I was going to suggest we head back to the house—I had an escape to plan—Annette turned to me with a curious frown and asked from halfway across the table, "You went to bed with your boots on?"

I blinked at her. "This is just hitting you?"

"Why would you go to bed with your boots on?"

I opened my mouth to answer, but nothing came out. Instead, I scrambled for a plausible explanation that did not involve nibbling. Or, more importantly, the fact that I may have lit all those candles with my nonexistent powers. "I-I saw a mouse." It wasn't a total lie. I had seen one in Ruthie's chamber.

Annette's mouth flattened across her pretty face. "Please. Last time you saw a mouse, you named it Howard and tried to catch it so the two of you could be together forever."

Gawd, did she forget anything?

She narrowed her eyes to accusatory blades of silver. "There is only one thing on Earth that would have you running and jumping under the covers like a kindergartener afraid of the monster under the bed."

The rest of the table paid rapt attention to our conversation, as though hanging on our every word. Thank God this one was fairly innocuous. Compared to most.

"Maybe I *am* afraid of the monster under the bed."

"After what happened in the attic? You're not afraid of anything. You're like a superhero, only braver."

"You didn't see my exit."

"Either way, that's not it." She pointed a finger at me in suspicion.

"Fine, then. What is it?" I asked, the challenge in my voice blatant.

She leaned toward me.

I leaned toward her.

She glowered.

I glowered.

She studied me for a few suspenseful seconds, trying to summon her nonexistent psychic powers, before her bow-shaped mouthed formed a perfect circle. She reared back with a gasp. "You hooked up with Roane!"

Every pair of peepers at our table—and a few not at our table—landed on me. Some in shock. Some in curiosity, their grins reflecting their desire to hear more. And some in a poorly disguised fit of jealousy. Well, one, actually. The skittish one biting her nails, Minerva.

"I most certainly did not."

"You totally did! If you hadn't, you would've denied it with regret not indignation."

Holy hell, she was good. Maybe she really was psychic. "Define hook up."

"Defiance Dayne," she said, her voice edged with a warning. Not that she could do a freaking thing, but it was adorable just the same.

"Okay." I caved. "Maybe just a little."

"How little?" Cupping her chin, she rested an elbow on the table, her expression turning dreamy.

The fact that we were discussing my love life in front of the entire coven, after only just meeting them, would not fully sink in until later.

I hedged. A lot. And I wasn't a hedger. "We just... you don't understand. He set up this test, and there were candles everywhere, but I told him I wanted to test him first, and he was like *bring it*, and then he gave me cake."

She grinned. "I bet he did."

"No. Not like that. There was some nibbling, but that's as far as it went."

"Nibbling?" She clasped her hands together. "You guys are at the nibbling stage?"

"Is that a real stage?"

A male voice intruded into our heart-to-heart just when it was getting good. A male voice edged with impatience. And derision. And a hint of disgust. "Are you Defiance Dayne?"

We turned to a large man, with thinning brown hair, standing beside our table. He wore tan coveralls, a ruddy complexion, and a toxic frown.

"I am," I said, not offering any more than that.

"I've left you three messages." His voice reminded me of the edge of a dull knife.

Annette bolted to attention. "Sorry. Defiance has been under the weather—"

"Yes," he interrupted. "Until yesterday."

How could he possibly know that?

"I called seven times."

"Oh, I'm so sorry," she said. "The phone was ringing off the hook, and it's so loud. I unplugged it for a couple of days to allow Defiance a chance to rest."

I reached over the table and set my hand on top of hers. She had zero reason to apologize or explain anything to this man. His demeanor spoke volumes.

He stopped and scanned the table as though just realizing we weren't alone. "I have a situation I'd like your help with." He changed his attitude, though not by much.

"We aren't taking on clients just yet." Annette squeezed my hand.

"I thought you took over for the witch," he said to me, his earlier frown marching back.

"I haven't done anything of the kind."

I could practically hear his teeth grinding when he bit down. "It won't take long. I have money, since that's all you people seem to care about."

I was just about to launch into a tirade—one I had no hope of nailing, since I had no clue who this man was or what he wanted—when a calmness came over me. I looked past the giant and saw Roane walking toward our table, his stride full of purpose.

He didn't stop when he walked up behind the man. He strode past him, leaned down, and pressed his lips to mine.

The kiss lasted barely the span of a heartbeat, but it was enough to steal my thunder. And my breath. And my complete train of thought.

He kept his face close to mine. "Ready?"

"As I'll ever be."

He rose up and addressed everyone at the table. "Ladies, gentlemen, lunch is on me, but I need to steal these two away if you don't mind."

They shook their heads indulgently. A few gazed lovingly. Serinda gave him a wicked grin. "Thank you, Mr. Wildes."

He took her hand and kissed her knuckles. "Anytime, Ms. McClain."

She shook her head. "Incorrigible."

After gracing her with the sexiest wink I'd ever seen, he helped me to my feet and led me and Annette away without so much as a glance at the man.

I risked a quick peek just in time to see ire spark around him as he watched us go. "I'm going to lose count," I said, as Roane held open the door.

"Count?"

We walked toward a public parking area. "How many times you've come to my rescue, especially considering the fact that I've only known you five days. If you leave out my six-month dream-a-thon."

"How many times has it been?" Annette ticked them off on her fingers. "He rescued you when your ex and his horrible mother were trying to weasel Percy away from you."

"And when my powers emerged," I said, remembering how Roane had held me under the cold shower while my powers burned me from the inside out.

"And when he got stabbed saving our lives from that guy who wanted to kill his girlfriend for leaving him." She added another finger.

"If we keep going at this rate"—I weaved through a group of tourists—"you may not live much longer."

"You're worth the risk." He kept his hand on the small of my back as we walked. His warmth seeped through my sweater and blouse.

"Were you following us?"

"Not us," Annette said. "You. General's orders."

"What?" That threw me. "What general?"

Annette grinned. "That would be the silver-haired vixen living in the basement."

I rolled my eyes. "Roane, you do not have to watch me."

"Because it's so taxing?" he asked.

"Yes. You have things to do, I'm sure."

"Not today, I don't."

A rush of excitement laced over my skin.

"So..." Nette glanced over her shoulder at us. "About the nibbling."

Leave it to Annette to douse that excitement with a hefty dose of humiliation. Thankfully, we got in the car alone, and Roane followed us home on his Harley. I was nigh hyperventilating from watching him in the rearview. Muscle looked good on him in every way imaginable.

"You know"—Annette adjusted the mirror yet again —"some drivers like to use the rearview for their own, selfish purposes."

"Are you catching this?" I pulled down the sun visor, trying to see him in that mirror. "He's riding that Harley in his kilt."

"Duh. That's the selfish part. I want to see too." She'd brought her car from Arizona at some point in the last six months, a ruby-red Dodge Charger with a blacked-out hood. We'd had a lot of good times in that car. And a lot of tickets.

We pulled up to Percy and parked next to my vintage mint-green Volkswagen Beetle, aka the Bug. Annette didn't trust me to drive, as though I'd lost the ability in six months of abstinence.

Our neighbor, Parris Hampton, was out gardening. Which was ridiculous. Judging by her wardrobe and nails, Parris had never gardened in her life. Also, she paid a nice man named Rocko a small fortune to keep her yard looking pristine. If not other things. Rocko was built.

Bottom line? She was spying. Waiting for Annette and me to get back so she could get the scoop on where I'd been.

She waved when we got out.

"Hey, Parris!" I walked to the edge of Percy's property.

Parris lived in a mansion on one side of Percy. Her husband, Harris, lived in a mansion on the other side of Percy. It was weird, but I guess it worked for them.

"You look fantastic." Parris gestured toward me with her never-used trowel.

I wondered if she knew what it was for. "Thank you."

Roane must've parked behind the house. We heard his motorcycle growl and then shut off.

She pulled a wide-brim hat lower over her eyes. "I dropped by a couple of times, but you were asleep."

In the last two days, I had yet to ask my family what they'd told people. Frankly, there just weren't that many to tell, so it hadn't occurred to me to inquire. "Yes, they told me," I lied. "I appreciate it."

"Well, Ebola is a hard disease."

I blinked. "Ebola?"

Annette walked up and patted my back. "Doesn't she look great, considering?"

"She does," Parris agreed. "When you're feeling up to it, I'd love to share another bottle with you two. I don't get to girl talk often."

"Absolutely," Annette said. "But I think we should get Deph back to bed for now. Don't want to overdo it."

"Of course. I should probably go in. It looks like rain."

We said our goodbyes and headed inside. "Ebola? Are you kidding?"

Nette cringed. "Sorry. She ambushed me. I panicked."

"No worries. I'm telling everyone you're trying to kick heroin."

"That's fair."

Roane walked in from the kitchen, drying his hands on a towel. "Coffee's on if anyone wants some."

Annette looked at me. "Does he know me at all?"

He grinned at her. A sweet thing. Innocuous and sincere. But the grin he gave me when she turned to hang up her jacket bordered on feverish. It was full of longing and desire, like the wolf in him was hungry. I'd never met a man who could communicate so much with a single smile.

We followed the kilt-clad hottie into the kitchen.

Annette's laptop was perched on the breakfast table along with the pocket folder holding the messages. An ancient phone sat on the counter by the table, which was why she'd set up shop there. The glow still seeped out of the edges of the folder.

Roane poured us each a cup and joined us at the table.

I about ovulated. He never just sat with us like that.

Annette took a few sips and opened the folder. "I want to know who that man was," she said, suddenly determined. She brought out dozens of messages and spread them over the table.

"The man in the café? I do too."

"James Vogel," Roane offered. "I went to school with him."

It was so strange to imagine Roane growing up. Roane

as a teen. Roane in school. A school for humans. It was like he was above it all. But maybe that was only in my mind.

"He's an ass," she said.

"He always was. He was what one would call a nemesis."

"What?" I asked him, surprised.

"At first, he was just a bully, but it became much more than that over the years. Much more... volatile, until one day I had to..."

When he didn't finish, Annette asked, "Kick his ass?"

"Something like that."

"I'm sorry, Roane." No idea why, but I somehow felt responsible. He'd been made human from a wolf. I had done that to him. He didn't know the language or the customs or how to behave. Statistically, children with social challenges were bullied much more often, though I couldn't imagine he'd been bullied long. Still, how would I know? Maybe he went through hell. So many kids did. The unfairness broke my heart. The thought of Roane going through something like that threatened to swallow me whole.

The look he gave me hovered somewhere between gratitude and curiosity, as though he was trying to read my thoughts.

That would be so bad. I dropped my gaze to the messages.

"Here they are," Annette said. "James Vogel. He did call. I remember him now. He said he had a situation he would only discuss with you."

"When was this?"

She fanned through them again. "Okay, three messages. The first one was about a week ago. Then he called again the next day and again the day after that. That was a couple of days before you woke up. He was very determined but never would give a reason."

"Why would he stop calling after I woke up?"

"His niece," Roane said.

"His niece?" Annette and I asked simultaneously.

"The squirrely one. Minerva."

"From the coven?" Annette asked, appalled. "Only the coven knew about you. She was keeping tabs and told him you'd woken up?"

I tilted my head in doubt. "If that's so, why was he calling in the first place? He would've known I was asleep."

"True. But he didn't call for two days before you woke up. Maybe when you didn't return his calls, he asked her thinking that, since she was in a coven, she might know."

"Because all witches are psychically connected?" I joked.

She lifted a shoulder. "It would explain how he knew where to find you today."

"Or he's watching you," Roane said.

I gaped at him. "Is he?"

He paused and took a moment to scrutinize me. "He wouldn't still be alive if that were the case."

Please let him be kidding. Kind of.

"I'm just saying. You're very powerful. You need to pay closer attention to the vibes you're getting."

"Vibes?"

"Whatever you call it. The energies you feel. They could save your life."

I nodded. He had a point. "So, are we thinking this Minerva told him where to find us today?"

"She did seem really nervous," Annette said.

"She's always been skittish," Roane said. "But she doesn't usually chew her nails to the quick like that."

"You seem to know an awful lot about her," I said, ignoring the fact that it made me sound stupid and jealous. She was just a kid.

At least James Vogel's messages didn't glow. The one from before still did. Almost brighter now. More urgently. And another message glowed as well.

I knew it had to mean something, yet a part of me didn't want to know what. I couldn't get involved. I was leaving soon. I should be packing. Then again, where would I go? I didn't really want to drive all the way back to Arizona. Maybe I'd stay with my dads in Ipswich for a while. It was only a half hour away.

As Annette scooped up the messages again, one of the two that glowed fell from her grasp. Slowly, the letters started to glow too, like when I made a symbol in the air.

"What is that one?" I asked, pointing without touching it.

She picked it up and flipped it over. "Oh, yeah, it's from a man who wants a remedy for male pattern baldness."

"Seriously?" I leaned forward.

"Leonard Quinn." She held it out. "For the record, do we do that sort of thing?"

I shrugged.

Roane watched us way too nonchalantly, probably taking notes for Ruthie. The traitor.

"Wait, why that one?" she asked, eyeing me carefully.

"No reason." Why would a message about male pattern baldness be glowing? My powers made no sense sometimes.

"Yeah, right. We need to talk about Love's reaction to you in her shop."

"Who says?" I asked.

"Who says what?"

"We need to talk about her reaction."

A knock sounded at the door just in time.

I lifted a shoulder. "It'll have to wait either way."

"Fine. But we still need to talk about it."

I stood and started for the door just as something brushed past me. I looked down and smiled. "Samuel."

He ran up to me and raised his arms like he wanted me to lift him up.

I knelt to him and held out my hand.

He put his in mine, but it slid through.

"I wish I could pick you up more than anything in the world."

When another knock reverberated through the house, he pointed toward the foyer. "Sir."

I followed him. "Is that who's at the door?"

He shook his head. When we got to the foyer, he turned to point up to the balcony.

I didn't see anything.

Neither did he, I guess, because he frowned and gestured for me to follow him.

The knock came louder this time.

"Let me answer the door real quick, okay?" By the time I got the sentence out, his attention had shifted to the cat that sauntered by like he owned the place.

Samuel tried to pet Ink, but the animal darted off. The boy followed. Even a battle-scarred cat like Ink didn't stand a chance with a ghost child taking a shine to him.

Laughing, I opened the door to a familiar face, clenched in a gruesome mess of anger and derision. "Your phone is still unplugged," said James Vogel as he wedged his way inside.

SEVEN

When people are dead, they don't know they're dead.
It's the same thing when people are stupid.
—Meme

At least, James Vogel *tried* to wedge his way inside.

The door didn't budge. He pressed a hand against it to open it farther. When nothing happened, he tried again, harder, this time with his shoulder. Nary an inch gave under his command.

I peeked behind the door to find Percy had barricaded it. I gave him a quick thumbs-up behind my back.

When James Vogel stepped closer, trying to barrel through me, I held my ground as well. "Mr. Vogel, if you'll just tell me what it is that you need—"

"Minerva said you're different." If his reddening complexion was any indication, his anger was well on its way to a reprisal.

Seriously, how could anyone live with such volatile

emotions twenty-four seven? Maybe it was a hormonal imbalance.

"She told me you could do things the rest of them can't."

Or an alcohol imbalance.

"You can do anything."

He reeked of cheap whiskey.

"You can bring people back from the dead."

And the cologne he wore... Wait. What did he just say?

"I lost someone."

Did he just say I could bring people back from the dead?

"There was an accident."

Like, literally?

"I want her back." His glare made it clear that saying "no" wasn't an option.

After a moment of speechlessness, I asked, "Your niece told you I could bring people back from the dead?"

"Yes. She said you did it with Ruthie."

What the hell? Weren't covens supposed to be like Vegas? What happened at the crossroads stayed at the crossroads? I just figured it was an unwritten rule.

Minerva made my decision not to help him that much easier. I'd make sure the girl would never join another coven as well, and I would tell Ruthie that as soon as I could. But first I had to get rid of Jason Voorhees lurking on my front porch. For reals, he just needed a hockey mask.

I did the only thing I could think of on such short notice. I laughed. "And you believed her?"

Laughing was, apparently, the wrong approach when dealing with the self-absorbed.

He shoved on the door. When it still didn't give, his face morphed into an angry version of the Jason Voorhees mask.

With a glower that could stop traffic, he reached for me, whether to push me back or to pull me out, I didn't know.

I stepped back and speared him with a glare. "Mr. Voorhees—"

"Vogel."

Oops.

"You need you to come with me." His voice sharpened into a scalpel.

"Even if I were practicing right now, which I'm not, and such a thing were possible, which it's not, I certainly couldn't do it."

His beefy hands curled into fists. But before he could do anything with them, something on the ground caught his attention.

We glanced down and watched as vines slithered across the porch like snakes. They curled up the walls and up my legs. To the regular joe, they had to be like a bad acid trip, but James Vogel seemed a little more knowledgeable than most.

He stumbled back with a scowl.

My cue to close the door. I slammed it shut, then peeked around the bay window.

He backed off the porch and studied Percy like he was trying to figure out a way around him. Definitely the creepiest Jason Voorhees I'd ever met.

"Thank you, Percy." I turned around.

Roane was behind me in the foyer. He'd knelt to pet Ink, but I could sense the tension from where I stood, as though his muscles were coiled, ready for a fight. He smiled at Samuel.

"You can see him?" I asked.

He nodded. "Of course."

"Thank goodness." I knelt with him, partly to pet Ink

but mostly to get closer to the blond-haired, blue-eyed angel I wished desperately to hold. "I was worried he was a figment of my imagination." I left out the part where I'd wondered that very thing when I'd first met Roane. For about half a second, anyway.

"He's not going to give up." Roane tipped his head toward the door.

I released an annoyed sigh. "He thinks I can bring someone back from the dead."

"You can, but that's not the point."

"Ruthie was different. I didn't do that on purpose. I wouldn't even know where to start."

"Still not the point."

"Okay, Mr. Know-It-All, what is the point?" I tore my gaze off the kid and repositioned it on the deity stroking the cat.

If not for Roane, Ink would've bolted. He wanted nothing to do with the kid. In all fairness, Samuel's touch was a little cool. But the poor kid just wanted to pet the creature. I understood the desire. Sometimes, I just wanted to pet Roane.

"He's not going to take no for an answer." He stared at the door, which was now vine-free.

I could see the wheels in his brain spinning. "He'll get the message eventually." But like Roane, I didn't really believe that.

Something brushed past me, and Samuel disappeared.

I glanced up to see Ruthie waiting quietly near the staircase, elegantly draped in a new dress that was no less magical than the first. She didn't look a second past sixty—if that—though I knew her to be closer to eighty.

I jumped to my feet. "You're out."

Roane stood too.

"Did you feel that?" She gazed up at the balcony.

"Did you just brush past me?" I asked her.

Confused, she turned toward me. "Where were you just now?"

"Here. We went into town, but—"

"What did you do there?"

Annette wandered out. "We met with your coven."

"You brought something back with you." But Ruthie wasn't looking at Nette, she was looking at me. "Something very dark."

"Oh, well, Jason Vorhees came to the door. He was very angry."

"No. Not that," she said absently, missing the reference entirely. Did ghosts even watch horror movies? "Where else did you go in town?"

Roane was eerily silent.

"We went to the Witch House," Annette said.

"That's it." Ruthie's expression turned grave. "Did you open the witch bottle?"

"Yes." Nette's warning came back to me in the form of pins and needles pricking the back of my neck, but I brushed it off. "Why?"

"Defiance, you never open a witch bottle."

"Ruthie, I can't imagine I'm the first person in four hundred years to open that bottle." And I hadn't been. Karl told me so."

"No, but you're the first witch. Certainly the first charmling. You set them free."

Them? Them who? "If you mean the men and women persecuted during the Salem Witch Trials, they were hardly real witches."

"A witch bottle captures all sorts of malevolent spirits.

Not just witches. And they are bound for all eternity to any witch who sets them free."

Nette gave me an I-told-you-so look.

Which I ignored. "What does that mean?"

"It means," Ruthie said, "that any spirit you set free is now attached to you."

"Great." Like I didn't already have a behemoth of baggage to drag around.

"If there were any malevolent spirits in the bottle, they'll come after you. You're the only thing anchoring them to this plane."

"See?" Fed up, I stalked past her, taking the other set of stairs. "And you wonder why I'm done with all of this."

Somehow, Ink beat me to my room and lay sprawled out on the bed.

I took out my suitcase and started packing while he watched. I'd come to Salem with exactly five outfits. But while I'd been KOed, my dads had the rest of my belongings shipped here, so at least I had a few outfits to choose from.

"Defiance." Ruthie stood at the threshold to what was essentially her room. "What's going on?"

"Nothing. I just need to get away for a few days to a place that's not filled with magical powers or malevolent beings that want me dead."

"Sweetheart—"

"If nothing else, I'll stay at a hotel for a few days. I just need to get my bearings." I tossed underwear and a couple of T-shirts into my suitcase. "I'll decide what to do from there."

"Sweetheart." She was beside me, her hand on my arm. "First, you can't go anywhere that doesn't have a magical presence."

"Of course I can. Most places on the planet don't have magic hanging in the air like string lights."

"No, I mean, *you* can't. Personally. Because just your being there will change everything. You are the magical presence. You change every place you visit."

I sank onto the bed next to Ink, holding two bras in one hand and a sock in the other. "I told you, I lost my powers."

Annette knocked on my open door. "Can I join you?"

I waved her inside with the bras.

She climbed onto the bed to pet the cat, who was not in the mood to be fondled. Not that she let his grumpy disposition deter her.

Ruthie sat beside me. "And second, if there are malevolent beings after you, there's no safer place on Earth than this house."

I dropped the bras and socks on the bed and moved to get up.

Ruthie took my hand to stop me. "What is all of this really about?"

I couldn't decipher exactly what I'd seen in my dreams, but I knew it was bad. I also knew I had to tell her. It was bound to come out, so why not now? Glancing over my shoulder, I worried about Annette's take on what I was about to say.

"Defiance," Ruthie said.

I turned back to her. "Something tried to get me while I was"—I waved toward where I'd been suspended above the bed—"out."

Annette stilled.

"And before you try to convince me I was only dreaming—"

"What kind of something?" Annette asked.

"A dark kind of something searching for me, and I had

to hide." I shifted on the bed. "I think Percy kept it at bay. I think he fought it off."

"I know." Concern knit Ruthie's graceful brows. "That was why he wouldn't let any of us in."

"Not even you?" I asked her.

"No." She dropped her gaze and shook her head, and I had the strangest feeling she wasn't being completely honest. "He was probably focusing all of his energies on keeping you safe. On keeping the warlock out."

A cold dread crept across my skin. "It was a warlock?"

"It had to be." She stood and paced, her jaw jutting out in anger. "Those sons of bitches."

I'd never heard her curse, but I liked it. Based on Annette's struggle to keep a grin in check, she did too.

"Did they find me?" I wilted at the thought. "The spell we did? It didn't work?"

"It worked. It worked like a charm, for lack of a better phrase. They did, however, find you in the dream world and tried to glean information as to your physical location. But they obviously have no idea who you are or where you are, or they'd already be here. They don't know you're my granddaughter. They don't know to look here. So clearly, they didn't get much." She looked up at the vines. "Thank you, Percival." Then she turned back to me. "And you. Clever girl."

"Damn straight, she is," Annette said.

I shook my head, adamant they were wrong. "I didn't do anything but hide."

"That was all you could've done." Finished pacing, she sat beside me again. "I don't know how you managed to keep them away for so long, Defiance, but..." She tucked my hair behind my ear. "Is that why?"

I bristled. Not at the hair tucking. That was sort of nice. "Is what why?"

"Is that why you're insisting you've lost your powers?"

"I'm insisting I've lost my powers because I've lost my powers."

"And why you're leaving?" she continued, completely ignoring what I'd said.

I decided to study my boots. In great detail. The curve over the toes. The stitching. The buckle at the ankle. After a long moment, I said aloud what I'd been afraid to even contemplate. "They're coming for me."

She squeezed my arm. "I know, sweetheart. I also know that if you leave, you'll be a thousand times more vulnerable."

Samuel came in and sat on the bed, right beside an oblivious psychic, and tried to pet Ink again.

Ruthie melted and put a hand over her heart. "He is adorable."

He struggled to get a good grip on Ink, who twisted and turned right out of his hold. It was like watching a wrestling match where the underdog never even had a chance. Poor kid.

"Samuel, when you asked me to open the witch bottle, was it because someone was inside?" Because along with the warlock—or seven—after me, I had a malevolent being—or seven—from the witch bottle attached to me. For all eternity. And I was feeling a little overcommitted.

Samuel nodded.

It was interesting that while he seemed to understand everything I said to him, he didn't talk much, his verbal communication skills clearly still emerging. "Samuel, who was inside?"

"Sir," he said, before scrambling after Ink, who'd gotten fed up and raced off.

"Hold up there, mister." I rushed around the bed before the boy vanished again. "There was only one man inside the bottle?"

Giggling at my audacity, he stopped short. "Mm-hm. Sir."

How bad could one malevolent being be? Even if his name was Sir. "Did Sir tell you to have me open it? The bottle?"

Samuel nodded, feigned to the left, then rushed around to my right.

I tried to grab him, genius that I was, but he disappeared through the wall, genius that he was. "Holy cow, he's fast."

"The little boy?" Annette asked, looking on longingly. "I want to see him."

"Well, as soon as I get that supernatural camera I ordered off Amazon, I'll set up a photo shoot pronto."

Annette shot me a fake glare. "At least you haven't lost your powers of smartassery."

I laughed and sat on the bed again. "Okay, so let's do inventory."

Ruthie sat on a chair that had my robe and a pair of leggings thrown over the back.

"If nothing else," I said, "I have at least one warlock after me. At least one malevolent being attached to me. And at least one unstable human wanting me to raise the dead. Oh, and let's not forget the creepy dungeon. We need to figure out where it came from. I mean, is Percy in danger of caving in?"

"I don't think so," Ruthie said. "It had to have been there when they built the house."

"Then why are we just now finding it?"

"Because of you." She graced me with a patient smile. "You're the finder of lost things."

"No." I held up an index finger. "You are the finder of lost things. That's what you did for the people of Salem for decades."

"And now it's passed to you. I never even knew that cavern existed. You're the finder of lost things on steroids."

Nette laughed at Ruthie's choice of hip words.

"Okay." I threw my hands up. "Let's table that for now. What do we do about the other two?"

"If you had your powers"—her emphasis on *if* couldn't have been heavier—"I would say we need to do a little casting." She got up and strolled to the door. "But since they're gone, possibly forever, and you're leaving anyway, I guess there's nothing we can do."

"You're funny." I crossed my arms. "By the way, what in the ever-loving hell is in the attic?"

She whirled around, her lids rounding for a brief second before she recovered. "What do you mean?"

I pursed my lips. "There's a darkness in one of those rooms, and I'm willing to bet you know what it is. Is it a warlock?"

"A darkness?"

"Yes. A very angry, very aggressive darkness. It almost knocked down one of the doors. I didn't check the other rooms, but—"

"It can't get through. There's no reason to worry about it."

"Why can't it get through?" Annette asked at the same time I said, "*What* can't get through?" I mean, it was the more pertinent question.

"I don't know," Ruthie said. "I never knew there was anything in those rooms. I can feel malevolence like you can, but I've never felt anything from the attic. We've tried opening those doors several times over the years."

"Did you try a locksmith?" Nette asked, trying to be helpful.

Revisiting her place on the chair, Ruthie looked at both of us. "We've tried everything. Locksmiths. Plasma cutters. Sledgehammers. We even tried small-charge demolitions. The doors are magically sealed. Nothing can get in or out, and I rather think there is a good reason for it, so we stopped trying."

"Holy crap, Ruthie. Who lived here before you did? Were they witches too?"

"This house has been in our family for generations, so yes."

"Okay, let me rephrase. Who was powerful enough to cast a spell like that?"

"To be honest, no one. None of our ancestors ever possessed the power or skill to create a spell that would remain absolutely impenetrable for decades."

"Then who could've done it? Someone who lived here before our family took possession? You know, in a non-ghostly way."

"This house was built in the early 1800s, and it's always belonged to us. We're one of only a handful of families in the entire state to have kept control of a property for over two hundred years. And we've owned the land even longer."

"Then who?" I asked.

She bowed her head. "You."

I frowned at her. "I don't understand."

She came over to the bed and sat on the edge with me.

Annette scooted closer, caught up in the intrigue.

"You're a charmling, and your lineage goes all the way

back to Mesopotamia," Ruthie said, as if that cleared it right up.

"Still not processing."

"I think that you somehow went into the past and sealed those rooms."

The hairs on the back of my neck perked right up. "And I think you've seriously overestimated the scope of the abilities I no longer have."

Nette inched even closer, until she was practically sitting on my lap.

"You may think I'm crazy, Defiance, but I just know it was you," Ruthie said. "I think I know how, but I don't know why."

"How?" Nette's eyes widened.

"My theory is that Defiance has access to all of the witches in her direct line going back thousands of years."

"Access?" I tugged absently at my earlobe.

"Yes. You can, how should I say it, *summon* them to help you out when you need it?"

"How do you know?"

"Research. There being so little known about charmlings, I've had to dig. But I found a few accounts from eyewitnesses. It's the only way to explain how you were able to pull something like that off."

In all honesty, we didn't know for certain I'd pulled off anything. "And when would I have done this?"

She lightly tapped her lips in thought. "If my calculations are correct, you did it when you were three."

"Three," I said, even more doubtful than I'd already been.

"Yes."

"As in years old?"

"Exactly."

"And I did this because...?"

"Like I said, I never figured that part out. But the presence you felt could explain a lot."

"Ruthie," Annette said, clearly having some trouble with this as well. "What makes you think she did it?"

"It's all in the book." Ruthie looked at me like I was the crazy one.

I felt very attacked. There were levels of crazy. Layers. It wasn't like I was the absolute worst. And hey, hadn't she just claimed crazy for herself a few seconds ago for even bringing all this up? I mean—

"And it's in the video," she added. "You never finished either of them, did you?"

My hackles rose. "I've been a little asleep."

"You woke up days ago."

"Yesterday," I reminded her. "Evening. Literally twenty-four hours ago."

"And we needed mani-pedis," Annette added, ever so helpful.

"What video?" I asked. When her only answer was to purse her lips, I turned and slid my laptop off the nightstand. "I was just finishing them." Honestly, it was like high school all over again with all the homework she assigned. "That's why Annette came in here. To finish watching them with me."

"Yep." She backed me up. Then ruined it by whispering, "What videos?"

"*The* videos," I said from between clenched teeth, as though Ruthie couldn't hear me.

When Ruthie died, she had left me a series of videos to watch. Then I pulled her out of the veil. I just figured I didn't have to watch them anymore with her being back and all. I was wrong. Apparently, in Fraulein Goode's class, you watched all the videos whether Fraulein Goode was dead or not.

I opened the laptop and clicked the folder I'd colored pink. It opened to four files. One was the link to Ruthie's message, which basically was her chatting with us from the great beyond, because apparently they have Wi-Fi there.

"Okay, we watched that one," I said, pretending to check it off. "And that one." I checked off the one titled *Missing Child*. It was the one of me finding a boy—finding Roane—for his grieving mother. It was an amazing video. I'd learned how to use my power to find things by watching it.

There were two more videos: *Goodbye* and *Licked*.

"Pick *Licked*," Nette begged. "Please pick *Licked*."

Out of the two, it did sound the most promising. I moved the cursor—

"Watch *Goodbye*," the Fraulein said.

—and double-clicked on *Goodbye*. "Fine, but it doesn't sound nearly as fun." I scooted against the headboard, and Annette snuggled close.

The last video we'd watched, the one of me saving Roane, had been filmed at night. It had been hard to get a sense of the colors and the environment. This one had been filmed during the day. Early morning, if I had to guess.

Sun shone brightly through the huge plate glass in Percy's front parlor, where two men stood. My dads and their handsome faces. Forty years younger, with horrible haircuts, but still, they were the same.

A younger version of Ruthie, probably in her early forties, walked into the parlor carrying a sleeping little girl—aka me. I recognized myself from the earlier video. She handed me over to them along with a duffle bag. "This has her favorite stuffed animal, a cat named Clam Chowder, her pajamas, and her favorite sippy cup." Her voice broke.

Tears burned the backs of my eyes. This was the big day. The day she had given me up.

"Gigi?" I woke up in the video, though sleep still clung to my face. "I haduh lock the doors for a long time ago so Bead-uh couldn't get out." Laying my head against Dad's shoulder, I fell back asleep.

"Okay, sweet girl," Ruthie said.

I remembered none of this.

"I've got you, cariña," Dad said.

Papi rubbed my back and lifted a blanket to cover me all the way over my head.

"These are all the documents." Ruthie handed them a folder. "You adopted her through Sacred Heart Adoption Services." Her voice cracked again.

Dad gave her a minute before asking, "You did the spell?" in the same soft accent he still had now.

"I did." She dabbed her nose with a handkerchief. "They won't find her as long as I'm alive."

"Ruthie," Papi said. "You can't imagine what this means to us."

"I can, actually." Her shoulders shook as Papi drew her into a deep hug.

"We will protect her with our lives," Dad said.

As they walked to the front door, Percy shook beneath their feet, clearly not wanting me to go. Tiny me poked my head out from under the blanket and waved sleepily at him.

I wanted to curl into a ball right then and there. Did they realize just what they'd promised my grandmother? Did they understand the dangers that awaited them had I been found? I didn't know. But I did know that they probably had no idea what happened after Ruthie closed Percy's door.

She sank to the floor, her heart clearly broken, and cried.

Trying to get control of my own emotions, the ones cinching my throat closed, I glanced over the screen at Ruthie. "Who's filming?"

The shy smile that spread over her face told me everything. It was Chief Houston Metcalf. They'd been seeing each other for decades, and she clearly still had feelings for him. Which was why it made less than zero sense why she'd banish him from her life now. Something else was up with that.

In the video, the chief laid down the camera and went to her. The only thing in the frame was a shot through the front window out to the driveway. I watched Dad strap me into a car seat before car seats were mandatory while I listened to Ruthie cry in the background.

The current Ruthie made a similar sound near the end of the bed.

I handed the laptop to Annette. "I'm sorry, Gigi." The old endearment just slipped out. But it was time.

Ruthie pressed a hand to her mouth as she took in what I'd said, then threw her arms around my shoulders, and I fell into her hug. "None of this was your fault, sweetheart. You were born to greatness. It wasn't a choice."

"But you did everything to keep me safe. I'm so grateful for you." I looked up, over her shoulder. "And for you, Percy."

Ruthie pulled me in tight for a long moment, then leaned back to look at me. She brushed a strand of hair off my face.

I swiped at a stray tear and struggled to stay focused. "In the video, when I said I locked the doors, you think that meant I went back in time and did it with a supernatural spell to keep *Bead-uh* inside?" Whoever Bead-uh was. The mysteries wouldn't stop piling up. At this rate, I'd need a pair of supernatural waders.

She nodded. "I do."

"Why? I mean, how could you possibly come to that conclusion?"

She lifted her head. "Because, before that day, sweetheart, there was no attic. There were no doors. There were no gables."

I stilled. "And then there were six? Just out of the blue?"

"Yes. If you look at pictures of when the house was first built, there are six gables. Even the original plans show them, yet I couldn't remember them being there until that day. And neither could Percy."

"What about the chief?"

"He remembers them. He even had a memory of the first time he saw the house. He was riding his bike past it when he was a kid, and he fell in love with the gables."

"Wow. Maybe you just, you know, overlooked them."

She laughed, not even bothering to entertain the idea.

"You realize that doesn't actually prove anything."

"It does to me. And it did to Percival too. Oh, and just in case you needed one more witness, do you remember meeting Serinda today?"

"Yes. She's amazing. Fiery and funny and elegant like you."

Ruthie's expression shimmered with surprise. "She remembers as well. That's how we met. She stomped up to the house and demanded to know what magics I was doing to put six gables on a house of witches where anyone could see them."

"Sounds like her. Did she think the *muggles* would suspect?"

"Oh, no." Ruthie waved a dismissive hand. "She didn't care about that. She was upset that I'd used six gables instead of five. That I'd created a Star of David instead of a proper pentagram. Said it was an embarrassment to the witch community." She grinned as she thought back. "We've been best friends ever since."

"Did you tell her what you think really happened?"

"Oh, goodness, no. Not for years. Remember, I had you in hiding. I wasn't about to tell anyone about you. But after a couple of decades—"

"Decades?" Annette asked.

"—I knew I could trust her completely."

"And she remembers the house without the gables even now?"

"Yes. Exactly like me."

"It must be a witch thing," Annette said.

Ruthie agreed. "Whatever or whoever Bead-uh was, it was bad enough that a charmling summoned a witch from her past to cast a spell on the house just to lock it up. And, Defiance, you did all of that while in a state of suspended animation."

"After I changed Roane?"

"Yes."

"Okay," Annette said, obviously unsettled. "I think we should change the subject, being as Bead-uh lives right above us. Let's watch *Licked* now. As a palate cleanser."

Ruthie dove—a dive worthy of the Olympic swim team —toward the laptop. She slammed the lid closed.

Annette barely had time to save her fingers from being crushed alive.

"You know what?" Ruthie said, taking the laptop from her. "How about we save that one for later?"

I looked at Annette. "Oh, hell no," we said simultaneously.

Giggling like schoolgirls, we wrestled an old lady for a laptop that may or may not have porn on it.

"Okay," Ruthie said through our giggles. "But you have to promise me something."

"Anything!" Annette shouted, refusing to release her death grip on the laptop corner she'd claimed.

I had a corner too, but Ruthie had managed to retain control of two of the coveted triangles, making her the victor thus far. But the battle wasn't over. "Defiance?" she asked.

"I promise. Anything. What am I promising?"

Ruthie tightened her hold, her knuckles white. "That no matter what you hear, you will not let this sway your decision to stay."

I grinned. "Who says I'm staying?"

"You can't leave now," she said. "You have a gorgeous little boy to take care of."

I almost gasped aloud. I did. Then again... "Samuel followed me here. Who's to say he won't follow me wherever I go?"

She sobered, wiped her eyes, and sat up, relinquishing controlling interest of the laptop to smooth her hair and dress. Vanity had struck again. "Because..." she said, a sadness coming over her. "Because of what this house is made of."

I bolted upright. "I knew it! It's the salt, isn't it?"

She nodded. "This house was built with wood from several retired ships that spent years at sea, soaking in the salt and brine. Your ancestors repurposed them before it was a thing."

"Is that why they did it? The salt? The spirits?"

"It is. They used every kind of ship they could get their hands on. Wrecked merchant ships, a few fishing vessels, even a pirate ship confiscated by the government. But my favorite was an ancient Viking ship your ancestor bought from a tobacco farmer in Virginia."

I leaned back against the headboard. "Percy, I knew you were cool. But daaaang."

He hummed happily beneath us.

"Ruthie?" Another thought hit. "Could there have been spirits already attached to the ships before they became part of the house?" It made sense. Especially if the wood had come from shipwrecks.

"I would bet my life on it. Only I already lost it once, and I don't want to tempt fate."

"Is that why you can't leave?"

Percy hummed again.

"Most likely," Ruthie said. "And when a spirit somehow finds its way in, which is almost impossible without a host, it can't get back out."

"I'm the host. I brought Samuel in."

"That's my best guess, sweetheart."

"Okay." I thought about it for a bit but eventually promised, "I won't let this video sway me either way."

"Then I give you my permission to watch it. Just know, you may find it a little disturbing."

"Pfft." I blew out a breath, reclaimed my precious from Nette, and opened it again. "Try not washing your hair for six months. I'm a rock. Nothing fazes me now." I exchanged excited glances with Annette. "Ready?"

"Ready," she said with a naughty gleam in her eyes.

Gawd, we were such pervs. I clicked on the video.

"This happened right before we said goodbye that day," Ruthie said. "That's the only reason Houston got it on video."

Onscreen, Ruthie was bundling tiny me up. I was still

groggy from being in what I assumed was suspended anima-tion after performing the spell that changed Roane into, well, Roane. That meant it was soon after my mother had tried to take my powers. And Gigi had taken her life instead.

Ruthie's movements were hurried as she tried to button my pajama top and slide on my bunny slippers. She was an emotional mess. How could she not be? Losing both her daughter and her granddaughter in a matter of days. Possibly hours. I would've been a wreck as well.

"He's not a real boy anymore," the me in the video said, half asleep. "He only finks he is."

Was I talking about Roane?

"Who, baby?" Ruthie asked.

"The boy who died. He keeps licking me."

Ruthie stilled on the video.

I stilled in real life.

"Sweetheart, what do you mean? Who keeps licking you?" she asked.

"The boy who finks he's a boy, but he's not."

Ruthie looked back at the chief, who wasn't the chief quite yet, as he filmed, her face full of concern. "And he licks you?"

I nodded. "He licks my fingers when I'm asleep, because he's not a boy anymore. He doesn't remember he's dead. I keep telling him, but he keeps forgetting."

Ruthie looked up again. "I'll have Mark and Kerry keep an eye on her," she said, referring to my dads. "We can't put this off. I've already cast the spell."

Houston agreed, and the screen went black.

"That's it! I am so out of here!" Pushing the laptop toward Nette, I jumped off the bed and sprinted back to my suitcase.

EIGHT

If I'm ever known as the one who got away,
it will be from an asylum.
—Meme

Five minutes later, the suitcase temporarily forgotten, I stood in front of the bathroom mirror, my lungs still stuck in overdrive. "You're a rock, remember? Nothing fazes you." Not a lie when I'd said it to Ruthie earlier. Definitely a lie now. "Dead children licking my fingers? No, thank you. No. Nuh-uh. No siree bob."

Annette stood beside me, Lamaze-ing me through my panic attack.

"I didn't understand what you meant at first." Ruthie stood on my other side. "Not until I met a certain young man who could shapeshift into a wolf. Who'd once been a wolf."

"Roane," I said his name, calming just a little. The man had two polarizing effects on me. He either soothed my nerves or spiked my adrenaline. Most often it was the latter.

"Think about it," Ruthie said.

I was thinking about it. A two-ton truck couldn't stop me from thinking about it. Yes, I'd turned a wolf into a boy. But he'd been alive. "In the video, I said the little boy was dead."

"True. But I have a theory." She always had a theory. And, more often than not, it was right.

"I have a theory too," Annette said.

I looked at her expectantly.

She immediately backtracked. "Oh, no. I want to hear Ruthie's first. See if mine holds water."

"Then I shall proceed," Ruthie said. "From what I've been able to gather, to create a living being from something no longer living, you need spirit and flesh."

"Like when I brought you back from the veil."

"Yes."

I drew in a deep breath. "Okay."

"You did save that boy that night—something I didn't even consider until you saved me."

I squinted. "I'm kind of following you."

"Me too," Annette said. "Kind of."

"I think you unknowingly pulled his soul out of the veil. But that was only half the equation. You needed flesh. You needed a physical mass."

"The wolf cub?"

"Exactly." Her gaze held a hint of astonishment, like I was some amazing being she was just getting a glimpse of. Just beginning to understand. "You extracted the boy's spirit from the veil and used the wolf cub to recreate him."

"But why didn't Roane remember who he was? He only remembered being a wolf."

She crossed her arms. "Trauma."

"Of course," Annette said. "Think about what happened to him just before you changed him, Deph."

It was a horrible story. Roane's parents were in a violent custody battle. His father, in an unforgivable act of depravity to make his mother pay, to make her regret ever leaving him, killed his own son. By the time my magics found them, Roane the boy was already gone, so the magics turned the wolf into the boy. Or so I thought. Maybe there was more to it than that.

"It makes sense." Rather astonished myself, I turned and leaned against the sink. "Especially knowing what we know now with you. That pulling a spirit from the other side is possible."

"There are spirits wandering the Earth veil-free all the time. So why am I flesh as well?"

I chewed a thumbnail for a moment. "I had to use something living to create you." I could almost see the pride swelling inside her. "But if that's the case, Ruthie, what are you?"

The grin that lit up her beautiful face had Annette and I both drooling. "Are you sure you can handle it?"

"Yes!" Annette shouted a little too loudly, her excitement echoing off the walls.

"I think?" I was a little more wary. Live and learn, right?

"You used the closest living creature near us."

"And that would be?" I braced myself. Literally. Against the sink.

"A mouse."

I blinked.

"There must have been one under the stove or under the floorboards." Nette almost squealed.

It had happened in the kitchen, so that made sense. "I made you from a mouse? Because the laws of physics—"

"Don't apply," she said.

"Good thing Ink wasn't around." Annette snickered. "Oh! Can you shapeshift into a mouse like Roane can a wolf?"

"I've had a couple of very long conversations with Roane about that. It took him years, and I think something triggered it.

"Probably puberty," I teased.

"I think that's it exactly."

"He told you that?"

"Not in so many words. He just said he was thirteen the first time he shifted."

"Poor guy. To go through all of that alone, not knowing what happened to him."

"I think we're all forgetting something very important here," Annette said.

Ruthie and I looked at her.

"What does any of this have to do with a dead boy licking Deph's fingers?"

"I think it was Roane," Ruthie answered.

Okay, there was some potential here for the whole dead boy thing becoming less disturbing. "What makes you say that?"

"After you brought me back, I was connected to you in your dreams as well. I still am."

I turned toward her. "You were the light. You helped Percy keep the warlock from finding me."

"I did. Only a little. Your grandfather did most of the heavy lifting."

"So, you think Roane came into my dreams and licked my fingers."

"Of course," Annette said in an a-ha moment. "He thought he was still a wolf cub. He would absolutely lick you to show affection."

We all stopped and let that sink in.

"Is it just me or is this room a little warm?" I asked. "And a little crowded?"

They both fanned themselves, feeling the heat as well.

Ruthie led me out of the bathroom and back to the bed, and we both sat.

Annette tagged along. "Did you think like a mouse when you materialized, Ruthie? Because that would be crazy."

"No, but a part of me knew, if that makes sense."

"I think the real question is"—I narrowed my eyes—"did you crave cheese?"

A hiccup of laughter escaped her before she could stop it. "I did have a sudden desire for Cheez-Its."

After a solid round of teasing, Annette left for her room, which I had yet to actually see. We'd decided to order take-out, but not till later, still satiated from our delicious lunch.

After telling me the chief was dropping by to check on things, Ruthie retreated back to her chamber under the stairs.

I'd wanted to ask her what was going on, why she didn't want to see him, but she'd seemed tired. No, exhausted. I could only hope bringing her out of the veil hadn't damaged her in some way. Although the fatigue had only hit when she'd mentioned Houston.

As for me, I went into the bathroom again. Looking into the mirror, I gave up on the pep talk and studied my reflection. My dark hair, only mildly ravaged after the girls-gone-wild session earlier, fell back to reveal skin that was ghostly pale, eyes that were feverishly bright.

But that wasn't why I barely recognized myself. I'd aged twenty years over the last twenty years. It was so unfair to feel like a late-twenty-something and be stuck in a forty-something body. I leaned forward and whispered, "What kind of woman are you, Defiance Dayne?"

Was I the kind of woman who ran from a fight?

Yes.

Yes, I was.

Was I the kind of woman who let down her family and friends? Who abandoned them and put their lives in danger? Was I the kind of woman who ignored other people's suffering? I thought about all of those messages. All those people asking for my help. Then I lifted my chin.

No.

No, I was not.

After yet another shower—I just couldn't seem to get the stench of lethargy out of my hair—I donned my favorite black maxi dress, an oversized button-down that was barely one step up from a robe, and threw on a pair matching black slouch socks. It was getting cold out, and I needed to snuggle up with a good book and a cup of hot chocolate as the fall weather demanded.

One quick hair check later—wet with an eighty percent chance of tangles—I descended the stairs in search of a big bad wolf. I wanted to know more about what happened to him. What it was like to suddenly become a boy. Or a wolf, depending on one's perspective. Did he know his spirit was the boy's? Did he recall his previous life as a human? Did he remember stealing into my dreams? Crawling close to me? Licking my fingers?

Something brushed past me again on the stairs. Closer this time. More aggressively.

Slowly but surely, I was learning to pay closer attention

to the little things. For example, did whatever brushed past me seem to want to rip out my soul and sup upon my guts? The answer to that question was a disturbing and resounding yes.

"Get in line, buddy."

And yet there was nothing magical about the energy from the entity that had, if Ruthie was correct, followed me from the witch bottle. It was more like a shadow. A poor replica of what it had once been. An echo. Either way, Sir was angry and wanted my blood. Ingrate. I'd set him free, after all.

I found Roane on the back porch, feeding wolves of all things. Watching him from the glass door, I started to step out until I saw the wolves emerge out of the trees and into the low light of dusk. Done filling a huge bowl with raw meat and bones, he set it down and backed up toward the door.

Without looking away, he reached behind him, opened the door, and took my hand.

Clearly, I wasn't as stealthy as I thought.

He tugged, encouraging me to come out.

The wolves padded forward, heads down, gazes wary.

"I'm sorry," I whispered, mesmerized. "My presence is worrying them."

He pulled me beside him and draped an arm around my waist. "Just give them a minute."

"They're beautiful." Five in all, they were all shades of gray. A couple had patches of black. "I didn't think there were any wolves left in the state."

"There weren't. Not in the wild. These are escaped wolves."

"Escaped?" That wasn't suspicious at all. "Escaped from where?"

He lifted a muscular shoulder. "Here and there. Mostly zoos. Possibly from people who obtained them illegally."

"And are you one of those people who obtained them illegally?" I slid him a sideways glance.

He, in turn, gave me a once-over. "You wearing a wire?"

"An underwire. It gets horrible reception, though, so you have nothing to worry about."

"Maybe I should frisk you."

Maybe he should. An exhilarating heat pooled in my abdomen. I looked back at the wolves. "What if someone tries to trap them?"

"I've told them what to watch out for. When to come out. When to stay hidden."

"You... told them?"

"Yes," he said, his voice whiskey smooth.

"You speak their language?"

"Only when I'm in wolf form. And it's more like a system than a language. Warning growls and such. I've simply trained them on what to watch out for. Not that they didn't already know most of it before I came along. They're smart."

A couple of the wolves hung back while others came into the circle of light coming from the porch to eat.

"I should go. I'm making them skittish."

"Just give them a minute to get used to your scent."

I resisted the urge to lift my wet hair and sniff. According to the bottle, I was supposed to smell like a Brazilian rain forest. Not sure if that was a good thing or a bad one.

"It'll mix with mine. They'll be okay."

Sure enough, the last two came forward after a couple of false starts. They would ease closer, then jump back and study us until, slowly, they inched toward the bowl, took out a meat-laden bone, and tore off into the dark.

"I'm still worried someone will hurt them. Humans can be such dicks."

"Me too. Your grandmother protected them for me. But when she died, I'm assuming the protection spell she had over them evaporated the way the one she had over you did."

"Has she re-upped it since her… reawakening?"

"Nah. She's got a lot on her plate right now."

I made a mental note to talk to her. Then I made another mental note to pay attention to my mental notes. I so often ignored them. "Has she told you her theory about the boy? About you?"

After a long pause, he answered. "Yes."

"Do you think she's right?"

"Yes."

I turned to him. "Really? So, in a way, the boy did survive?" Somehow that made the whole incident slightly less soul-crushing.

"I think so. I had instances growing up where I remembered things. Things I couldn't have known. It had to be him. I have to be him."

"You didn't talk until you were seven."

He seemed to bristle.

I squeezed his hand. "Roane, I wasn't judging. I would never."

He dropped his gaze. "I know."

"No, you don't." I needed him to understand. "I can't imagine how hard that must've been for you. I only meant that perhaps the reason your speech was delayed was not because you were a wolf, but because your father… well, killed you."

The muscles in his forearms flexed as he curled and uncurled his hands into fists.

"Maybe that's why the boy withdrew, and the wolf emerged as the dominant personality. The ruling psyche."

"From trauma?"

"Yes." I stepped closer. "Roane, you were literally killed by your father. That had to leave a mark."

He nodded.

"Hey." I elbowed him in the name of camaraderie. "My mother tried to kill me too."

His gaze traveled back to me at last. "I'm sorry."

"Don't be." I ignored the pang in my chest. "I don't remember it."

We watched as the last wolf ran into the dark, his jaws full of a late-night snack.

"Now that I think about it, how did the boy's father trap you? Wolves haven't inhabited this area in decades."

"He trapped me on the outskirts of a wolf sanctuary near Ipswich."

"For real?"

"For real."

"See? Dicks."

The air took a decidedly chilly turn, so he grabbed the bowl, checked a water tank near the back porch, and headed inside.

I followed.

Without looking at me, he set the bowl in the sink. "Does it make me more palatable?"

"I'm sorry?" I leaned against the counter. Our counter. The file folder with the messages still sat on the table, the seams glowing brighter than before.

When he turned, his olive gaze was harder than I'd ever

seen. "Does knowing I was once a real boy make me more palatable? More acceptable?"

He started to walk away. This perfect being. This stunning entity who'd lived a life I could hardly imagine.

I stepped in front of him.

He kept his gaze downcast.

Was he embarrassed? Again? We'd gone through this when I had first discovered what he was. "Don't you dare." I whispered the threat, hoping to soften the delivery.

Other than his jaw flexing under the pressure of his ire, he didn't move. A dark-red lock of hair brushed a wide shoulder.

"Don't you dare think me so shallow." I reached up and pressed a palm to his stubbly beard, and he let me. It was softer than I'd imagined. "Don't you dare believe you are ever unworthy because of your incredible past. Do you know how many people would kill for such an existence? The fact that you are the boy as well as the wolf? Icing on the cake, but only because, in a way, he lived. His mother did get to see him grow up. Her dream came true. And you would honestly think me so shallow, Roane Wildes, to be repulsed by your heritage?"

He winced, but just barely.

"You've clearly never met a female. Of either species. There's not a single one of us who would be repulsed by you. Quite the opposite. Or did you completely miss the longing gazes today in the café?"

"Why?" His glittering olive gaze locked with mine.

His question felt genuine, like he honestly couldn't understand how I would not only *not* be swayed against him due to his history but would find it appealing. And it was the most adorable thing I'd ever seen.

I looked down at his ankle. Or, more precisely, at the

scars on his leg above the top of his work boots. Where the trap had been. Where his life had taken a drastic turn. I dropped my hand to his abdomen.

It hardened beneath my touch. And yet, he made the softest, softest sound.

Encouraged, I stepped closer, rising onto my toes. It was my turn to nibble. When my mouth reached his ear, he wrapped a large hand around the back of my neck and held me to him. His other snaked around my waist. Pulled me closer. "I just have one question," I whispered.

He backed me against the counter. A place I was growing very fond of. "What would that be, Ms. Dayne?"

"Do you remember licking my fingers in my dreams?"

He leaned back, the look of surprise on his handsome face undeniable. "That was you?"

"You mean it really *was* you?" I stared in wonder. "You're the finger licker?"

He started to step out of my embrace.

I tightened my hold until he gave in with a heavy sigh.

"I was a dog," he said, embarrassed once again. "And you have delicious fingers. You can't blame me."

With a grin I constructed from sin and mischief, I revisited one of my favorite vacation destinations by nipping at his ear.

He inhaled sharply.

"I don't blame you, Mr. Wildes." I pressed my lips to his ear. "I worship you."

A desperate groan wrenched from his chest. He tangled his fingers in my hair, pulled my head back, and covered my mouth with his.

I wasn't a schoolgirl. I'd never been prone to fits of euphoria. I knew lust was simply a psychological force producing an intense desire for an object, circumstance, or person.

So when his tongue dove past my lips and explored my mouth with exquisite precision, the fact that raw, unadulterated lust fueled my reaction didn't lessen the impact of the adrenaline spike. Didn't slow the acceleration of my pulse. Didn't stop the flood of warmth between my legs. Didn't make his kiss any less overwhelming. Any less exhilarating.

He released my hair and sent both hands in search of my breasts. In a move Houdini would've been proud of, he had the dress unbuttoned and off my shoulders and my bra on the ground at our feet in a matter of seconds. My breasts spilled into his hands.

He sucked in cool air between our mouths. The prickle of desire when his palms cupped the weight of them, when his thumbs brushed across my nipples, was instantaneous.

His mouth left mine to trail scalding kisses across my jaw and down my neck, each one rippling through my body in rising quakes.

And suddenly, I was on the counter. Like lifting me had been effortless. Either he had enhanced strength due to his werewolf status, or I'd lost a crap-ton of weight while out.

He moved his hands back to my breasts and watched as he kneaded each one.

"Shirt," I said, wanting to do the same to him.

With a quickness born of desire, he lifted his shirt over his head and returned to the task at hand. And there was nothing—nothing on Earth, above or below—as sexy as a shirtless man covered in ink, wearing a leather kilt, and gazing at me like I was a bottle of bourbon and he was a connoisseur.

The art on his body was nothing short of haunting. A giant skull spanned the entire length of his torso, its eyes penetrating and surreal. The work that blanketed the rest of him was a combination of symbols and sayings and the edges of a map of old Salem.

The full map took up his entire back along with one giant symbol. A spell, actually. The spell I'd used to create the magic that transformed him into what he was today. Somehow, he'd remembered it and drew it for his incredibly talented artist.

He licked his lips and pulled the lower one in through his teeth as he studied me. But he didn't reach for my breasts again, to their great disappointment. Instead, he went for my knees.

He spread them. Slowly. Giving me time to think about the gravity of the situation. The significance of what we were doing. The reality of what more he wanted to do.

Anticipation thickened the air around me.

His hands slid up my thighs, and I clutched his sinuous forearms, but he didn't stop until he got to my hips. Taking a firm grip, he wrenched me closer, molding me around him until I could feel the evidence of exactly how interested he was through the thin leather of his kilt.

When he leaned in, I wrapped my arms around his wide shoulders. Pressed my breasts against his chest. Covered his mouth with mine.

Curiously, I heard drawers being pulled out on either side of me.

Just when I was about to break the kiss and demand he put his hands back where they belonged, he lifted my legs. Taking an ankle in each hand, he gently placed each of my feet inside a drawer.

One was filled with dishtowels and the other with utensils. I couldn't have cared less, because his hands traded their places at my feet for the space between my legs.

Pulling aside my panties, he slid two long fingers inside me in one smooth thrust.

Gasping, I broke off the kiss. Buried my face against his neck and my hands in his hair. I grabbed fistfuls of auburn locks and pulled. Wanting more. Willing to beg for it. How long had it been since I'd felt this way? Never. Honestly, before him, never.

He put his mouth to my ear and said, "Spread your legs, Ms. Dayne." Wetting his fingers, he pulled out to circle my clit, the process painfully slow and deliciously precise, sending out vibrations that rocked me to the core. He dipped his fingers again.

I bucked, my knees squeezing him in response.

"Wider," he said more forcefully, sending an arrow of molten lava straight to my girl parts.

And I tried, but a pressure was building between my legs, like a dam about to burst in a storm.

His thumb brushed my clit, so softly it throbbed with need. I wanted his cock inside me. He leaned close again. "More," he demanded in a husky voice.

"I can't," I said between pants.

"You can," he insisted.

It took enlisting the help of the gods, but I spread my knees, forcing them apart, tightening my fists in his hair.

"I'm going to kiss you here," he said, massaging my clit, thrusting his fingers inside me. They were still deep inside when he knelt and found my clit with his tongue.

I whimpered.

Soft and hot and wet, his tongue feathered over me before he pressed his lips there and suckled, almost lifting me off the counter in ecstasy as he milked me to climax.

I couldn't hold back the floodtides any longer. I forced myself to relax, and the dam burst, the orgasm rocketing through me so fast, so unexpectedly, I cried out and screamed a few choice words as well.

I rocked forward, drawing his fingers deeper. Squeezing them. Kneading as the pulsing slowly ebbed into the sound of my heavy breaths. My soft sighs. My generous use of the F-bomb. Because nothing said "Fuck yes" like the words *fuck* and *yes*.

He kissed me there again, then stood and took my mouth, the taste of salt and sugar fresh on his tongue. "Fuck," he mumbled against my lips and broke off the kiss.

"What?" I asked, more than a little dazed.

His face held utter disappointment. "Did I mention that I also have very good hearing?"

"What?" I asked again.

He had my dress over my shoulders a microsecond before my dads entered the kitchen, their faces shock incarnate.

NINE

...if you get a link called "free porn" don't opin it. It is a virus wich deactivates your spelcheck and fcuks up you riting. I also receibed it but lukily I don't uatch porn so I dint opin it. Plaese warm yu frends. Wanks.
—PSA

My feet were still in the drawers when my dads walked in. And Roane's shirt was still on the floor. Right next to my bra.

"What the hell?" Dad asked, his hands full of takeout. "Cariña! We prepare food on that counter."

"Defiance!" Papi said, bringing up the rear and pretending to be appalled. He didn't fool anyone.

I scrambled off the counter, scooped up my bra, and rushed past them with a soft "I'll get dressed."

Before I got too far, however, I heard Dad say, "So, Roane..."

Crap. I had to hurry.

Annette stood on the landing above me, her mouth unhinged as she looked me over and said, "No. You did not."

"Not now, Nette."

"Yes now, you saucy minx. Where? In his pad?" She wriggled her brows.

I rolled my eyes in humiliation. "The kitchen."

The gasp that erupted out of her throat would become known the world over as the gasp that launched a thousand dust bunnies. I could've sworn dust filtered down from the ceiling and into my freshly washed hair.

I hurried past her. "The same kitchen my dads are in now. Please, go down there. I'll be there in a jiff."

When she wanted to, Annette could move with the speed and grace of a jaguar. This was not one of those times. She lost her footing more than once racing down the stairs and almost face-planted at the bottom, but she was still in the kitchen before I'd even gotten to my door.

Percy opened it for me. "Thanks, Percy," I said, grateful for the help and the lack of judgment.

By the time I got changed and returned to the kitchen, the food was spread out on the island, and my dads were busy eyeing Roane like they were counting the ways they could kill him in his sleep.

I didn't know why. It wasn't like I was in high school and the local bad boy had taken my virginity. Though thinking about it now, I wished he had. My first time had been the disaster of disasters. I'd never looked at a penis the same way again. Not that I'd looked at any before that point. Maybe that had been the problem. Maybe if I'd had Roane's penis filling my—

"I see the gang's all here," the chief said as he walked in, scanning the room, trying to cover up the fact that he was crestfallen when he didn't see Ruthie. He also sensed the tension instantly with a quick perusal of the dinner guests.

"Hey, Chief," I said.

He gave me a quick hug. "Hey, daffodil. Feeling better?"

"Much."

"I wonder why," Dad said, and my face heated.

"Probably the shower," Papi said, joining in.

"Or the mani-pedi," Annette offered.

Even at forty-five, the thought of my dads catching me in the act was mortifying.

"Oh, Chief," Annette said, "we might have a problem with a Mr. James Vogel."

"A lot of people have a problem with a Mr. James Vogel." The chief filled a plate with pasta from Bela Verona. "What's he done now?"

Annette and I exchanged hapless glances before she said, "Does being rude and obnoxious count?"

"Legally?"

"We aren't really sure he's done anything," I said.

"But," Annette added, "he wants Dephne to bring someone back from the dead."

That got the handsome man's attention. He sat down and waited for us to bring our food to the table. "Tell me everything."

We explained what was going on with Mr. Vogel, whom I'd almost called Mr. Voorhees not once, not twice, but three times throughout the conversation before it was all said and done.

Scraping the last of the pasta from his plate, the chief said, "I'll look into it."

"Thanks, Chief," I said, avoiding yet another near miss with Roane's burning gaze.

From there, the evening devolved into small talk, which included Annette's version of what happened at the psychic's and with the witch bottle. I ignored the pocket folder that had been moved onto the toaster oven and the fact that it glowed now. Not just the seams, but the entire folder, clearly calling to me. Insisting I pay attention.

"I just want to see him," Annette said, talking about the curtain climber we'd apparently adopted.

The chief asked if I had my powers back, and Annette had to explained in great detail how, in her humble opinion, they were still there, buried deep inside me, rather like I wanted Roane to be.

Not that I said that out loud. But the hungry glances he kept casting my way were making me squirm in my chair. He was a talented, talented man. Part of me wanted to know where he'd learned his powers of seduction and if I could send off for the correspondence course so I could pull a reversal on him.

One thing I hadn't considered during our little tête-à-tête was Samuel. Thank God he hadn't come into the kitchen. He was still a tad young for sex ed. The boy Nette was so desperate to see tore through the kitchen, searching for a certain battle-scarred cat named Incognito. Ink wanted spaghetti. Samuel wanted Ink. Giggling, he laughed and chased the poor animal off the table before Roane could get him off.

I giggled as he dashed by. "That poor cat. Samuel's going to kill him."

Roane chuckled softly. "It's good for Ink. He's become entirely too complacent. Have you seen how many mice we have?"

"We have mice?" Annette asked, suddenly wary.

Dinner was lovely. My dads listened with rapt attention

to all of Annette's tales and even a couple of the chief's. Ruthie definitely had some skeletons in her closet. And not just actual ones, but metaphorical ones as well. The evening was nice. And soothing. And normal, if one didn't count the werewolf at the table.

Right before everyone got up, I looked at the handsome men who'd raised me. My gratitude for them had no bounds. "I saw the video of the big day."

Dad graced me with a look of pure, unconditional love. "Which day, cariña?"

"The day you guys came to get me."

They exchanged surprised glances. My dads were always perfectly groomed, and today was no exception. Dad with his olive skin and thick gray hair and Papi, the Viking, the silver-streaked blond fox who still worked out every day and had the biceps to prove it.

"You gave up so much for me. I just wanted to thank you for everything you've done. Everything you've given me." The room fell silent. "Mostly your time and attention when you didn't have to."

Papi took my hand and mimicked Dad's soft accent when he said, "Always, cariña."

Dad laughed softly. "It has been an honor, *mi corazon*."

We stood, and they pulled me into a deep hug that lasted longer than it should have but was shorter than I'd hoped.

Dad joined the others as they cleared the table and wrapped up leftovers, and Papi scooted closer to me.

"You saw the video?" he asked.

I nodded, knowing this was going nowhere good.

He leaned closer. "How was my hair?"

I laughed and gave him another hug.

"Your hair smells good," he said, burying his face in the top of my head.

"Really?" I asked, far too desperately. "It doesn't smell like lethargy? Or failure? Or six months of indolence?"

It was his turn to laugh when Dad walked up. "So..." he began.

Here it comes.

"... the wolf."

"Sorry about that."

"Please," Papi said with a scoff. "It's about time you found someone decent. We just want to make sure his intentions are honorable."

My gaze darted to the subject at hand, who was at the sink, rinsing off dishes, his wide shoulders and lean waist so visually stunning it mesmerized me. But triangles had been my favorite shape since kindergarten, and now I knew why.

I wondered if he could hear us talking about him, figured he could, and decided I didn't care when I said, "I don't know about his intentions, but his tongue makes up for any discrepancies."

"Cariña," Dad said, fighting a grin tooth and nail while Papi high-fived me.

But my question was answered when the wolf tossed a smile over his shoulder so wicked that I almost climaxed again. In my defense, it had been months.

We said our goodbyes under the light of a bug zapper, then I went inside to help finish cleaning up. The chief was just leaving.

He gave me a hug. "Can you tell her hey for me?"

"Absolutely." I set a hand on his arm.

He headed out the front door.

I ran to stop him. "Chief, don't give up on her."

He nodded, his expression grave and anything but hopeful.

"You know her. You've known her far longer than I have. She's not doing this for herself, although she is part mouse now, so who knows how her brain works."

"Come again?"

"Either way, I promise you, she's making this great sacrifice for you." I spread my arms wide to emphasize the greatness of it all. She loved him. I knew she did. She knew she did. He knew she did. But for some reason, she felt she could no longer give him what he needed when all he needed was her.

He studied the wrapped plate of leftovers in his hand. "Then she's doing it for the wrong reasons."

"I know, but she needs to figure that out. Just... just don't give up on her."

The impassioned gaze he speared me with told me everything I needed to know. "Never."

"Thank you."

He left, and by the time I got back to the kitchen, it was deserted minus a single slice of leftover pineapple upside-down cake arranged on a dessert plate with a single bite taken out of it. I hopped onto the counter of coitus and delighted in every last crumb.

The decision to go back to my room was a difficult one when all I wanted to do was visit the wolf below. But I figured he'd had enough of me for one day. Still, he hadn't gotten to experience the same pleasure as I had. Surely, he'd want to finish what we'd started. Then again, if that were the case, wouldn't he have stuck around?

I almost locked the back door, then realized Roane may have gone out to check on the wolves. I left it unlocked and started for the stairs when the damned pocket folder piqued my curiosity.

After sliding an oven mitt over my right hand, I grabbed the bright folder. The whole thing glowed. I figured it would burn when I touched it like the message had, thus the insulation. Precautions were definitely in order.

I opened the flap and scooped out the messages with a set of salad tongs, worried they would all be glowing now. Thankfully, the only two glowing like they burned with some kind of supernatural eternal flame were the same ones from before. The little girl who'd lost her dog and the man wanting a remedy for male pattern baldness. But why those? Neither seemed particularly life-threatening, yet my magics seemed to think they were important enough to set them aflame.

I ran upstairs, grabbed my laptop, then hurried back down. The little girl had left no address and no phone number. The only clue I had to go on was her name and the fact that her dog was a bull. That could mean anything from a French bulldog to a boxer to a pit bull or any number of breeds in between.

After searching the local papers online for her name, I found a Clara Thomas from Peabody, Massachusetts, in the second grade, who'd won a pumpkin carving contest last Halloween. The caption listed her parents as Bernie and Hope Thomas. From there, it wasn't terribly difficult to find an address.

Sinking back into the chair, I wondered if I should do what I was about to do. A lost dog was one thing, but if the girl's message was radiating light like a glow stick made of sunlight, something else had to be going on.

I thought about enlisting Annette's help, but it was past eleven. I didn't want to bug her if I didn't need to.

I made up my mind. I'd just drive by. See if anything felt amiss.

After changing into warmer clothes, I hurried to the front door. The front door that was no longer visible. Percy had covered every inch of it with vines and dark roses and razor-sharp thorns that could easily open a vein.

"Percy," I said, putting my hands on my hips. "I'll be safe. I'm just going to drive by and get a feel for what's up."

He still didn't budge.

"Look." I held up my phone. "Help is just a phone call away."

The vines shrank back slowly, and I stepped to the door. "Thank you."

But when I put my hand on the knob, he wrapped a vine around my wrist. At first, I thought he was going to lock me there, but the vine broke off. I looked down at the tiny delicate buds decorating it, black with a deep crimson underlay, and wondered if he still controlled the rose cuttings.

I got my answer when the vine tightened softly around my wrist then relaxed. I smiled up at him as though he'd just given me a diamond bracelet, only this was so very much better. Diamonds had nothing on enchanted roses.

I ducked out before he changed his mind and hurried to the Bug. She started up on the first try, Goddess bless her.

Thanks to the wonders of the modern smartphone, I found the address easily. It sat on a quaint side street with close neighbors on either side. An old blue Taurus sat in the driveway, along with a yellow panel van. Apparently, Mr. Thomas owned a janitorial service. The house had white siding with dark trim, a color I couldn't quite make out, both cracked and peeling and in bad need of a fresh coat.

But that wasn't what captured my attention. It was a

feeling, a niggling at the back of my neck that kept me from stopping in front of the house. I cruised down the block and parked in front of a small colonial.

"Ready?" I asked the vine on my wrist. It tightened again, and I wondered just how much of the vine was Percy. Like, could he be in two places at once? Could a part of his ghostliness, his essence, break off and still be conscious? And how was even a part of him able to leave the house? I thought the salt kept him locked inside.

Not that any of that mattered at the moment. I had a glowing message to investigate.

I stayed down when I exited the Bug and crept toward the house until I realized how creepy and suspicious I must look, so I straightened and walked like a normal human bean. But something told me not to knock on the front door. It was probably the sign that read, *Do not knock on this fucking door.*

Okay, then.

At least I knew what kind of person, or people, I was dealing with. I couldn't imagine Clara's mother putting the sign there, but who knew? I would totally put that sign on Percy's door if I thought it wouldn't get me kicked out of the neighborhood. Faster.

I used the flashlight on my phone and walked around the house, curious if I would feel anything or see anything or hear anything. Who the hell knew how these magics worked? Not me. That's who.

The scent of rain and fireplaces filled the air, and wet leaves insulated my footsteps, but the sound still seemed too loud no matter how softly I tried to walk.

Sure enough, when I got to the back of the house, I felt something. Two somethings, actually. A darkness and a pull. The pull was one of innocence and fear, and I knew instantly something was very, very wrong.

"Any thoughts?" I asked Percy.

In a movement full of grace and beauty, the tip of the vine formed a question mark against the paleness of my skin.

"This is officially the coolest bracelet I've ever owned."

He squeezed again.

I kept walking until the pull grew stronger. So strong, in fact, it felt like I'd been ensnared in the Death Star's tractor beam. But the hot spot, the area I felt the most pull, was toward a basement window.

The rectangular pane had a vertical bar over it and sat at ground level. No light seeped out.

I filled my lungs with crisp New England air, got down on all fours, and tried to peer inside as the knees on my jeans soaked through. I saw a lot of blackness and little of anything else, so after reciting the Lord's Prayer—because it was the only prayer I could think of at the moment—I shined the light from my phone inside.

A small face stared back at me, a haunted expression on her face.

I yelped and fell back onto the wet ground.

The window opened out, though just barely. The bar kept it from opening far.

I crawled back to a mop of brown hair that looked like it hadn't been washed in days—I knew the feeling—and huge brown eyes that gazed up at me.

We took each other in for a long moment, then I asked, my voice low, "Are you Clara?"

She glanced back over her shoulder, then nodded. She reeked of fear, and my heart broke for her.

"I'm Defiance Dayne. You left a message for me about a lost dog?"

She nodded again.

"This isn't about a lost dog, is it?"

Her grip tightened around a stuffed turtle, and she shook her head.

I tried to see inside, but it was too dark. My light simply didn't reach that far, and trying seemed to distress the girl. "Sweetheart, what's going on?"

"My dad," she whispered. "He's mad at my mom and won't let us leave the house. He has her in his room and"—tears pooled between her thick lashes—"he's so mad."

"I'm sorry, sweetheart. Did you call the police?"

"My mom already tried. She wrote a note on a pizza receipt to get help. The police came, but Dad was holding me behind the door. He threatened to kill us all if they came in. So, my mom told them I did it as a joke, and that she was fine and that she would give me a good talking-to." She hiccupped with emotion, trying to stay brave.

"Oh my god." Why would the cops not insist on seeing Clara? On questioning her? I reached a hand through the narrow slit.

She grabbed it and held on for dear life.

"Okay, I'm going to get help."

A jolt of panic shot through her. "Please don't leave me."

"I'm not going anywhere." I turned my phone over to dial the chief.

"Wait," she said, a tear finally escaping its cage. "If the police come, he'll kill us."

I pocketed my phone, got onto my stomach, and reached through with my other hand to wipe away her tears. "I have a friend who is very good at this stuff. He's a policeman, but it's okay. He'll know what to do. Can I call him?"

She thought about it, her tiny brows knitting before she finally nodded her consent. "But you won't leave me?"

"Never," I promised, hoping I hadn't just lied to her. The chief might need me to move away from the house.

I took back my hand and called him.

"Daffodil?" he said, his voice thick and groggy. "What's wrong?"

I explained the situation as quietly and succinctly as I could.

"No sirens," I warned. "No lights."

"Got it. I'll call the police chief in Peabody. He's good people. And I'll be there in thirty."

"Thanks, Chief."

"Don't thank me yet. I want you away from that house right now."

"I can't do that, Chief. I promised Clara."

"I don't care. I want you away from there or... or I'll have Ruthie put a hex on you."

"You wouldn't."

"I would."

A grin fought its way to the surface. "I'm not scared of my grandmother."

"Then you don't know her as well as I do. Please, daffodil."

"I'm in the back, Chief. I'll be the blue one soaked head to toe and shivering from hypothermia if you don't hurry."

"I'll arrest you," he said, lobbing his last Hail Mary.

"Chief." I *tsked* him. "You know I have a thing for handcuffs."

"Damn it." He hung up, but I'd watched enough TV to know what happened next.

If the cops came in with guns blazing despite what the chief advised the Peabody department to do, this would turn into a hostage situation. I had to get Clara out.

I studied the bar. Hinged at the top, it was bolted to the wood frame above and below the window to keep someone from opening it as it swung out. Unfortunately, I didn't have a wrench. Or a hacksaw. Or a plasma cutter. But I might have a tire iron. Didn't most cars have those? Then again, if I tried to pry the bars off, it would be too loud.

Clara's small hand kept a death grip on mine. We heard footsteps overhead, and she stilled, her gaze snapping up, her lungs seizing.

"Hey," I whispered to take her mind off of the imminent danger, "how did you know to call me? Did you really lose your dog?"

She blinked back to me, and it took her a moment to process what I'd asked. "No," she whispered. "My dog ran away when I was little. My dad said it was my fault, so he never let me have another one."

"I'm sorry."

"It's okay. My mom told me if I ever needed anything ever ever to call you."

"Me? Do you mean my grandmother?"

"I don't know. She made me memorize your phone number and said if I was ever in trouble, the person at that number would help. She said you're magic."

As I lay shivering in the wet leaves, I was once again struck by how many people Ruthie had helped over the years. How many people knew they could count on her. That they could trust her.

Another round of footsteps, and Clara gasped.

"What are you standing on?" I asked, trying to take her mind off the monster upstairs. My jaw ached from biting down to keep from chattering. I really was soaked. And shivering. And probably blue.

"My bed." She looked down and bounced for me. "Can you come get me?"

"Help is coming, sweetheart." I examined the bar again and realized something. She was right. I *was* magic. I could do this. "Step to the side, hon."

She did but didn't dare let go of my hand.

What to use? I only knew a couple of symbols. They just seemed to pop into my head as I needed them, but nothing was coming to me. Then I remembered one that might work.

I lifted two fingers and drew it on the air. It was like a charmling version of *open sesame*. Normally, when I drew a symbol, the lines glowed, much like the messages had. As though the sun was bleeding through them.

But nothing happened.

I racked my brain. That was it. That was the right symbol.

"Did I really lose my powers?" I whispered aloud. Panic shot through me like an arrow. Then I remembered the attic. I'd drawn a symbol then. Maybe I was shivering too much. Maybe I didn't draw the symbol right. Wait. I'd felt a resistance. I looked up but could only see the eaves and the storm drain. Was the house enchanted?

Then it hit me. I looked at the vine around my wrist. "Percival Goode," I said, talking to my wrist like a secret agent. "Are you blocking me?"

Clara simply watched, possibly afraid to interfere with the crazy lady. I couldn't try to get him off without releasing her hand, and I was worried she'd panic too. Best if only one of us was as useless as a flounder in a gunfight.

Headlights from a car slid along the trees behind the house as it turned into the drive.

"That might be them," I said to her, relief flooding every cell in my body. I looked at the vine and said through clenched teeth, "You and I are going to talk later."

He squeezed my wrist gently.

"No. It's too late. If this goes south, it's on—"

Before I could finish my tirade, the back door swung open, flooding the area with light. A thin man in a dirty tank top stepped onto the back porch and turned toward me.

I shrank back and held my breath. Mostly because it was creating huge clouds of vapor.

I'd been too loud. I put Clara's life in danger so I could threaten a plant. Not to mention her mother's.

But instead of coming after me, the man walked down the three steps to the ground and carried a garbage bag to a bin on the other side of the house without a care in the world.

This was my chance. If I could keep him out of the house, it would give the cops time to go in and get Clara and her mother out.

I heard a knock from the front of the house. He was going to be back up the porch steps and in the door in no time. I had to stall him. I had to keep him from going into that house and creating a hostage situation.

When he cornered the side of the house, I had no choice. I ripped my hand away from Clara's, stood, and hurried over to him, trying to wedge myself between him and the porch steps. I couldn't tell if I was shaking from the cold or the massive adrenaline dump.

He stopped and frowned at me. "Who are you?" He looked around, suspicion coloring his face, narrowing his lids. He clearly hadn't heard the knock. "And what the hell are you doing in my backyard?"

I rubbed my hands together, trying to stop the shaking. But my teeth chattering violently when I spoke couldn't be helped. "I'm going door to door, talking to people about their car's extended warranty."

He crossed his arms over his chest and looked me up and down. "You look more like a drowned rat than a door-to-door salesman. And it's almost midnight."

"We're trying to accommodate people's schedules."

"Yeah?" He eased closer.

Another knock sounded. That one he heard.

He grabbed my hair, and not in a sexy way. At all. He jerked me toward him until we were nose-to-nose. "What the fuck is going on?"

Just then, a male voice shouted, "Police! Open up!"

Great timing.

He jerked my head to the side, throwing me to the ground face-first.

I slid across the freezing earth a total of two feet as he took the stairs in one jump.

Without thought, I threw out my hand and drew the symbol that was the exact opposite of the one I'd tried earlier.

It happened faster than my eyes could see. The spell blinded me, and by the time his hand was on the knob, the door was locked up tight. He couldn't have gotten through that door with a wrecking ball. Not until I released it.

He tried it again. Shook the handle. Kicked the bottom. Threw his shoulder against the door. "What the fuck?" he said, pounding on it. "Clara! Clara, let me in!"

"Isn't she locked in the basement?" I said sweetly.

He whipped around, his face the picture of rage.

I heard the men in the front breaking down the door. At the same time, someone was running around the side of the house toward us. Either the chief had told the police I was back here, or it was the man himself.

Clara's dad heard him too, and stalked forward until he towered over me. And the man really liked my hair. He grabbed a handful and ripped me off the ground.

"Bernard Thomas!" the chief shouted.

We turned.

The chief had a gun pointed at Clara's father. Except there was one little problem: The man was using me as a shield. He pulled a knife from his pocket and held it to the back of my neck while keeping his head ducked down.

The tip dug into my skin, and I felt a tiny trickle of blood. Yet it didn't hurt. My head should've ached as well, his grip was so tight on my hair, but the adrenaline must've been doing its job. I was no longer cold. My scalp didn't throb. I was no longer afraid, which was odd considering the knife.

A uniformed officer ran up behind the chief, his gun drawn too. "We got them out."

A beautiful, sparkly kind of relief flooded my body. My knees almost gave out. In fact, they would have had Bernard Thomas not been holding me up by the roots of my hair. It had been through so much lately.

"Stay the fuck back!" he shouted, as he backed me toward the woods. Then he said for my ears only, "You are dead, bitch. No matter how this goes, you are fucking dead."

Hold a grudge much?

"Let her go, Thomas," the chief said, advancing slowly.

"One thrust." He pushed the tip of the knife further into my skin. "I'll sever your spinal column and disappear into these woods." He kept backing me toward them.

We were still thirty feet from them, and the knife went a little deeper with each step he took. He bobbed and weaved, keeping me in between him and the gun. "I know this forest better than anyone alive. They'll never find me."

A warmth came over me as I watched the chief. He was worried. Worried what this would do to Ruthie. Worried what Roane would do to him. Worried he would be the one to get a charmling killed. And still, a warmth covered me like an electric blanket.

Either I was going into shock or—

No way.

—Roane was nearby.

A low rumble cut across the chill in the air. Then another. And another. They came from all sides.

Thomas stopped. He glanced around, his breaths coming in quick, panicked gasps. "What the fuck?"

I risked a glance to the side and saw a wolf. One of the wolves Roane was feeding earlier. Then another emerged from the shadows, its sleek coat glistening under the hushed light of the moon.

Thomas pulled me against his chest and wrapped an arm so tight around my throat, he cut off my air supply.

I might be in trouble. Even with his head exposed, it was simply too dark for the chief to risk a shot.

I looked over at the lead wolf, who'd emerged from the trees directly behind us. He was much larger than the others, his fur red with a black undercoat. I knew that because I'd seen him before. Roane. His teeth were bared, the snarl he wore vicious. He stopped, lowered his head, waited the span of a heartbeat, then snapped his jaws.

The wolves attacked. They jumped from all sides, their growls and snarls the stuff of nightmares. Thomas screamed as they tore at his flesh. Roane stood back and watched. Not a single wolf bit me. In fact, one knocked me to the ground and stood over me as her packmates ripped the man to shreds.

Then, with another snap of his jaw, they stopped and tore off into the night, including the one guarding me. But he stayed. I lay on the ground and watched as he walked forward, his movements slow. Full of purpose.

He gazed at me, his olive eyes shimmering, before he bent his head and licked my neck. He whimpered and nudged my jaw with his nose. I reached up and drew my hand back, realizing I was bleeding worse than I thought.

Naturally.

I collapsed onto the grass and looked back at the chief. He was upside down. The uniform trained his gun on Roane. The chief lowered the man's weapon for him and said in a low growl, "Don't you dare."

The uniform raised his hands in surrender and went to check on Thomas, who lay sobbing, holding an arm they'd ravaged. The arm that tried to suffocate me.

The bad arm.

Then I felt it. More licking. Only this time, the sensation was familiar.

I looked over and watched as Roane licked my curled fingers. His tongue molded to each digit, tickling them like when I had been a kid. Then he moved to my thumb. My palm. Up to my wrist, bathing it in warmth. Luckily, it was the Percy-free wrist. Had it not been, I wasn't sure how that would've ended.

He put a massive paw between my arm and rib cage and bent to my neck again, his cold nose nudging me.

I reached over with my other hand and buried my fingers in his thick fur. It was much softer than I'd imagined it would be.

The next time, he went for my ear, gently nipping the lobe before taking off and vanishing into the darkness.

I sucked in a soft breath and grabbed my ear.

"I'm going to assume you're okay?" the chief said, standing over me.

"I'm pretty good right now. Thanks, Chief."

He knelt beside me. "You're soaking wet."

"I know. He's so hot, though, even as a wolf."

He grinned, unfazed. "You probably saved that woman's life. Possibly the girl's too."

"Good. Hope Thomas had so much faith in Grandma, how could I let her down?"

"I've called for a paramedic and a stretcher."

"What?" I asked, rising up and bringing half the leaves of the forest with me. Honestly, my poor hair. "I can walk, Chief. I swear." I stood. It took a while, but I managed it.

"Are you sure?" He took my arm. "'Cause you look a little wobbly."

"I think the mass of leaves on my back is throwing me off balance."

"Yeah, that's it for sure."

TEN

If each day is a gift, I'd like to know
where I can return Monday.
—Meme

After a tearful goodbye and a thousand thank-yous from Hope and Clara, I left them in each other's arms, safe at last. I felt wonderful. And I wanted a shower, but that was nothing new. The chief had a uniform drive my car home while he drove me.

"Thanks for believing me, Chief," I said when we pulled up to Percy. "You didn't even question it. You just came."

"Of course I did. I am very aware of what you're capable of, daffodil. I'm retiring soon, but I'll make sure my replacement is just as aware, as long as Ruthie thinks it'll be okay to bring him or her into the fold. It's ultimately up to you, however."

"Retiring?" I asked, as though he'd just pulled the rug out from under me. "Why are you retiring?"

"I'm too old for this shit."

"That's silly."

"Daffodil, I could've retired almost ten years ago. It's time."

I knew he was a good twenty years Ruthie's junior, which would place him in his early sixties, while at the same time making her a bit of a cradle robber. But damn, he looked good. I could hardly blame her. I was beginning to wonder if Ruthie had an anti-aging spell, because I wanted it.

"Well, I'm going to wash my hair, but I really think we need to talk about this retirement nonsense."

He laughed softly. "Promise."

I jumped out of his cruiser and waved to Parris, who'd seen us pull up and stepped onto her porch, her busybody tendencies getting the better of her. After running into the house, I started for the stairs and a hot shower. My clothes were muddy and wet and ice cold. Not a good feeling. Before I reached the first step, however, a light from the kitchen caught my attention. A glow.

Was it on fire?

I ran toward the back of the house only to find the entire kitchen alight with a luminous yellow-orange glow. I searched for the source and found it sitting on the breakfast table where I'd left it.

The message.

It glowed so bright, it made the kitchen look as though it were on fire. I almost grabbed it but pulled back. The last time I tried that, the message burned my fingers. I searched for the salad tongs and pulled the message out of the pile I'd left. It was the one from the balding man.

What in the world could make a fear of male pattern baldness so urgent? A little girl trapped in a house with a sadistic, controlling asshole, I could understand. But a man worried about his receding hairline? Not so much.

Still, it was obviously important.

I tried the number to one Mr. Leonard Quinn of Ipswich to no avail. Then again, it was a tad late. Or early, depending on one's perspective.

After biting my lower lip for a few seconds and weighing my options, I realized I had to change before I could even think about checking on the man. The sense of urgency I now felt had me flying up the stairs. Well, flying if I were a T-rex. Slow and ungainly with more weight than any wings could feasibly lift off the ground.

Breathless, and not in a good way, I tore off my clothes, wondering yet again if I should wake Annette to come with me. It was her idea to do all of this. To take all of those messages. To start a business. But it was now after three in the morning. I couldn't do that to her.

Come to find out, peeling off water-logged clothes was not as easy as I'd imagined. Gazing longingly at the shower —and the bottle of shampoo inside—I dried off, threw on the warmest sweater I could find, brushed most of the dirt and leaves out of my hair, and flew down the stairs. This time I resembled a less flighty bird. Something along the lines of a penguin. Or possibly an ostrich during a mating dance.

I slid to a stop at the front door, remembered my keys in the Popsicle jeans I'd just peeled off, did the T-rex-ostrich dance again to fetch them, then tried to open the door, my legs and lungs burning from climbing all those danged stairs.

Like the first time I'd tried to leave tonight, it wouldn't budge.

I stepped back to examine it. No vines were blocking it. It just flat out wouldn't budge. I tried again, pulling harder on the knob. Nothing. I checked the lock that I knew I hadn't locked. I locked and unlocked it for good measure. Nope.

Was Percy blocking it somehow? He was pretty much the house itself. Maybe he didn't need the vines to block the door.

I looked up. "Percy, the message is glowing. I feel an urgency, like this guy's hairline is in serious trouble. I have to go check on him." I pulled again, then sagged against it. "Percy, you are not helping."

The vine on my wrist tightened softly.

I turned full circle. "What does that even mean? Are you blocking the door?"

The rosebuds on the bracelet opened up.

"Okay, open for yes. Close for no. Will that work?"

They opened farther.

"Are you blocking the door?" I asked my wrist.

Even more, their petals spreading gracefully.

"Wait, really? Why?"

Nothing.

Okay, yes/no questions. "Are you blocking the door because, I don't know, you're worried about me?"

They opened more, the swirls in the middle revealing the filament tucked inside.

"Is this guy a jerk?" I'd already dealt with a couple while trying to help people.

Nothing.

"You don't know. Then why?" I asked again. "You're just being cautious."

They didn't move.

"I'm going to take your silence as a yes. Percy, I need to check on this guy. You have to let me out."

The tiny roses folded into themselves like ballerinas, closing once again to create the beautiful little buds that dotted the vine.

A resounding no.

Frustrated, I tried the door again, groaning through gritted teeth, then I stepped back. "You know what? Fine. I give up. I'll just take a shower and go to bed, then. But if something happens to Leonard Quinn, it's on you, buddy."

I trudged up the stairs, sliding my jacket off as I went. I kept an iron grip on it as I entered my bathroom and lifted my sweater over my head. As nonchalantly as I could, I went to hang them both on a hook on the side of the shelves. The shelves that led to a super-secret, super-cool passageway.

Roses blossomed in the corner where the wall met the ceiling.

I slammed the sweater over my decolletage. "Percy, I told you. Out of the bathroom."

The vines shrank back, and I tried not to let the astonishment I felt show on my face. He fell for the oldest trick in the book. Or the second oldest. I couldn't be certain.

I grabbed the hook—and the jacket off the hook—and pulled the shelves open, jumping into the narrow passageway before he caught on.

Which he did pretty quickly, unfortunately. He tried to close the shelves, but it was too late. I was mostly through. In my haste, however, I fell. Of course. My foot was still inside the threshold when the shelves shot toward me. I gasped, thinking my ankle had been crushed when the shelves stopped suddenly, like they had been frozen in time.

They hadn't.

The shelves immediately opened again, and I wondered why until a vine wrapped around my boot.

Uh-oh.

Percy jerked me toward the bathroom as I released a screech worthy of a barn owl.

"Percival Goode!" I shouted as he slid me inside. He was like Jaws. Or the plant from *Little Shop of Horrors*. Or —gasp—Jason Voorhees!

I anchored my other foot against the doorframe and pushed. My resistance must have surprised him because I got far enough out into the hall that parts of him shriveled and shrank back. He immediately let go, and I boomeranged into the passageway, hitting my head on the other wall.

Grabbing it with both hands, I lay in a fetal position for a solid twenty-three seconds before shaking it off and struggling to my feet. I looked back at him. The threshold was sprinkled with black dust.

I knelt down and picked some up. "Percy, I'm so sorry."

He'd withdrawn all the way back into my bedroom, and I didn't dare peek around the doorframe to check on him. I lay my head against the wall at an angle where I could see much of the vines in there. They were okay. Only the part that was pulled across the threshold had withered and died.

With a soft intake of breath, I checked my wrist. The bracelet was gone. I looked at the wood floor beneath my feet. Black ash dusted a small area. I must have flung it off me when it withered and died.

Surely there was more than just salt at work here. What would do that? Magic was certainly a fickle thing. Like when it wouldn't work on the bar covering Clara's window.

So many questions, so little time.

Reaching for the jacket I'd flung inside the passageway,

I put it on. Then I scooped up what ash I could with my hands, cupped it into my palm, and transferred it to my jacket pocket. For what, I didn't know, but it broke my heart that I hurt Percy, who'd protected me so fiercely.

"I'm sorry, Percy," I said again, angling my head.

Percy slid back into the bathroom.

"Are you okay?"

Roses blossomed, black and bloodred, dark and gruesome and beautiful.

I rubbed my wrist. "I didn't know that would happen. I'm sorry."

The vines curled languidly like a cat's tail before he closed the shelves behind me.

I stood there a solid minute, fighting the anguish of what I'd just done to him. Had it hurt? Had I physically hurt him?

After a moment, I snapped out of it and continued my mission. The only way out that I knew of from the passageway without going through the house, of course, was through the cave. I became lost almost immediately and took any stairs I found going down. Thirty-seven thousand flights later, I emerged in the cavern. I heard water dripping to my left and water running to my right. I went right.

The flashlight on my phone helped me navigate the rough floor, but not much. It had more water in it this time, clearly tethered to the tide. My boots soaked through instantly, and I was wet once again. Not in a good way. Not in a Roane way.

I followed the water for seven miles. Or possibly a quarter of a mile. It was hard to tell. I came to an iron gate that had been pushed aside as though someone had entered it, or exited it, recently. Metal hinges had been cut through with something either very sharp or very hot. I ducked through a small opening and emerged through a grouping of vines and bushes in the middle of nowhere.

I had no idea where I was, but I followed the GPS back to the house, my toes frozen. I didn't want to call anyone. It was nearing four in the morning. The more I walked, the warmer I got. I took more turns than a Stephen King novel. I ended up on Lafayette, then Dodge, then Normal, until I was finally back at the house and, more importantly, the vintage mint-green Volkswagen Beetle.

After fishing my keys out of my pocket with fingers that had lost all feeling about ten minutes into the walk, I tiptoed to the Bug, then stopped and listened. When I heard nothing but the sound of my own wheezing, I inserted the key into the lock as slowly as I could, unsure of how far Percy's domain reached, and turned.

That was when I saw them. The vines. Coming at me en masse like a wall of black razor wire.

I ran.

He followed.

"Percival Goode! You stop this right now! Oh, hi, Parris!"

Parris, the human drama detector, had stepped onto her front porch again. A part of me couldn't help but be impressed. Did she ever sleep? Was she a racoon? An owl? A vampire? At this point, nothing would surprise me.

"Hey, Defia— Are you okay?" she asked, her hand freezing in midair.

"Wonderful. Thanks." I ran past her walkway, but I could still feel him nipping at my heels. "Percival, damn it!" How could he come this far? Wasn't he bound to the house? Or, at the very least, our property line?

I was just about to run past Parris's driveway when a

huge black truck pulled into it. I slammed into the side. It was loud. And not the least bit pretty.

The window rolled down, and a very angry wolfman by the name of Roane Wildes glared at me. "Really?" he asked. "You're going out alone again?"

I brushed myself off. "It's late. I didn't want to wake anyone."

"Anyone like me?"

I heard heavy breathing behind me and turned to see five feet of fury hurrying up to us.

Annette was wheezing too. It made me feel better about my own inability to fill and empty my lungs while partaking in strenuous activity without making a whistling sound.

"You were going to leave me again?"

"It's late," I repeated. "And how do you know I left you in the first place?"

"You mean when you almost got killed saving that little girl and her mom without me? Everyone knows!" She waved an arm to demonstrate the totality of it all. "Percy woke up the entire house!"

My lips parted in surprise. "I am so sorry." Then I looked behind her. Percival was nowhere near me. He had indeed stopped at our property line, but I could've sworn...

"I'm not mad about him waking me up." She poked me softly in the chest. "I'm mad that you didn't. And that you almost got killed without me."

Oops. "Fine, next time I almost get myself killed, I promise to almost get you killed as well."

"See?" She held up her hands and shrugged. "That's all I ask." She bent at the waist, still gasping for air. Goddess, we were out of shape.

I decided to turn the tables on her. "This is all your fault, anyway."

"How is this my fault?" she asked Parris's sidewalk.

"You took the messages. Now they're, like, summoning me."

She bolted upright. "How?"

"They're all bright and summony. I don't know."

"So," she said, crossing her arms over her heaving bosom, "you haven't lost your powers after all."

"I can see glowy things. That's not power. That's most likely an aneurism waiting to happen."

Roane spoke up. "And you're sneaking out at four in the morning because...?"

"I told you. The messages. One of them is glowing, and I think something is really wrong with male-pattern-baldness guy. I think he's in trouble, and Percy wouldn't let me out of the house!" I turned and yelled at Percy through clenched teeth before refocusing on the wolf. "So I had to sneak out. Also, my hair."

"Really?" Annette said, alarmed.

"Yes. It was basically dragged through mud. I brushed it, but—"

"No, male-pattern-baldness guy," she replied. "What happened to him?"

"No clue. I think the real question here is: Are you two going to help me or not?"

"Get in," Roane said, his deep voice causing a delicious heat to coil low in my abdomen.

We went around and, after a quick wave to Parris, who was still gawking at us, climbed in.

I scooted next to him in the seat so Annette could sit beside me. "How many vehicles do you have?" I asked.

"Just the one. This one is a shapeshifter like me." When my eyes rounded, he laughed softly, his gaze appreciative despite my naïveté.

I nodded, accepting the fact that people often found my gullibility humorous. My dads said it made me adorable. I disagreed. "That was mean," I said. "After everything I've seen lately, a shapeshifting truck is well within the realm of possibility."

We sat idling for a solid thirty seconds before I raised a questioning brow.

"Seat belts," he commanded.

"Oh." We scrambled to get them on, then I gave him the address. He knew the area.

"I still can't believe you went on a mission without me," Annette said.

"I didn't want to wake you."

"That's so incredibly lame."

Brutal honestly had never been an obstacle for her. The question of how Roane knew where to find me hadn't even occurred to me until that moment. "Did Percy tell you?" I asked him.

"Tell me what?"

"Where to find me?"

"He was there, too?" Annette asked, now thoroughly miffed.

I smiled. "In wolf form."

Roane cast us a sideways glance, then another when we both gazed at him dreamily. "No, I was... already out."

Annette gasped. "Running with your pack?"

"Something like that."

"Wait." A thought occurred to me. "Do you have, like, a wolf mate?"

One corner of his sculpted mouth slid up. "Jealous?"

I snorted. "No. Maybe. How's her hair?"

"Fur. And, no. I do not have a wolf mate."

Relief flooded my chest cavity. I would never be a

homewrecker. Or a den-wrecker. Either way. I sucked in a soft breath when another thought occurred to me. I turned to Annette and whispered, "I wonder if he can have cubs."

She pointed at me and nodded.

"Wolf," he said, reminding us. "Excellent hearing."

We winced and shut up as he turned onto a side road. "It's just up here."

I felt it before we stopped. Cold. Pain. Fear.

Roane pulled onto a dirt drive. It was so dark, the narrow column of foliage seemed to go on forever, but a few seconds later, we pulled up to a rustic house.

I didn't wait. I unbuckled my belt and was over Annette and out the door before he'd stopped completely.

"Defiance!" she yelled, but I took off, tripping on the uneven ground as I went.

After fumbling with my phone, I finally managed to get my light on and held it out as I followed the pain. It stole my breath.

"Defiance," Roane said, following behind me. He caught up easily, took my arm, and pushed me behind him. "I smell blood."

"Oh my god. He's hurt."

We eased around an old detached garage that was probably a barn at one time. An old muscle car sat out back with a small crane that lifts engines.

"Can you see?"

"Everything," he said.

"That's so cool," Annette said.

We stole around the car, and there he was. Mr. Leonard Quinn lying on the ground with a seven-hundred-pound engine on his leg.

I rushed over and knelt beside him. He was unconscious. "Mr. Quinn?"

His lashes fluttered open. Though his cinnamon hair was indeed thinning, he was much younger than I thought he would be. Stocky with a boyish face, he was probably in his late thirties.

I quickly assessed the scene around me as Roane examined the motor. The chain on the small lift had broken, and somehow the motor ended up on top of him. I could see by the disturbed ground on his left that he'd struggled, possibly for hours, to get to a phone that lay nearby, a phone just out of his reach. It must have been beyond frustrating.

I pointed. "Annette, his phone."

She took her hand from her mouth, grabbed the phone, and handed it to me, then took out her own phone, and said, "I'm dialing 9-1-1."

"Thank you. Mr. Quinn, can you talk?" I took his icy hand in mine.

He smiled, clearly in shock. "I knew an angel would come for me, but I had no idea she would look like you. Makes it... all worthwhile." His voice was hoarse. It had to be from both the cold and the fact that he'd probably been yelling for help for hours.

I grinned and, after pocketing his phone, wrapped both of my hands around his. "Sadly, I'm no angel. How long have you been here?"

"I-I'm not certain. What time is it?"

"It's a little after four in the morning."

"Then a long freaking time. I'd only been... been working a couple of hours when this happened. Maybe... maybe ten?"

"This morning?" I asked, shocked.

He nodded. I was amazed he was even still alive.

"First responders are on the way," Annette said. She knelt beside me.

"I was rebuilding my motor." He pointed to the massive hunk of metal on his leg.

Roane spoke in a low tone. "I can lift it off him, but I don't know the extent of the damage. This could be the only thing keeping him from bleeding to death."

I nodded to him, then spoke to the backyard mechanic. "I can see that." His lashes drifted shut. "Leonard—"

"Leo," he corrected, blinking back to me.

"Leo, stay with me, okay? Can you stay awake until rescue gets here?"

"As long as I get to look at you, I can."

Annette brushed a lock of hair off his brow, fibers from her fingerless gloves grazing his nose. He reached up and rubbed it. The fact that he had the strength to move at all was a good sign.

"We need to cover him," she said.

He glanced up at her. "Wow. Two angels for the price of one. This must be my lucky day." He flashed a nuclear grin.

She offered him her best grin in return. "Damn straight it is. Can I get into your house? Grab some blankets?"

"Are you trying to get in my bed?"

"You're feisty," I said, trying not to giggle. "That's a good sign."

A thought hit him. He tried to rise but sucked in a sharp breath of air through his teeth and laid back.

"What is it?" I asked him.

"Work. I was supposed to be to work at three. I need to call in."

"How about I call for you tomorrow?"

He answered, but his words were garbled.

"We need to cover him," Annette repeated, worry lining her face. "We need to get him warm."

"Isn't there a thing about warming someone with hypothermia too fast?"

"Yes, but it's just blankets. I don't think he'll—" She stopped herself, but I could imagine what she was going to say. She didn't think he would survive much longer.

"What's that?" I asked, pointing into the trees that acted as a barrier between Leo's house and his neighbor's. Annette looked over while I raised two fingers and summoned the spell for warmth.

Having given up on lifting the motor off him safely, Roane knelt on his other side. The symbol I drew sparked to life, light exploding out of the lines to draw heat from above and below. Not a lot. Just a steady flow to keep the cold at bay.

"Wow," he said, gazing up at me. "How did you do that? Are you really an angel?"

Annette gaped at me.

My gaze shot to Roane's. Only powerful witches, supernatural beings, and a segment of the population with certain mental illnesses could see the light from my spells. The everyday mundane could not. Leo Quinn just got a lot more interesting.

Annette continued to gape. "You did a spell and tried to hide it from me."

"Did not," I said, throwing in my best scoff for good measure. I'd bought it in a little shop in Sedona, so I knew it was good. They sold quality stuff there.

"You totally did too."

"I totally did not."

"Are her spells like staring at the sun?" Leo asked, not helping at all.

She glowered at me. "They are exactly like that.

Well"—she looked down at him—"to certain people, they are. Say, you're not a homicidal maniac, are you?"

The last guy who could see one of my spells tried to kill us, so her question was legit, albeit poorly timed.

He laughed softly, then coughed, the act causing pain instantly. He bit down and threw back his head. I twirled a finger out of Miss Nosy Britches's line of sight. Just a little spell to ease the pain a bit. His blood pressure had to be either dangerously high or dangerously low. It could go either way.

He relaxed and tried to go to sleep on us.

Annette started telling him stories of her childhood—no idea why—when a police cruiser pulled up, followed by fire and rescue and an ambulance.

"You ordered the whole cavalry," I said to her.

"Yes, I did."

It took them a while to tourniquet his leg, get the motor back on the chain, and lift it off him. Roane helped with that, making sure the cold metal didn't break again. His muscles bulged in places I didn't know they could bulge, like this one muscle behind his biceps that looked really handy if he should ever need to support a woman's weight while... helping her change a lightbulb, and it took a lot not to drool.

"He wouldn't have lived much longer," an EMT told me after they got Leo loaded. "I can't believe you found him."

"That's her specialty," the chief said, walking up and shaking his head. "Didn't I just drop you off?"

"You did," I said. "But there was a glowing message, and then Percy wouldn't let me out, so I had to sneak down to the cave and follow the water out, then he almost caught me when I tried to get in the Bug, but Roane and Annette showed up, and I'm pretty sure I dented Roane's truck." I looked at him. "My bad."

"How about you go get some rest and try to stay home for a few hours. Let me catch up with my paperwork."

"You got it, Chief." I turned toward the EMT. "Can we ride with Leo to the hospital?"

"Yeah," Annette said. "Make sure he's okay."

"We've got room for one."

Annette deflated. "You go, then. Do your nonexistent magic on him if you need to."

I did a tiny sample of my nonexistent magic, twirling my finger behind my back, and the EMT said, "You know what? We can fit you both. Hop in."

She clapped her gloved hands, her curly hair bouncing with joy as well, and climbed inside. With some help. Her legs were not what one would call *lengthy*.

I looked at Roane. "We'll, um, meet you back at the house?"

He'd leveled a knowing smirk on me that held so much more than the average smirk. It was filled with, well, knowing. Appreciation. A little come-hither to soften the edges. And a shimmering dose of desire that shot straight to my nethers. He nodded and watched as I, too, tried to climb into the ambulance. So much harder than it looked on TV.

As we drove to the hospital, Leo looked over his oxygen mask and asked, "What are you?"

It felt wonderful. Doing good. Saving a life. I felt much like the EMTs must have, and a little guilty that I hadn't listened to the glowy thing sooner.

I leaned forward and whispered, "The real question is, what are you?"

ELEVEN

It was almost eight in the morning when we got home. Hopefully, Roane was sleeping, but I knew Ruthie would be up. I marched straight down the basement stairs and knocked on her door to tell on Percy.

Annette followed, only to tell on me instead.

Ruthie was dressed in her usual angelic gauze dress, this one a soft gold with midnight-blue edging.

We sat at the high table in her arts and crafts room. It was only then I realized there were a couple of doors in the room, and I wondered if one was a bedroom. Surely, she slept. Unless she really was a zombie.

For a moment, I thought I heard a soft whimper come from one of the rooms, but Ruthie didn't seem to notice. Instead, she made tea and insisted on the lowdown.

And the lowdown she would get. "First, he wouldn't let me do a spell to unlock the bar on the basement window."

"Which I wouldn't know about," Annette said, "because someone went without her sidekick. And I thought you lost your powers."

"Right," I said, busted. "I was trying to get them back, and Percy blocked me."

"Sweetheart"—Ruthie placed her cup in her saucer just so—"Percy can't possibly block your magics. You're simply too powerful. Was it iron?"

"His will?"

"No, dear." She stirred her tea absently. "The bar on the window."

"Oh. I have no idea. Why?"

"Witches can't manipulate iron or anything with a lot of iron in it."

"It had to be iron, then," Annette said. "Not that I would know since I wasn't there."

"I'd just assumed with your charmling status," Ruthie continued, "that rule wouldn't apply to you." She bowed her head in thought. "Interesting."

Annette and I looked at each other. "Did you know about the iron thing?" I asked her. She was much more knowledgeable about all things witchery than I was.

She put down her cup. "Yes and no. I mean, there are a ton of myths surrounding different metals with different preternatural beings."

"Like werewolves and silver," I said.

We exchanged glances again.

Her gray irises glistened. "You totally have to test Roane."

"Yeah, but I can't shoot him with a silver bullet. That just seems wrong after everything he's done for us."

Annette nodded. "Okay, well, how about stabbing him with a silver letter opener?"

"Oh, hey, that might do it."

"Like just a little poke," Annette added. "Don't go in all the way."

"That's what she said."

We burst out laughing, and at some point in the conversation, I realized I was delirious with all the adrenaline dumps and just a general lack of sleep. I needed to state my case quickly and find my bed. So, back to the complaining.

"Second," I said, "he tried to stop me from leaving the house. That's called false imprisonment, by the way, and it's illegal." I looked up and glared at Percy, wherever he may be.

Ruthie laughed softly. "I believe he was doing what he does best."

"Kidnapping?"

"Trying to keep you out of harm's way."

"Ruthie, I am not a child."

"Then act like it," she said, seeming to get irked herself.

"Wow," I said, taken aback. "Tell me how you really feel."

"You should never have left this house alone if you knew it could be dangerous. You are not immortal, Defiance."

"It was late." I regurgitated the same excuse I'd been using all night. "I didn't want to wake anyone. And how could I have known it would be dangerous?" I had to wonder what kind of tea had she made because I was feeling a bit woozy.

"Your magics will guide you in all things. You must learn to trust them."

"Well, it was still late. Percy didn't have a right to wake people up on my account."

She wasn't buying it. "Do you know why Roane is here?"

"Because I turned him into a shapeshifter so he could escape his murderous father?"

"No, after that."

"Because he looks great in a kilt and he's good at fixing things?"

"No, before that. I found him. Once I realized what he was, who he was, I searched for him for the same reason he's here now."

"Is this spiked?" I pointed to the tea, getting sleepier.

"He's here to protect you, Defiance. That is literally his job."

"I thought his job was to fix Percy's pipes?"

"That sounded kinky." Annette giggled.

I giggled too, and felt more than a little loopy. "Is there something in this tea?" I asked again.

"Of course not," Ruthie said. "It's just chamomile."

"You dosed me?" I asked, appalled.

Her expression flatlined. "You haven't slept, and you used your powers."

"I knew it!" Annette said.

"Naturally, you're going to feel a little woozy."

"I don't have any powers," I insisted, stubborn to the bitter end, as my dads would say. "So, you pay Roane to watch my every move?"

"Yes. Well, no. That's not what I meant. I pay him to be with you, and should the need arise—"

"He's a gigolo?" I asked, double appalled this time.

Annette rested her head on her arm. "Have you guys done it already?" Her words were slurred.

And I was the lightweight. Either chamomile worked way better than I thought, or Ruthie had tossed in a little rum for good measure. Except, usually, my BFF could drink me under the table. I would have to talk to Percy about him waking everyone up for no reason. It was taking a toll.

"No, we haven't done it," I said.

"Then he's not a very good one."

"Ha!" I laid my arm across the table too, rested my head on it, facing her, and whispered, "He's spectacular."

That hit her like a shot of espresso. She jerked upright. "You did him?"

I straightened too, only slower. "Not exactly. More like he did me."

"I probably shouldn't hear this," Ruthie said, then stayed right where she was and listened intently.

"And you didn't tell me?" Annette draped her body over the table again. "It's like I don't even know you anymore." Her last words faded out as her eyes drifted shut.

"For real, Ruthie, did you dose her?"

"Defiance, a lady never doses unless that lady intends to kill, and she'd better have a damn good reason."

"Good to know." I started to take another sip, then thought better of it. Still, the allure of sleep called to me. My eyelids felt thick and scratchy.

Ruthie cleared her throat and asked from behind her cup. "How was Houston?"

I put my cup down. "Oh, no you don't. If you want to know more about the hottie you've been banging for the last four decades, you're going to have to find out for yourself."

She pursed her lips. "Banging makes it sound so crude."

"What would you call it?"

"Shagging." A smile as warm as a summer breeze softened her face.

"Well, there you go." I was just about to grill her on the hows and whys of her sudden detachment from the tall drink of water that was Chief Houston Metcalf, when I heard the whimper behind her door again. "Ruthie, are you keeping someone locked in your bedroom?"

She turned, curious as well. "No."

She stood.

I channeled the desire to finally see her apartment beyond her arts and crafts room and used it as motivation to push myself up and off my chair.

She opened the door to a small bedroom, sparsely furnished with only the bare necessities. It was like Ruthie was punishing herself. She had an entire house full of lovely rooms, and she chose to live in squalor. Well, *squalor* may have been a bit of an overstatement, but I couldn't help but wonder why. Why live in the basement? Why cut ties with the love of her life?

The sound I'd heard was coming from the other side of her bed. And this being Percival, there was simply no telling what would happen next.

Wishing I had a baseball bat, I eased around a twin bed topped with a sage-green bedspread and found a little boy curled up in the corner.

"Samuel." I rushed to him.

His little blond head popped up, and he looked at me with huge blue eyes from behind folded arms. And he had tears—real tears—streaming down his handsome little face.

"What's wrong, sweetheart?"

He pointed over and up. "Sir."

I sat down next to him, my arms aching to embrace him. "What happened with Sir?"

"Him mad."

"He's mad at you?"

He nodded and scrunched up his face in what I thought was a demonstration of Sir's anger.

The cuteness caught me off guard, but the fact that anyone was angry with this sweet baby lit a fuse, igniting my own anger.

But what he did next—clawing at his arm and baring his teeth—stunned me. Had Sir hurt him? Was that even possible?

Percy grumbled above us.

Right there with him, I took a deep breath and pretended the fury rushing through my veins didn't feel like my blood had caught fire. "If Sir is mad at you," I said melodramatically, "then I'm mad at him."

He tried to put his hand on my face, and my heart shattered.

"Is he here now?" I asked as nonchalantly as I could.

He nodded and pointed again.

I followed his finger. Since walls didn't hinder him, I tried to decipher where, exactly, Sir might be hiding. From this position, he was either in the broom closet on the first floor or on the balcony landing between the staircases.

I looked back at Ruthie, who'd been watching us the whole time. "What can I do about this?"

"You're a charmling. I'm sure there are any number of things you could do."

"Let me rephrase. What would *you* do?"

She lifted a shoulder. "It's a remedy almost as old as we witches are, but the tried-and-true witch bottle works wonders. You could cast him off this plane, of course, but only you would know how to do that without a witch circle. And those can be a bit shaky, even with the strongest of witches."

"Witch bottle it is. How do I get him back inside of it?"

"You don't understand. There is nothing special about witch bottles, other than the fact that they're darned near unbreakable. On purpose, naturally. People were afraid they would break and release the witch, so they were usually made of very thick ceramic or even metal."

I looked back at Samuel as he tried to play with the zipper on my jacket. It seemed to fascinate him. "Interesting, but what am I not understanding?"

"The fact that any bottle will do."

"Oh." I remembered what went into a witch bottle. "I don't have to pee in it, do I?"

A breathy laugh escaped her. "I would highly advise against it."

"Yeah?" I asked, watching Samuel grab at the zipper, only to have his fingers slip through again and again. But he never grew frustrated.

A vine grew down the wall, and one stem brushed over his cheek.

He watched in wonder as a rose bloomed in front of him. As he leaned in to smell it, I realized he could touch and feel the vines and the roses.

Percy led one of the vines around my wrist, curling it around multiple times as he had before, and Samuel played with it. His touching the vine almost felt as though he were touching me. One end twisted around his finger, and he laughed and patted it before trying to eat it.

I pulled it out of his mouth as Ruthie sank onto the bed and wiggled her fingers at him. He tried to hide his face in my jacket, and I cast her an expression that told her exactly how adorable I found the kid.

"Witches are hardly stupid," she said, keeping her smile steady. "Not that any of the accused were actually witches back then, but a few real witches got together and created a sort of revenge, which, unlike what modern films would have you believe, is rather unlike us."

"What kind of revenge?"

"They created a spell that reverses the effects of a witch bottle. Whoever creates one and urinates into it to try to trap a witch will instead trap his own soul upon his death."

"I like it," I said with a grin. "Savvy and deserving."

"It has to be done on an individual basis, bottle by bottle, so it makes me wonder who in this area would have known to do that back then."

"So, Sir was very likely a persecutor of innocent people."

"Very likely."

"And now he abuses children."

She lowered her head. "It looks that way."

"Ink!" Samuel said, clearly able to see through walls as well as run through them. Ink was probably next door with the wolf. Samuel hopped up and vanished through the wall.

I climbed to my feet. Not an easy task. "What do you say we pay Sir a visit?"

"Sounds good. I've been trying to pinpoint his location. So far no luck, but I don't have nearly the power you do."

I walked back into her arts and crafts room, which would normally be a living room in the small apartment, and looked around at all the books and potions and maps on the table she'd pushed aside for tea with the girls. Potions were of particular interest to me, but now was not the time.

Annette was still over and out, but she was the one who'd wanted to be in the thick of it. I didn't dare go on a ghost hunt without my illustrious sidekick. Not anymore. Not ever again. She would get what she asked for.

Her glasses sat askew on her face, her mouth pressed

open with her arm, and a thick lock of curly chestnut hair lay across her nose. I snapped a pic for posterity's sake, then tried to wake her with a gentle tap on the shoulder. When that didn't work, I shook her softly. When that only garnered a groggy moan of annoyance, I shook her harder. Nothing.

"Well," I said to Ruthie, much louder than I needed to. "Guess I'll go ghost hunting by myself."

Annette bolted upright. "Ghost hunting?" she asked, morbid little being that she was. "You're hunting ghosts?"

"Are you in or are you going to sleep on the table all day and wake up with one hell of a crick in your neck?"

"I'm in." She swiped at the drool that had dripped down one side of her mouth. "I was born to hunt ghosts."

Somehow, I didn't doubt that.

We said our goodbyes to Ruthie and headed upstairs after a quick, longing glance at Roane's door.

"Do you know where this *Sir* is?" Annette asked me.

"I have a good idea where he's hanging out if Samuel's directions are any indication."

"Oh, good. Do I need anything? Like salt? A cross? Garlic?"

I chuckled. "We aren't hunting a vampire. Wait." I stopped in the hallway and turned toward her. "Given everything we've learned, do you think vampires are real too?"

Her lids rounded behind her turquoise cat-eye glasses.

"You know what?" I said, continuing the journey. "Let's not worry about that right now."

She followed. "Right. Good idea."

A knock sounded as we headed across the foyer.

I groaned, and Percy grumbled, making me wonder who it was.

Annette went to the door and pulled it open. "Oh, it's you."

I walked up behind her. "Mr. Vogel." I was none too pleased that the burly man was gracing our doorstep again.

"You still haven't plugged in your phone."

"Or we have caller ID," Annette offered.

He glared down at her, his ire turning his pasty skin a bright scarlet.

His presence felt like acid on my skin. I found that many people only seemed distant or antagonistic, but deep down they were nice people. Vogel didn't fall into the nice category. He was aggressive and volatile all the way through to his cold, black heart. I also had the feeling he'd hurt people in his past. I would be looking into that past as soon as I had a chance.

I pushed past Annette to take first position at the door. "Mr. Vogel, what can I do for you? Besides bring someone back from the dead, that is."

"Can I talk to you alone?" He stepped back, expecting me to follow.

The darkness that overwhelmed me in that moment took my breath away, as though his intentions had manifested into a physical sensation. Even if I'd wanted to follow, Percy wrapped his vines around both of my ankles. To some degree, it didn't matter. I wasn't about to follow Vogel anywhere. He had a peculiar smell about him. An off scent I couldn't quite place.

Oh, yes. There it was.

Death.

But to a larger degree, Percy keeping me glued to the spot did matter. I looked down and whispered through my teeth, "False imprisonment, mister."

He didn't care. He tightened his hold, clearly no longer

trusting my judgment. If he ever did. We were going to have to talk. Soon.

"I'm on a case at the moment," I said to Mr. Vogel.

"I just need a minute."

"I'm afraid I don't have one. And I'm not sure we would have anything to talk about even if I did. I told you, I lost my powers."

He stepped close again. "I'm pretty certain I don't believe you."

"Be that as it may..." I started to close the door.

His hand shot out, and he grabbed my arm and yanked none too gently.

"Hey!" Annette shouted, trying to get past me and at him. Little firecracker.

His audacity stunned me. The razor-sharp thorns from the vines that twisted around his hand stunned him. He jerked his hand back, and we both stood there with our mouths agape as Annette harumphed in satisfaction.

He backstepped to a safer distance before stabbing me with that lethal glare of his. "I wanted to do this the easy way."

"What does that mean?" I asked, stunned by his audacity again.

His gaze darted past me to something over my shoulder.

I was not about to take my eyes off him. The man was quicker than he looked. He tossed me one more glare for good measure, then turned and strode down the walk to his pickup.

I finally turned and saw what I knew I would, because a calmness came over me anytime Roane stepped into my orbit.

He stood behind me, hair a mass of tangles and arms crossed over his wide chest, in a rumpled maroon T-shirt, leather kilt, and work boots he'd crossed at the ankles. All the things a growing girl needed.

"Did Percy wake you?" I glared up at the entity as though I could actually see him, though I had appreciated the intervention with Vogel.

"I was up," he lied, his voice thick with sleep, and his lashes crumpled together like he'd been in a deep state of slumber.

"I'm sorry."

"That I was up?"

"No," I was quick to correct. "Never. It's just... Roane, Ruthie told me you're basically paid to keep an eye on me. It's unnecessary. Please don't feel obligated to, I don't know, be my bodyguard."

The grin that stole across his face seized my lungs. "Ms. Dayne, there is little on Earth I'd rather do than guard your body."

Every bone I owned, and even a few I didn't, dissolved. It was the mischief in his smile. The glistening in his eyes. The promise of things to come in his expression.

A sigh echoed through the foyer, and we turned to see Annette standing close by. Like really close by. Like at our shoulders. She had difficulty with respecting personal space.

"Either way"—I fidgeted with my wrist, missing my bracelet—"it's not your job."

"Are you firing me?" His deep voice sent ripples of pleasure over my skin.

"Please don't fire him," Annette said, her expression pleading, and it took everything in me not to crack up.

Something moved in my periphery. The shadow I'd been seeing. The entity from the witch bottle. Sir.

"There he is," I said to Nette and Roane.

They looked up at the balcony overlooking the foyer. Percy released my ankles, and I sprinted upstairs, even though I only saw the barest hint of a shape. I stopped at the balcony and walked toward the wall.

"I would like to have a word with you." That was when I realized I had no plan whatsoever. Then I saw it. Him. A stocky man with puffy bags under his eyes and a bulbous nose. I had a similar look once when I'd first discovered mudslides. The morning after had not been pretty.

He glared at me, but his glare was more disgust than the acidic, hate-filled glower of toxic waste that was Vogel's infamous death stare. Sure enough, Sir was dressed in Puritan garb. A wide white collar and cuffs, a form-fitting black coat, breeches that gathered at the calves, stockings, and black loafers with a metal buckle. He was the real deal.

I was rather impressed. "Dude, you've been trapped in a bottle for, like, hundreds of years. Maybe take a breather. Get to know the people a little. Stop being a dick to a little boy one-tenth your size."

"You can see him?" Annette called up to me.

"Yes." I turned back to her. "Hey, aren't you supposed to be by my side? Isn't that where a sidekick lives?"

"I'm okay." She kept her feet firmly planted downstairs.

I turned back to the Puritan. "Did you know there's a line of supplements named after your pride?"

"Thou art a witch." His sneer could freeze Hawaii.

"You guys legit said *thee* and *thou* and *art*?"

His watery gaze turned into a livid glare. "Thou shalt not suffer a witch to live."

"Wow. Seriously?" I stepped closer.

He grew opaquer but just barely. We stood eye to eye, our heights evenly matched, which was perfect. I could glare right back. "I don't mean to rain on your parade, buddy, but that's pretty cliché. Is that all you assholes had to work with while you were persecuting innocent people back in the day?"

The smirk he wore spoke volumes.

Oh, yeah. He was going down. But apparently not before me.

A wrecking ball hit me square in the chest. At least, it felt like a wrecking ball.

I heard a crack, the breath whooshed out of my lungs, and I went flying back. Literally flying. I soared over the railing, my trajectory forming less of an arch than a seven, sharply changing from horizontal to vertical, which kind of defied the laws of physics as I understood them. The ceiling rocketed away from me as the floor rose up. I couldn't imagine how much this was going to hurt.

"Defiance!" Annette screamed.

While the stop was sudden, it wasn't as skull-crushing as it should have been. Instead of slamming into the ground, soft tentacles captured me and slowed my descent before bringing me to a full stop. Rather like a thrill ride at a fair. I was not, however, thrilled. Not in the least. I couldn't breathe. Really couldn't breathe. Something was very, very wrong.

As Percy lowered me to the ground and faded back, I doubled over and gasped, clutching my chest. My vision blurred. Tears amassed. There was a loud ringing in my ears. The pain shooting through my chest was not in my heart but in my bones. My collarbones. My sternum. My rib cage. They all felt shattered. Sir had broken me.

Suddenly Roane was by my side, and I was off the ground again. In his arms. Against his chest. He carried me to the kitchen as pain thundered through me and laid me on the table.

And then Ruthie was there, shoving tea down my throat again. Gawd, that woman loved her tea. But I couldn't swallow. Couldn't talk. Couldn't hear Ruthie when she got in my face and spoke. She ran out of the room and came back holding a drawing. "This," she said, as though underwater. "Draw this."

A pain so sharp, so overpowering that it suffocated me, wracked my body. Nausea and dizziness decided to join the party, and I was almost blinded by the agony. I felt the bones in my chest crack and scrape against one another, like a puzzle in a puzzle box before someone put it together. The pieces were all there, they were just in the wrong place.

She held my left hand as I tried to draw the symbol, but crushed bones sucked.

So.

Bad.

I realized she was arguing with both Roane and Annette. After a lengthy discussion, Roane turned away, angry, then she encouraged me to draw again, holding up the picture.

I tried to catch my breath but only managed short, excruciating gasps.

She yelled to get through to me.

I couldn't make out the words, but I could imagine what she wanted. However, I'd learned early on that if I didn't know what a spell meant, it was difficult to infuse it with power. I just didn't know what power to infuse it with.

Still, I tried. I slowed my breathing and concentrated, trying to remember what the spell meant, wondering how Ruthie, who didn't know the language, could be aware of its meaning. When I raised my shaking hand, it seemed to upset the wolf.

I concentrated on him. On his calmness. The steely

resolve in everything he did. Even in his agitated state, it helped. I examined the symbol again, tearing through my memories, trying to spot the right one like a facial recognition program trying to match a face to a name.

There.

It sat on the fringes of my memories the way a child sat in a corner after being scolded. I pulled it forward. Drew it on the air. It blinded me with light for a split second.

Roane shoved Ruthie aside and took my hand. Wrapped his long fingers around mine for a better grip. Twisted our hands together. And held on.

The spell worked. The pain began to leech out of me, and I could draw in a slightly deeper breath.

I felt Roane squeeze my hand. His face, so near mine, was simple perfection. Ruggedly handsome. Five o'clock scruff. Sparkling olive irises. Lashes to die for. Or kill for.

But then, as I watched him, his shoulders went stiff.

"Stop!" I heard Ruthie in the distance, the ringing in my ears ebbing at last. "Defiance, stop!"

Roane kept his gaze locked on mine, but his face tightened into a mask of barely controlled agony, his irises shimmering with unspent tears. He bit down and closed his eyes, pushing a tear past his lashes.

Ruthie and Annette were both yelling at me. Annette shook me. "Defiance, stop!"

I snapped to attention. Pulling my hand out of Roane's grip, I tried to sit up. But the pain, while manageable, was still there.

Roane dropped to his knees, then fell to the ground.

I gaped at him. "What happened?" I asked Ruthie. "What did I do?"

"Now's not the time. You need to ease his pain. Hurry, love."

He gripped a table leg with one hand and clutched his chest with the other. What did I do?

"Hurry, sweetheart."

I rolled over and drew the symbol that practically burst out of me, perhaps putting a little more energy into it than I'd planned, and pushed it over him like a blanket.

Light enveloped him. Embraced him. Saturated every molecule in his body. It took a moment, but his muscles relaxed. His panting slowed.

I eased off the table, despite the pain, and lay behind him. "I'm sorry," I whispered into his ear. Scooting next to him, I brushed his hair off his face. "Roane, please be okay."

He turned over and buried his face in my hair. "I'm okay, gorgeous," he said, but he said it through clenched teeth. Slowly, the spell worked, and he relaxed more and more.

I lay my head on my folded arm and petted his hair. Kissed his cheek. Marveled in the fresh scent of him. And fell.

TWELVE

Sometimes I wonder if all of this is happening
because I didn't forward that message to ten other people.
—Meme

I heard a clock ticking down the hall. Felt a weight on my waist. Warm covers over that. I pried open my lids to see a beautiful red wolf in human form.

His lashes fanned across his cheeks as he slept, his breathing deep and even. An arm tucked under his head.

I started to move, but the vines that embraced us tightened gently.

"You're awake," Annette whispered from a nearby chair. She'd been working on her laptop. She closed it and eased closer.

"Am I?" I asked, my mouth full of cotton. "This isn't another dream? Because damn." I gestured toward the man candy wrapped around me.

She giggled behind her hand.

My dads sat beside her, draped over the table with blankets wrapped around them, snoring away.

I heard a soft purr and leaned up to see Ink on the other side of Roane, the cat's head tucked against the wolf's neck. "Why is Percy suddenly into bondage?"

"To support your weight," she whispered. "You were both still healing."

"Like a cast?" I whispered back.

"Exactly."

I reached over Roane, and Percy pulled back the vines so I could scratch Ink's ears. Poor cat had been tortured the last couple of days. I could only hope he'd get used to it. There was no telling how long we would have Samuel with us. If I had my way, it would be forever, but I wasn't sure how Ink would take that.

"Now that you're okay..." Nette leaned forward. "You are okay, aren't you?"

I nodded.

"Then, oh my god, that was so cool. What happened on the stairs? You just flew, *vroom*." She reenacted my flight over the railing with her hand. "And then *whoosh*." She showed my descent in detail. Apparently, my legs had been kicking and my arms flailing. "And then *bam*." She wrapped it up by showing my sudden stop by stopping suddenly. Then her hands floated down like feathers landing softly on the ground.

"A riveting portrayal."

"Deph, it was... it was magical." She hopped off her chair. "Can I get you some water? Coffee? Wine?"

"Please. In that order."

She snickered and got a glass down.

"Are you sore?" She handed me a glass of water with a straw.

I drew deep from the cup, my throat scorched. "Not terribly." I couldn't imagine how Roane would feel. So far, I'd dented his truck, gotten him stabbed, and shattered every bone in his chest. I was such a great dating prospect. It was no wonder he liked me.

"Percy," I kept my voice low.

A rose blossomed near me.

"Can you let me out without disturbing the wolf?"

He went to work instantly, loosening his grip here and tightening it there, until Roane was secured, and I was free.

"Thank you," I said to him. "Again."

Roses all around the kitchen blossomed, filling the room with a rich, fragrant scent.

With Annette's help, I eased onto my feet, trying not to disturb Roane, but parts of me creaked. Literally creaked. I wondered if there was a spell for that.

Annette draped a blanket over my shoulders.

"Thanks, Nette," I said softly. Once I'd straightened, I turned and looked behind me.

Ruthie was sleeping in a wingback they'd pulled in for her from the parlor, her sandaled feet propped on an ottoman.

I examined the takeout bags on the table as quietly as I could. "Ruthie is basically a ghost, right?"

"Yeah." Nette pointed to a bag that had takeout from one of our favorites, Kiki's.

"Oooo." I grabbed the chicken fried rice. "And she can't leave the grounds, right?"

"Right." She motioned for me to hand her the rice to heat up.

"It's okay. It's just as good cold. If she's a ghost..." I paused to take a bite and roll my eyes in ecstasy. "Why does she need sleep?"

She nibbled on a crunchy roll she'd dipped in sweet-and-sour sauce, her plastic chopsticks held expertly. "This is your world, my lurve. I only take messages in it and do research."

And I wasn't sure how much more of this world I could take. "What time is it?"

She took another bite, held up a finger, and reopened her computer to check. "It's almost three."

"Holy crap. We've been on that floor all day?" Hopefully, no one had come to visit, what with us sprawled on the floor like drunken teens.

"Yep. Your dads, of course, freaked, but Ruthie assured them you'd be fine. Just so you know, they weren't just a little freaked. Like it really got to them this time."

I looked over at their sleeping forms. They sat right next to each other, Papi's arm thrown over Dad. They were going to be so sore when they woke up. "I think they're traumatized. After my six-month stay-cay, who can blame them?"

"I wish they'd adopt me," she said softly.

"They still can. You're only"—I blinked in surprise—"forty-five."

"So are you," she said defensively.

"No, I mean, I missed your birthday too."

"Oh, pfft." She waved a dismissive hand. "It was uneventful. You didn't miss anything."

"We always toast on your birthday."

"I still toasted. Just, you know, by myself."

I put down my fork. "You didn't celebrate?"

"I did, actually."

"Good."

I started to take another bite.

"With Percy."

"You celebrated your birthday with Percy?"

"Yes."

I pointed up. "This Percy? Our Percy?"

"Yes. And you, actually." Her mouth slid into a side-ways grin. "He let me into your room so I could toast with you."

After beaming at her, I looked up. "Thanks, Percy."

The vines rustled.

"Only I got a little wasted, and the next thing I know, I'm back in my room with no recollection of how I got there."

"Really?"

"Still, it's not every day one gets to toast one's birthday with a floating witch in a state of suspended animation."

"True. So, I need to wash my hair."

"Wait, what?" she asked.

"I need a shower. Then I'm going to try to get everyone into a real bed."

"There is no way I'm going upstairs. Not with that *thing* up there."

"Okay. But I need a shower."

She jumped to her feet and grabbed my arm. "There is no way you're going upstairs either."

"Nette." I gave her my no-arguments face.

"Deph." She gave me hers right back.

"En."

"Dee."

"You did not see what my hair went through in the backyard of Clara Thomas's house."

"You did not see what you went through on the balcony at Ruthie Goode's house."

"Well, I kinda did. You showed me." And I'd lived it.

"No. You don't understand. You didn't just fall. You were shoved with such violence, Dephne. Such malicious intent." She leaned close and looked at me from over her glasses. "He aimed to kill you."

"Well, then his aim is lousy."

"Not from where I was standing."

I took another bite and washed it down with cool water. "You're telling me I can't take a shower because the Puritan from hell is on the balcony?"

"I don't know where he is. I just know he's not in here, and here is where I'm staying." She popped an entire slice of the crunchy roll in her mouth and, well, crunched.

Draping the blanket onto the back of a chair, I rubbed my hands together. "I guess it's time for a rematch, then, because I am taking a shower if it kills me."

Annette did the deer-in-the-headlights thing.

"Excellent hearing," a voice came from below. Not, like, hell, but below us. And here we thought our whispering would be nigh indecipherable.

Roane rose, the vines falling away to let him. Ink scrambled away from him while I scrambled to the floor to help.

"I'm good, gorgeous." He managed a sitting position. He pulled a knee up and put an elbow on it, and all I wanted to do was look under the kilt. I had to know. "But *you* are in no shape to take on the revenant."

So that's what we were calling it now. So much cooler than the Puritan. "And you are in no shape to stop me. You don't know how bad I want a shower."

The grin that slid across his face took my breath away. "I didn't say you couldn't have a shower. You can use mine."

While the thought alone sent a warmth to my nethers, I shook my head. "It'll be fine. I challenged him. He fought back. I'll use the passageway to sneak up to my room and then deal with him when I smell better."

Roane surprised me and leaned close. Ran his nose

along my jaw. "You smell like midnight rain and jasmine," he whispered into my ear, his warm breath giving me goosebumps.

A single chopstick fell to the floor. We looked up at Annette, who sat watching us, transfixed, her chin cupped in her hands.

After a quick giggle, I looked back at the wolf. "I'm so sorry, Roane."

His thick lashes cast a shadow over the olive green in his eyes. "You said that already, but it was my decision."

"Your decision?" I was confused. "I didn't know what that spell would do." Not till after it was too late, and I'd literally transferred my pain to him.

"Why do you think we didn't tell you?"

Frustration coursed through my veins like sand. I stood and looked down at him. "You don't get to make those kinds of decisions without me anymore."

He stood to tower over me. Not fair. "Then you don't get to go out in the middle of the night without me anymore."

"Fine."

"Fine."

We only realized we'd raised our voices when my dads stirred. Papi snuggled closer, and they went back to sleep. Ruthie never moved a muscle, snoring softly. Ladylike.

Roane accompanied Nette and I through the passageways upstairs. He showed us where it opened into Annette's room, pressing and pushing aside a sliding door to reveal the back of a freestanding mirror.

"It's in my closet?" she asked.

"So that's how you unlock them."

Roane carefully moved the mirror aside, and we stepped in.

"This is your closet?" I marveled because it was marvelous. The thing was massive. While my closet was big, my room was ginormous. Her closet took up half of what would've been allotted to her bedroom. Not that she had it even half full.

"Why do you think I chose this room?"

"You need more clothes," I said.

"I agree. We have to get our business going ASAP. Baby needs a new pair of shoes."

We giggled, and she asked Roane, "Are you sure we're safe?"

"No." He looked at me. "But a revenant can't normally do what the Puritan did to you. I don't think he could hurt a mundane."

"Oy, you with the mundane thing again." She held up a hand in surrender. "I'm a witch. I swear."

He grinned. She melted. It was like his smiles had supernatural powers of their own.

We stepped into her bedroom. She had decorated it with all things witch. It was alarmingly similar to the décor at Love's shop, The Witchery.

Speaking of whom... "You never told me what you did to Love to make her so mad at you."

"What's Love got to do with it?"

"I don't know. You just never—"

"Love hurts."

"She hurt you?" I asked, alarmed.

"Well, love is a battlefield."

Ah. We were playing the song title game. "Have you tried love in an elevator?"

"No." She draped her jacket over her gorgeous cast iron bed. "I'm all out of love."

"Please." I examined an old photograph of Percy, my

grandfather, in her room. Man, he was a looker. "You're addicted to love." I fought both a giggle and the urge to ask her why she had a photo of my grandfather on her mirror. Probably because the guy was hot, but still. He had long since passed. And not peacefully.

"Tainted love, maybe."

I gaped at her. "You've always been lucky in love."

"No, I've always been a victim of love."

"You can't give up. People need love."

"I'm telling you, love stinks."

"Love makes the world go 'round."

"Love bites."

"Give love a try."

"Love don't live here anymore."

"You need to open your heart. You never know. One day you're walking along, trying not to trip over your own feet, and bam. Love walks in." I stepped closer. "Like the first time ever I saw your face." I reached up to brush my fingers across her cheek.

She slapped my hand away. "Space bubble."

"I never knew love like this before."

She ducked away from me and held up a finger to put me on pause. "Okay, the love game is over."

"Last night, I dreamed of loving you."

"No. That's wrong."

I wrapped my arms around her. "Lovin', touchin', squeezin'."

"Ew, stop."

After drawing in a deep breath full of melancholy and my lost will to live, I headed to the closet and ducked into the passageway. "Love will lead you back to me!" I yelled.

"Not in this lifetime!" she yelled back before closing her bathroom door.

Roane slid the door closed and followed me. "You two have some unique conversations."

"Thank you," I said, even though I was certain it wasn't a compliment. I only found my room in the passageway because of the camera setup. I pointed at it. "By the way, this needs to come down."

He grinned.

"I mean it, Roane. I know magic. I can do things."

When I opened the door-slash-shelf, I saw a little blond boy in the corner of my bathroom. I turned on the light. He sat huddled on the tile floor, his arms wrapped around his knees, his face buried behind them.

"Samuel." I rushed to him.

He looked up, his face wet with tears. And there was a mark. On his face. Like he'd been hit.

Before I could even wonder about the whys and hows of a ghost bruising—honestly, how hard did a ghost have to be hit before it left a bruise?—anger spiked within me like a lightning strike.

It was so hot and so fast, I didn't remember leaving my room or walking the mezzanine to the balcony that over-looked the foyer or Roane yelling at me from behind.

I didn't remember raising my hand. Or casting the spell in the air to summon the revenant. And I didn't remember dragging him into my palm. Curling him into my fist. Crushing him.

Until I stood there, my chest heaving, my knuckles white with a blackness seeping from between my fingers. That was when I panicked. "Gigi!" I yelled, afraid to move, like that time I'd captured a bee, and the fear of the sting I might receive if the thing got the chance had immobilized me.

Roane stood beside me, staring at my outstretched hand.

Then he folded his arms over his chest and leaned against the back wall like he hadn't a care in the world. As if to say, "You got yourself into this mess. You can get yourself out of it."

"Gigi!" I yelled again.

Annette came running, a towel wrapped around her, and skidded to a halt.

Spry for an eighty-year-old, Ruthie hurried up the stairs, my dads behind her, making sure she didn't fall. They needn't have bothered. She was quicker and more agile than me.

"What do I do with it?" I asked, imitating a marble statue. Some of the darkness leeched out. I slapped my other hand over my fist to hold it in.

Ruthie gawked. "Is that—?"

"Yes! It's the witch hunter!"

"I knew I should've brought salt," Annette said.

"What do I do?" I asked Ruthie.

Samuel stood a few feet away, his huge blue eyes as round as Jupiter.

"We need a container," Ruthie said. "Something that can't be opened."

"Then how do I get him inside?"

"I know!" Annette took off toward my room.

"Don't you dare pour out my Patrón!"

"You keep Patrón in your room?" Dad asked.

"Only the one bottle. I bought it in celebration of my divorce being final, but I never opened it. That stuff is too expensive to drink."

Annette ran back to us, her flapping towel dangerously close to revealing more about her than anyone needed to know. Too bad the Puritan was locked in my fist. He'd have a cow at how much skin she was showing. It would've been fun to watch.

"This." She skidded to a halt beside me. "It's a container and can't be opened." She held out the crystal ball.

"No." I frowned at her. "You bought that for me."

"You can still use it."

I glanced askance over my shoulder.

Ruthie nodded.

"Even though it's solid glass?"

"Glass is more porous than you might think," she said. "He'll fit."

"Okay, fantastic. So how do I get him in there?"

"How did you get him into your palm?" she asked.

"I don't know. It just sort of happened, like everything else I do." I never thought before I leaped. That was my problem. Well, one of them.

Ruthie stepped in front of me, a patient smile on her face. "Only you know how to do it." She put her hand over my closed fists. "Take deep breaths and think about it."

The pressure of holding him in my palm was starting to feel like tectonic plates rubbing together and creating friction. My hand was getting hotter and hotter. Like I'd disrupted some sort of cosmic balance, and the universe was trying to right itself again. "Deep breaths. Okay, I can do this."

Roane was still leaning against the wall without a care in the world, a gorgeous grin lifting one corner of his mouth.

Ruthie took the glass orb from Annette and held it out to me. "This way, no one can ever release him again. Even if it happens to break, he'll be scattered throughout the microscopic holes in the glass."

"Right. Good idea." Heat blistered my hand, but I concentrated, filling my lungs and slowly releasing the air.

Ruthie was wrong, however. I didn't know anything. The dozens of witches who came before me did. Those who were a thousand times stronger than I was. I tapped into that. I went back in time and asked my sisters how to stuff a malevolent spirit into a glass orb, as one does.

Naturally, they had an answer.

"Oh," I said aloud. "Duh."

The spell flashed in my mind, bright, hot, and excited. I risked the revenant's escape by releasing my left hand and taking the orb. I cradled it in my palm and drew the spell on the air with the orb.

This spell reminded me of a Josephine knot, intricate and interlaced. Closing loose ends. Tying them off. Binding that which needed to be bound. Instead of the air glowing with the lines of the spell, the orb absorbed the power and glowed as bright as a small star.

I brought my right hand to my mouth, the energy in it scorching my skin. I filled my lungs and opened my hand.

Annette gasped.

But I'd tethered the revenant to me as I blew softly across my palm. His molecules drifted like dust on the wind and penetrated the glowing glass. Even though it was solid, it absorbed the revenant, soaking him up and drawing him deep inside.

We would never know his name, but it didn't matter. I leaned closer to the glass as it began to solidify, and whispered, "You will never know peace."

The glow dissipated, and I could see beyond it again.

"Did you do it?" Annette hugged the front of her towel.

I turned and showed her the orb. "I did."

"Oh, wow." She walked forward and peered inside. "You can see him in there." She looked at my dads. "It was clear before. Now it has black sand in it." She tapped it like a kid at a snake exhibit, because that doesn't make the snakes nervous at all. I couldn't help but wonder what it would do to Sir.

My dads leaned in. "You did it, cariña," Dad said.

Annette beamed. "This calls for donuts."

"Isn't it, like, four in the morning?"

"Almost five. And Dunkin' opens at five. I should know. Worst two weeks of my life."

"Okay, but don't get pulled over." A teasing grin played about Roane's lips. "You're nigh naked."

"And you're nigh high if you think I'm going out for donuts in a towel." She turned on her heel and strutted off like only my BFF could.

"You did it," Ruthie said, her smile full of pride. "And without almost getting killed this time."

"That's a first, eh?"

She laughed.

I hugged my dads, raked my gaze over Roane as though he were in wolf form and I was a dog brush, and announced my intent to finally take a shower. Roane offered to help. My dads were not amused. But I was.

I walked over to Percy and pulled a rose as black as my heart closer to smell. He wrapped a new vine around my wrist since I'd burned the last one to ash. I had so many questions for him. For everyone.

"The offer still stands," Roane said. "About the shower."

I felt a warmth spread over my face. "Though I am dying to see under the kilt, I think since I've already tried to kill you once today, maybe we should give you some time to heal."

"You can look up my kilt anytime," he threw over his shoulder as he walked off.

Electricity arced through my body. I went in search of Samuel before I caved and took the wolf up on his offer.

Samuel had disappeared after I stuffed his friend into the orb. And now I couldn't find him. He must be torturing the cat. Wasn't there something about kids who tortured animals growing up to be serial killers? Sadly, I'd never know.

THIRTEEN

Today I'm wearing a lovely shade of
I slept like shit so don't piss me off.
—T-shirt

Fifteen minutes later, I had just stripped off my clothes in my bathroom when Annette came in through the passageway. I jumped and grabbed a towel.

"Please," she said with a scoff. "Like I haven't seen your sad excuse for a bosom before."

"What?" I looked down at the girls. They were showing their age a little, but all in all, they were still pert. Spirited. Dare I say perky?

"I'm posting it to our social media page."

I hugged the towel to me. "No one needs to know what you think of my bosom."

"We are back, baby."

"Who is we?"

"And the world is going to know it."

"But does the world *need* to know it?"

"I've already applied for the LLC. Breadcrumbs, Inc. is back in business."

"We were never in business."

"Right. But we are now. So... never mind." She hurried out. Hopefully to get the donuts. But who knew what hare-brained—inspired—scheme she'd come up with between here and there?

"Wait," I called down the passageway. "We have a social media page?"

An hour later—it was a long shower—I had squeaky-clean hair, polished skin, and sparkly teeth. In theory. With those three essentials checked off my to-do list, I went in search of someone I knew would have answers. It had taken me a while to learn his signature. His texture. But once I figured out where I'd felt him before, I knew exactly where to look for Percival Goode.

I took the basement stairs and headed straight for the door between Roane's and Ruthie's. I'd felt a presence every time I came down here, but it hadn't occurred to me until now that what I was feeling was my biological grandfather.

The door was locked as usual. Before he could stop me, I did a simple spell and unlocked it. The door opened to a completely empty room. Small with a dirt floor, it couldn't have been more than ten feet by ten.

I turned on my phone's flashlight and saw something glisten on the ground near the back wall. I stepped forward only to find my feet glued to the spot. Percy had put on his Sherlock Holmes hat and figured out my game.

"It's okay, Percy." I kept my voice soft. "I already know."

The vines shrank back but stayed close. They slid along the walls of the empty room like thousands of snakes. Watching me. Making sure I didn't get too close.

I stepped near the glistening object. A headstone. Percy's bones were underneath it.

Percival and Ruthie had split long before I had been born, though they'd never officially divorced. He'd grown interested in black magic which, at its core, was all about doing harm in one way or another for personal gain. He had quickly become addicted. Apparently, that was a thing. He'd fallen deeper and deeper into that world until his humanity had been almost completely stripped away.

After that, Ruthie didn't see him for years. Then, in a more lucid moment, he'd come to her, wanting to die. The darkness would not let him, so he'd begged her for help.

She and her coven had performed a ritual. They had to burn him in a witch fire and sear the flesh from his bones to accomplish the tragic act. Those bones were buried here.

I knelt in front of the headstone.

Percy covered it with vines before I could read it.

I smiled at him and brushed them away, and he let me, pulling back until I could see the black stone. I read the name that had been etched into the memorial. "Percival Channing Goode." I looked up. "That's an incredible name."

The room hummed around me.

"You keep saving my life." A soft vibration rippled over me. "I just wanted to thank you."

Brushing dirt off the stone, I looked for dates. There were none. But there was a saying at the bottom. *Igne natura renovatur integra.*

Since my Latin was beyond rusty, I cast a spell, drawing the lines of *reveal* on the air and pushing the bright hot symbol toward the stone. The letters transformed into *Through fire, nature is reborn whole*. They stayed that way until I released the spell.

I stood. He'd saved my life I didn't know how many times. He deserved his privacy. "I'm sorry I bothered you, Percy. I won't do it again. Just... just thank you. For everything."

An entity took shape before me. Vines rose and formed a human shape and then fell away to reveal a revenant. A man. Percival Channing Goode, in all his glory.

When I'd first seen a picture of him, the one Annette now had in her room, my initial impression was that Percy could've given Lucifer Morningstar a run for his money. And I was not wrong.

The man was nothing short of stunning. My grandmother sure knew how to pick 'em. Inky black hair. Full mouth. Strong jaw. His clothes were a little dated. Late sixties, early seventies. Not a great time for fashion. But he didn't just pull it off, he made it look good.

"Percival." I didn't try to hide the surprise in my voice.

He tipped an invisible hat. And just like I could tell Samuel's eyes were blue, I could tell Percy's were too. Startlingly blue. Brighter than the rest of him. The color impenetrable. His stance was guarded, but I stepped closer anyway.

And I suddenly had nothing to say. I rubbed my hands together and stuffed them into my jeans pockets. "So, how have you been?" I rolled my eyes inwardly. What was up next? The weather? Hockey? Did ghosts get into hockey? If Ruthie had Wi-Fi, surely Percy had ESPN.

A charming grin slid up to those beautiful blue eyes, and he lifted a shoulder.

"Can you talk?" I asked.

He pressed his mouth together and shook his head.

While I was burning to know why, I kept that flame to myself.

He put a hand on my face. Or tried to.

Just like with Samuel, I only felt a coolness where his fingers would've been. "We're going to have to learn sign language."

He smiled and nodded.

"Hey." I thought of something I could ask him. "Did you know there's a cave underneath the house?"

He nodded, put an index finger over his mouth to shush me, then cupped a hand over one eye. Which was weird until it sank in.

"Pirates," I said, astonished.

He encouraged me to take it further with a summoning wave.

"Smugglers."

He pointed at me, and I could practically hear him say, "Bingo!"

"Wow. Do you know what they smuggled?"

He spread his hands. A bunch of stuff, apparently.

He had a small scar on his face. I asked, "What happened?" before I remembered he couldn't answer.

He dismissed my question with a shake of his head, but I looked closer. It didn't look so much like a scar but more like one of the vines that covered the house. "Is that from when I pulled you across the threshold into the passageway?" My stomach clenched at the thought. It was the only time I'd seen him hurt. "When you withered and turned to dust?"

He didn't answer.

"Percy, I'm so sorry."

He stepped to me sharply and shook his head.

"But it's my fault."

Another shake, this one sharper. He pointed to the door. Was he kicking me out?

I started to leave, but he stopped me by blocking it with his arm. He lowered his head and pointed to himself, then pressed his palms together as though in prayer.

"You're apologizing to me?"

He nodded.

"You're asking for my forgiveness?"

Another nod.

"That's ridiculous. There is nothing you need to be forgiven for."

The smile he flashed me was blinding. Yep. Ruthie sure knew how to pick 'em.

"Thanks, Percy. I have to find Annette before she eats all the donuts."

He stepped aside to unblock the door.

"Would you mind if I come back? You know, from time to time?"

The smile that stole across his face was all the answer I needed. I tiptoed to him and made a soft kissing sound on his cheek. Bona fide dimples appeared at the corners of his mouth. What a heartbreaker he must've been in his day.

I turned and hurried up the stairs, but not before saying over my shoulder, "I love the bracelet."

He was already gone, but the vine on my wrist tightened ever so gently.

My life was so strange.

Leaving the basement, I strolled into the kitchen in search of sustenance in the form of roasted bean juice and fried rings of flour dipped in a sugary glaze. I found neither. At least I could do something about the roasted bean juice. I put on a pot of coffee, then ran upstairs to grab my laptop.

My dads had gone back to bed, sleeping in their designated guest room at Ruthie Goode's Broom and Boarding

House. I couldn't help but wonder where the wolf was. If he was resting too.

After retrieving my laptop, I sipped the bean juice and dug into Salem's murky past. That time in the Witch City that even Salemites regretted. A time when fear and superstition were at an all-time high. When the persecution of their own became the norm. Who knew? Perhaps I'd run across a drawing of the Puritanical revenant now residing in my crystal ball. Did that make my ball possessed? Was it okay to have possessed balls? A few choice, and inappropriate, images brought Roane to mind.

Two hours and three cups of bean juice later, I emerged from the rabbit hole with a veritable wealth of information but was no closer to finding the truth about the things I went in for: Samuel's family, the witch hunter's name, and the smugglers' cave underneath our house.

Generally, when I fell down a rabbit hole, I fell hard. Today was no exception. I'd fallen so far so fast, I'd failed to realize Annette never came back with the donuts. Alarm shot through me until I remembered I had to take three things into consideration.

One, Annette loved to shop and most likely found a little store full of baubles and trinkets to keep her occupied for hours.

Two, she'd worked at the donut shop for a couple of weeks. She could be hanging out, chatting with her acquaintances. Or, knowing her, helping with the morning rush.

And three, our lives of late were anything but normal. At this point, a freak rockslide or a vampire attack could've slowed her down.

There was a fourth option, as well. Annette could've tried to enter The Witchery again, and Love could've bludgeoned her to death with a jar of wolfsbane. But that one was a stretch, even for me.

I took out my phone and texted her. Then I looked out the window and got sucked into watching the wolf stacking wood in the backyard.

He wore a tobacco-colored hoodie with the sleeves pushed up to his elbows. His forearms corded as he worked. His breath fogged in the air. He must've felt me staring because he turned, his powerful gaze meeting mine. He nodded a greeting before going back to the task at hand.

Ink jumped onto the table.

I nuzzled him, and then texted Annette again—three times in a row to make sure she felt the vibration if she had her phone on silent, which she rarely did. My dads came in, and we chatted a while but even they noticed how fidgety I'd become. Well, when they weren't ogling my man.

"Dads," I said, appalled. "You can't lust after my guy."

"The hell we can't." Papi raked a hand through his thick silver-streaked hair.

Dad chuckled. "What's wrong, cariña?"

"Something's wrong?" Papi asked.

"Annette went out for donuts, like, three hours ago." I stood to get my jacket. "Would you mind calling the chief, just in case? See if there've been any accidents?"

Papi sobered. "Of course, sweetheart."

"I'm going to drive the route."

Roane walked in the back door, a gust of cool wind following in his wake. "Not without me, you aren't."

"Holy cow, you really do have good hearing."

He didn't react. He just stood there, staring at me like he'd caught me doing something bad. When I did something bad, he'd be the first to know. And the second. And the third.

"I'm not going out to save the world. I'm just driving to the donut shop and back. Maybe ask around. Knowing Annette, she's shopping for scented underwear."

"I'll drive," he said, his tone a rather firm brook-no-argument.

My girl parts noticed. An illicit ripple of desire spiked within them. "You can drive into me," I whispered to myself, about half a second before the excellent-hearing thing registered. Why did I keep forgetting that? Heat creeping up my neck, I pretended I hadn't said that out loud and continued on my way.

He chuckled behind me.

I chose to ignore that too. Before I got to the stairs, however, a knock sounded at the door. Naturally. "I swear, if it's Vogel—"

"It's not," Roane said.

"Oh." It was still frustrating. I walked to the door and swung it wide.

A brunette stood there, pretty, midtwenties, her face the picture of panic.

She opened her mouth, but I was in a hurry. "It's under the sink behind the towels."

She blinked in surprise. "But I already—"

I started to close the door, then paused. "Not that sink."

"Oh. Why would it be—?"

This time I did close the door. Only to open it right back up. "Because you bought the thing for the guy, and then he came over early, and you panicked, much like you're doing now, so you stuffed it under the sink behind the blue towels—not the white ones—and in the process, your bracelet snagged on a towel and fell off your wrist."

I'd apparently sent her into a state of shock. She stood,

unmoving, a little birdlike sound escaping her open mouth every so often.

"'Kay." I closed the door and ran upstairs for my jacket, which was way more effort than I wanted to put into avoiding hyperthermia. I'd have to remember to utilize the cloakroom off the foyer. And the detour took too much time.

A knock sounded again before I could escape.

After rolling my eyes so far back into my head I almost seized, I opened the door again. Still didn't have time for the explanation that was on the tip of the older woman's tongue. She did have a spiffy blue do, though.

"The neighbor's kid stole it. It's in a vent in his bedroom." I pushed on the door but changed my mind. "You really shouldn't leave stuff like that out in the open."

I shut the door just as a third knock sounded. I gaped at Roane. "Nette clearly got the word out. Breadcrumbs, Incorporated is officially in business."

He crossed his arms over his chest and leaned against the banister. "She's going to have a fit when she finds out you aren't charging these people."

"Oh, crap." I winced. "I didn't even think of that. Oh well. It's kind of her fault."

This time I opened the door to an older gentleman. A gentleman who did not deserve my assistance.

I pointed a damning finger at him. "Don't even think about making a request like that."

His jaw came unhinged, and he tried unsuccessfully to stammer an explanation that I had neither the time nor the inclination to hear.

Spearing him with my best glare, I stepped closer. "Serves you right for trying to hide that kind of thing from your wife. Two words, buddy: habeas corpus."

I was just about to close the door for the two hundredth

time when two teen girls wearing far too little clothes and far too much makeup started up the walk. What the hell had Annette done? Hire a skywriter?

"Seven!" I called to them before they even got close.

They stopped in their tracks. "Oh. Are you... are you sure?" one of them asked, looking away from her phone for a precious few seconds. Not that I had any room to talk, but still.

I gave her my best deadpan and waited for my answer to sink in.

They looked at each other, emitted a high-pitched radio wave, and embraced while jumping up and down in utter delight. Then the one with the phone shouted over her friend's shoulder, "Thank you!"

I waved and closed the door.

"What was that about?" Roane asked.

"You don't want to know."

"I do, actually." He led me to the back of the house so we could take his truck.

"Well, it involved stolen cherry schnapps, several rounds of spin the bottle, and ten visits to the coat check room at the country club."

"And the number seven?"

"A secret admirer whose only clue was the fact that he fell in love with her under a sea of coats."

He nodded.

"Coat check number seven."

"Got it." Dimples appeared on his cheeks.

"No accidents were called in," Papi said as we strode past.

"Thanks. We're going to drive the route now. I'll call if —" My phone dinged before I could finish the thought. Relief flooded every bone in my body. "It's Annette."

Roane leaned close to read over my shoulder. He smelled like soap and morning mist. I wanted to turn into him and breathe deeply but figured that would be awkward.

Um, so something happened, Annette texted.

What? I texted back, my pulse picking up speed.

I had a minor fender bender, but I'm okay.

"Oh, thank the gods," I said aloud, wondering when her texts had grown from teen hearts and emojis to middle-aged sentences, complete with punctuation. *Where are you?*

I had to get all of that taken care of, but I kind of did something else.

I stilled for a moment as my mind raced. I texted back, *Call me.*

That's the thing, she texted. *I can't make any calls. I broke my phone. Screen is shattered. I'm barely able to text, but for some reason, it won't let me call.*

Then why was she texting so much? A simple 9-1-1 would've done. *Is that the something else?*

Yes and no. I'm at Gulu-Gulu now. Come meet me for breakfast, and I'll explain. Alone. I'll die if anyone finds out.

What in the world could she have done? Then it hit me. "Oh my god," I said to Roane. "She really did go back into The Witchery. I have to go."

I made a U-turn to the front door.

Someone else was already there knocking.

Roane grinned. "Want me to drive you?"

Now that we knew what happened, kind of, there was no need. "It's okay. I'll sneak around the house and hop into the Bug before anyone sees me."

I passed Dad and Papi in the kitchen, searching through the drawers.

"What are you looking for?"

"Paper," Dad said. "You do not need people knocking

on your door at all hours. You need official office hours. This is ridiculous. I'm making a sign."

"Thanks, Dad," I said, leaning in to kiss both of them.

When I turned to Roane, he stood there, expectant, a challenge beckoning between his lashes. Since I was on a roll, I leaned in, albeit a bit hesitantly, and kissed his scruffy cheek as well.

He slid a hand to the small of my back and pulled me close, then let go and gazed down at me.

"I'll be back in a few." I said.

After a quick nod, he went to find paper for my dad just as the knocking started anew.

FOURTEEN

I'm not saying I drink too much coffee,
but I do believe my body will keep moving
forty-eight hours after my death.
—Meme

When I got to the café, the tourist crush had already begun, and it was barely nine in the morning.

I couldn't imagine what Annette had done to Love that would warrant such secrecy, but any excuse to eat at Gulu-Gulu, a local fave I'd been dying to try, was a good one in my book. I looked around at the people in the room. Curiously, she wasn't here, so I got us a table and sat stewing in yet another conundrum.

Everyone who'd come to my door today had needed something. A question answered, a problem solved, an object found. And I'd known exactly what their need was before they'd even knocked. How? Was that part of my calling? Was that what a charmling did? Help people? Like a magical PI?

Maybe I was more like Ruthie than I thought. A finder of lost things. Perhaps, because that was my ultimate purpose, I could read people and know instinctively what they needed most at any given time. Or perhaps I was simply losing what was left of my mind. It could go either way, because I couldn't read a single person sitting around me. How was that even possible?

The waiter came by.

I ordered hot chocolate and asked for more time since Nette had yet to arrive. He set it down a few minutes later, but before I could drink it, a woman approached the table.

Confident. Austere. Slender with long auburn hair, she had sparkly eyes like Roane's, only I couldn't tell what color they were. She wore jeans and a loose black sweater. "Are you Defiance Dayne?"

Seriously, Annette must've handed out flyers on the street corner with my picture on them. Or taken out one of the moving ads in *The Daily Prophet*'s wizarding news. Or filmed an infomercial.

"I am," I said.

"Oh, good." The woman sat down, even though she hadn't been invited.

After the onslaught at the house, I wasn't feeling very invite-y. And when Annette finally got here, she'd tear this woman right out of that chair if she had to. The place was packed, and it was the only available seat.

"I'm Belinda." She stretched out her hand. "You met my grandmother the other day. Serinda McClain?"

"Oh, yes." I relaxed. "She's a firecracker." I didn't want to assume she knew her grandmother was a witch—you know what they say about assuming—so I treated it like an unmentionable and, well, didn't mention it.

After a placating laugh, Belinda nodded. "To say the least. I'm glad I ran into you. My grandmother is… getting up in age."

"Okay."

"She seems to think your grandmother is still alive."

Well, that was unexpected. "She told you this?"

"Of course not. She tells us kids nothing."

Kids. *Sheesh*. Belinda was my age. "So, you eavesdropped?"

"My brother did. Anyway, he heard her talking to some of her cohorts. She and that ridiculous coven think you're some kind of"—she leaned in and lowered her voice—"allpowerful being."

"Ah. I wasn't sure you knew about… the lifestyle."

"I don't." She sniffed. "Not much. My grandmother swears I have talent, and that I'm wasting it, but I don't believe in any of that hocus-pocus nonsense." She wiggled her fingers.

"I didn't either until a few months ago."

"That's why I'm here. She's told me a few things about you, trying to lure me into the coven, no doubt. I need you to talk to her. I saw your grandmother's body." She leaned in again. "She wasn't alive. I'm so sorry for your loss, by the way." She covered my hand with hers for a split second before yanking it away, like she was afraid of catching something.

"Thank you."

"It's just, if my grandmother doesn't stop all this nonsense, we will have to put her in a home."

"Will you?"

"We'll have no choice." She picked up a napkin and

dabbed at eyes so dry I thought about offering her some drops.

"Who does she tell all of this to?"

"Excuse me?" Belinda said from behind the napkin.

"Does she tell your brother?"

"Goodness, no." She put it down. "He would've had her committed years ago."

"So, she tells you."

"Like I said, she thinks I'm... she thinks I'm a witch."

"Are you sure you aren't?" I took a sip of hot chocolate. "I never dreamed any of this was possible, either, but here we are."

"Oh." She folded the napkin and smoothed it on the table. "You're one of them. I'm sorry, I didn't realize you were a part of her coven already."

"I'm not." It hit me then. The thing she was searching for. And it certainly wasn't what I would've expected.

"Thank you for your time." She started to get up.

"You can ask me, you know."

"I'm sorry?"

"The thing you're searching for. You can ask me where it is."

She scoffed and shook her head. "I'm not searching for anything."

"That's just it." I leaned forward as though to confide in her, this utter non-believer. "You are. But I can't figure out how I know that. I mean, isn't everyone searching for something? Why can't I see his or hers or... well, hers I can see." I pointed around the room in a quick game of Duck, Duck, Goose, stopping at an ebony-haired police officer a few tables down. "I think she recognized me. But for the most part, nada. And then there are some that I just know."

She repositioned herself in front of me. "Okay, I'll bite. What am I searching for?"

"The crystal elephant your father bought you at the state fair. You were in... the second grade, I think?"

She went deathly still.

"It was clear, the glass smooth, with blue around the ears."

She swallowed hard. "My grandmother told you that."

"So, your grandmother knew?"

She dropped her gaze to the table in thought.

"Didn't think so. You were playing cars in the dirt with your brother. At the house on Elm? When you weren't looking, he buried it. It's still there."

"That's... you can't possibly know that." She looked up.

"It meant everything to you. You were clutching it after the accident as the first responders used the Jaws of Life to try to save your parents. You remember the smell of gas and burning plastic. The sound of running and shouting. The feel of the seat belt as it cut across your waist, suspending you upside down." I reached over and covered her hand. "They did everything they could, but it was too late for your parents."

Tears of astonishment and disbelief filled her eyes. She jerked her hand back. "Stop," she whispered.

"It's okay. You don't have to believe. But go find that elephant." I took the napkin she'd used and drew a picture of where it was in proportion to the house. Although my elephant looked more like a dying beetle than a magnificent beast. I offered the map. "This is where it is. Just... maybe ask permission before digging up the current owner's yard."

She took the napkin from me in a daze.

"And Belinda," I said, "your brother knew what that elephant meant to you. Food for thought."

The server came up. I went ahead and ordered something else, mostly because I felt bad for taking up the table when there was a line outside. In the process, I missed where Belinda hurried off to. Hopefully to dig up an elephant.

I checked my phone for messages from Annette. She was rarely late to anything.

A chair scraped across the floor, and I looked up into the face of James Vogel. He stole Annette's seat, the burly man barely fitting, and offered me a sneer.

"Yeah, that seat's taken, actually."

"By your little curly-haired friend?" He slid his phone across the table.

The screen showed a shot of a woman lying on a dirty blanket, blindfolded and gagged, the restraint so tight it cut into the sides of her mouth.

Annette.

Fear immobilized me. I cradled the phone in both hands, gazing at the photo, when someone reached over me from behind and snapped something onto my wrists.

I frowned at the black rings, two individual bracelets, and then watched as Minerva, the skittish witch from my grandmother's coven, walked around to stand beside her uncle.

She was young and pretty, even when she bit her nails, like she was doing now. Her dark hair hung in strings over her eyes, her clothes too big for her bony frame. "She can't do magic in irons," she said to Vogel. "Even the Puritans knew that."

"They knew nothing," I whispered.

According to Ruthie, discovering a charmling in the wild was rather like finding the holy grail in the witch world. We were often held captive by malevolent witches or even warlocks seeking to use us, to use our powers, for their own gain.

But if we were so powerful, if we were so capable, how were we forced to serve others? It made no sense. I glanced at the iron cuffs, wondering in the back of my mind if they would really work on me. If they'd really suppress my powers.

I turned my focus back to Minerva. She wore a look I couldn't wrap my head around. Had I done something to her? Did her uncle want her to have my powers? Only a female could steal them. Maybe he wanted to control her, but he'd said something earlier about bringing someone back from the dead. Surely, he wasn't serious.

I sat there, treading in a volatile sea of confusion. Her uncle didn't have a magic bone in his body. But he did have a sneer that sent my ire skyrocketing to Defcon 1. I wanted to strangle him. I actually wanted to do him real harm. Not for me, but because my best friend, my sister for all intents and purposes, was at his mercy.

I decided to test the legitimacy of the iron cuffs until... until I saw what Minerva was searching for. Her fondest wish. Her deepest desire. Her need for justice.

She wanted revenge on the man sitting beside her. He'd killed her aunt. The only woman who'd shown her kindness growing up. The only person in her family who hadn't made fun of her fascination with the occult. With witchcraft and magic books and spells.

She gazed at me from between her strands of hair. Fear consumed her. So much so, she bit her nails to the quick. Dried blood crusted her cuticles and stained her fingers. Her uncle had coerced her into helping him, thinking she could bring back his wife from the dead, the wife he'd killed in a moment of anger. If witches had that kind of power, they'd be driving Mercedes and installing helicopter pads. They could name their price.

"You make one sound"—Vogel opened his jacket to show me the butt of a gun—"and your friend is dead. Hear me, girl?"

When I didn't answer, he took my hand and squeezed it painfully.

I clenched my teeth and fought not to react.

"You hear me?"

I nodded. Just barely.

"Don't try none of that witch bullshit. There are three cops sitting at that table, and if they get the slightest wind something doesn't seem right, your friend is counting worms." He leaned closer. "Told you I tried to do this the easy way."

"Well, I've never been easy. What do you want?" I asked, even though I knew exactly what he wanted. Not because of him, but because of Minerva.

Her desire gave me access to everything. Everything he'd done. Everything she'd been through. Everything Annette had suffered since he'd grabbed her outside of the donut shop a few hours ago.

Minerva had been there. She'd tried to warn Nette, but he was keeping too close an eye on her. He forced her to text me instead of doing it himself, which was why the texts didn't sound like they'd come from a middle-aged male. Unfortunately, she hadn't seen where he'd put Annette— only that he'd said they'd never find her, and she'd be dead by ten that morning.

What time was it now? Minerva's fear fed my own, and I fought to stay focused.

"Need your help with a little problem is all. Nothing to get huffy about." He glanced around. "Now, you're gonna put money down for the food you ordered, and then we're gonna get up and walk out of here. You understand?"

I nodded and reached for my purse.

"Slowly," he whispered through his teeth when I lifted my purse onto the table. "And hand me that phone of yours while you're at it. Wouldn't want that pretty boy showing up to our party uninvited."

No. We wouldn't want that.

After we left the restaurant, Vogel shoved me into his car and put a bag over my head that smelled like onions. We drove a little while, then he yanked me out, ripped off the bag—thank God, because I was beginning to think I'd never be able to look another onion ring in the eye—and pushed me into his garage.

When he closed it, the door scraped loudly against the rails. Because I didn't know the city well yet, I had no clue where we were. All I did know was that the number ten kept flashing in my mind. I had until ten a.m. to find Nette. I racked my brain. Why ten? What happened at ten? It was just a number, and not a particularly scary one.

I blinked the room into focus.

Boxes stacked floor to ceiling filled the room with a small corner cleared out. It contained shelves and a deep freeze. Minerva stood in that corner, watching us.

Vogel opened the lid to the deep freeze, grabbed my hair, and jerked me closer. Nothing good ever lived in a deep freeze. And I wasn't wrong.

His wife lay inside, her body frozen, her eyes open and unseeing. Frost crystals had formed on her lashes, around her blue mouth, and over the huge gash in her temple.

"Bring her back," he demanded, like all I had to do was stand over her and say the word.

Even Gandalf couldn't bring back this kind of dead. "Mr. Vogel, I can't just—"

"Uh-uh-uh." He waved the gun at me. "I already know you've done it at least once. Minerva here might not be the brightest, but she's seen her. That grandmother of yours. Alive and kicking, like they hadn't just shoveled six feet of dirt on top of her."

I drew in a deep breath, trying not to throw up. "There are certain things I need."

"No, ma'am. Not you." He pointed at me. "You're different. When my niece couldn't bring my wife back, she told me all about you, missy." He hauled Minerva to his side, her face soiled with tears and dirt. "I didn't believe her at first. Thought she really was simple." He made the crazy sign at his ear with the barrel of the gun. "Funny thing is, she's more scared of you than she is of me. But since you seem to care so much about other people..." He pointed the gun at Minerva's head. "Even the stupid ones."

The sad part was that Minerva really was scared to death of me. I couldn't see why, exactly. On the other hand, she believed I could save us. Truth was, no one was making it out of this alive, including Annette, if I couldn't use my powers. I couldn't read minds, per se, but I could always read people's intentions. And James Vogel's were evil. "Where's Annette?"

"Safe, but not for long. You'll never find her in time."

In time. How much time? How close was it to ten? "I can't do this with the irons on."

Minerva's eyes held a hint of encouragement. She really didn't think the irons would work. Neither did I, but what did I know? I was stalling, trying to come up with a plan.

When he reached over to take them off, I looked at his

watch. It read 9:57. Panic closed my throat. What happened at ten?

"And before you even think about trying anything"—he waved the gun at me—"your friend won't survive the next ten minutes unless I want her to."

That was a lie. She barely had three.

He stood back and waited, but I didn't have time to do the same. I said a prayer to whoever would listen, looked at the once-vibrant woman in the freezer, and touched her face with my fingertips, asking for her help, for her forgiveness, because I was about to steal whatever energy she had left.

"What's she doing?" he asked Minerva.

She winced at the bark in his tone. "I don't know. Her magics are different from mine."

He looked between his late wife and me. "Why isn't anything happening?"

"Because she's frozen," I lied. "It'll take time."

He grabbed my throat, his fingers digging into my jaw, and yanked me closer, until we stood nose to nose. "You lie to me, and it'll be the last thing you ever do."

"I'm well aware of that, Mr. Vogel," I ground out. "I just needed you to touch me."

"What?" He squeezed harder.

My jaw popped, and pain shot through from the roots of my teeth to the tips of my fingers. I worried he was going to break it, but I'd needed him to touch me. I'd needed my skin to come into contact with his for the magic to seep out of me and into him.

His eyes rounded when he felt the magics begin to consume him, and his mouth slowly opened in disbelief. He pulled back, his fingers twisted and frozen in place. They turned a grayish blue as he looked on. He grabbed his wrist and watched in horror as crystals formed on his fingertips and spread through his hand and forearm. "What's... happening?"

"I only thought it appropriate you freeze to death, Mr. Vogel, since your wife was still alive when you put her in here."

"You... you bitch."

"She sends her regards."

As ice crystals slowly spread through his body, freezing him from the inside out, I drew the *reveal* spell on the air. I felt her instantly. Annette. But the terror coursing through her veins fought against the magics. Created a barrier. Made it difficult to pinpoint her location.

Minerva stumbled back as her uncle stiffened before her eyes, crystals sliding up his neck and over his jaw. His gaze darted around wildly, like a cornered animal looking for an escape.

"Minerva." My own fear made me lose concentration over and over. I squeezed my eyes shut and searched. "Do you have any idea where she could be?"

I heard her whisper, "I'm sorry."

But I saw something then. Annette buried under uniformly laid boards.

She'd managed to get her blindfold off as she struggled against the nylon ropes tying her hands behind her back, screaming through the gag, her throat raw. She wrestled with the rope until her wrists bled.

But this was more than just being bound and gagged. Sheer hysteria had consumed her. Once again, something to do with ten o'clock.

I pulled back on the visual, widening the frame.

She could see through the slats in the floor. A single

board missing on her right and a small opening overhead allowed a line of sunlight to cut across her face.

I pulled back even farther and scanned the building for a location, an address to give the chief. And then I saw it. Exactly where she was.

Vogel had put her in a crawlspace of the old printing factory. A factory set to be demolished at ten a.m. And her time had just run out.

An explosion thundered around her. And then another. And another. A daisy chain of perfectly timed devices designed to go off in a precise sequence to control the fall of the building.

Birds flew out of broken windows overhead as the building began to crumble. Smoke and dust billowed out of them. The birds were swallowed by it, but they burst out of the ash and scattered before the windows, too, fell to Earth. And in that instant, Annette stopped.

She stopped struggling.

She stopped screaming.

She stopped crying.

A calmness washed over her, and she let her lids drift shut, knowing she was going to die.

Every cell in my body flooded with adrenaline. The magics surged through me so sharp and so fast, I didn't have time to think. I drew the first spell that came to mind, thrust it out to her, and held my breath as thousands upon thousands of pounds of rubble began falling around her.

Then I waited.

And I prayed.

FIFTEEN

May the bridges I burn light the way.
—Proverb

"I don't mean to sound like an ingrate, daffodil," the chief said to me as he examined the frozen corpse in James Vogel's freezer. "But maybe you should stay home for a few days." He looked at Vogel's wife and shook his head.

I concurred. "I'm inclined to agree with you."

"How're we gonna explain this one, Chief?" the coroner asked. She'd clearly had the day off and used it to rack up some time at the spa. Telltale signs of a mud mask still framed her gorgeous dark face.

"That's a canister of liquid nitrogen, isn't it?"

The woman looked at a container of oxygen Vogel kept next to his MIG welder and nodded. "I do believe it is."

"Freak accident, I'd say." He turned to me and then glanced at Minerva.

Still huddling in the corner, she'd covered her face with her hands, looking almost as pitiful as her abused fingertips.

"It's a miracle you girls weren't caught in the blast when it exploded."

"It is." Minerva dropped her hands to her side, her face wary. She probably wasn't sure what to think of the chief's willingness to help us.

"Care to explain this?" he asked her.

Her gaze drifted to her aunt, and she hugged herself. "He killed her a couple of weeks ago and had planned on reporting her missing after he went through her papers. She'd inherited some money—a lot of money—but it was being held at a high-security bank vault in Boston. He knew it would take years to get the courts to declare her dead. For him to get access to the box. So, he needed Defiance to bring her back to life so she could get the money out."

"And then what?" the chief asked. "He was going to kill her again?"

A shiver ran through her. "I don't know."

He took off his police-issue visor cap and scratched his head. "When did you find all this out?"

"About a week ago. He knew I did magic. At first, he wanted me to figure out how to get to the money. But I have no idea how to do that kind of magic. If it even exists." She looked at me pleadingly. "I'm so sorry. I knew once he figured out I couldn't get to the money, he'd kill me. I knew too much. So, I told him... I told him what you did for Ruthie and..." Her voice cracked.

"Minerva, it's okay."

"I wanted to warn you," she said. "He took my phone and was watching every move I made. I had to pretend to be on his side. I was trying to tell you at the café, but he got suspicious." She buried her face in her arm, crying into her jacket.

I walked over to her and put a hand on her shoulder. "Minerva, who can I call? You need to be with someone."

She sniffed and shook her head. "No, I'm okay.

"Are your parents in Salem?"

"No, we don't... they don't talk to me. They think I've been possessed by Satan."

"I beg your pardon?" And then it hit me. "Because you practice witchcraft." And they obviously practiced witch discrimination.

She nodded as a sob shook her shoulders. "My aunt was the only one who was nice to me. She took me in when my parents kicked me out. I kept telling her it was time I get my own place, but she didn't want me to move out. I think..." She gazed up at me. "I think she really loved me."

I pulled her into my arms. "I'm sure she did." Over her shoulder, I spotted my ride across the street from all the flashing lights—a little flashy himself, leaning all *GQ*-like against his pickup—and had a sudden urge to leave. "Chief, can we go?"

"Sure. I'll stop by later for an official statement, but this looks pretty cut and dried. Witnesses saw him take you from the café. They alerted my officers there, but you were already gone."

I led Minera away, but the chief stopped me. "Hey, where's that fruitcake friend of yours? Your dads said she was missing?"

I smiled. "I'll tell you when you come by later."

Minerva saw where we were headed. Or, more to the point, who we were headed toward. "Yeah, I don't want to be a bother. I'm sure you two need alone time. Can you guys drop me off at a hotel?" She turned to me. "A really cheap one?"

"We can, actually. It's called Ruthie Goode's Broom and Boarding House."

Ruthie was going to kill me for bringing home so many strays. First Samuel. Now Minerva. Next, the entire population of the Franklin Park Zoo.

"Are you sure?" she asked, hesitant.

There was no way I was about to leave her alone. She was heartbroken and traumatized. Odds were, someone in Vogel's family—maybe even Minerva's jackhole parents— would get his house. I'd have to make sure to take her back so she could grab her things before the vultures descended, but for now, she needed rest. And maybe a manicure. "I'm positive. We'll get you sorted, love. I just want you safe for now, okay?"

"Thank you."

"Ms. Dayne," Roane said when we got to his truck, looking exceptionally tasty in his hoodie.

"Mr. Wildes."

He eyed me with a combination of lust and wicked intent. "Do you just start shit wherever you go?"

"'Parently."

BACK AT THE HOUSE, I smelled food the minute we walked inside. Before I got to any of said food, however, Percy blocked my path. I grinned and waited as a vine covered in little black rosebuds slid around my wrist. I hugged it to me. "Thank you, Percy. This is Minerva."

She watched him, mesmerized, as he shrank back and let us through.

I kissed my dads—who wanted the whole story *right now, missy*, asking *what the hell happened* and *why didn't you call*, then told me I was grounded forever and a day.

I told them that was a very long time. But that was fine, as long as I got to serve my punishment in bed with Roane.

After promising a show-and-tell of everything that had gone down, I took Minerva upstairs, grabbed some clothes for her, and showed her to a bedroom. "You'll have to share a bathroom with my dads when they're here, but they have amazing taste. You'll love their shampoo."

She laughed softly and promised to be down for something to eat after a shower.

I went back to my room. The suitcase I'd started to pack earlier still lay open on my bed. It'd been a while since I slept on that bed, what with the kitchen floor being so available and nearby. I was just starting to put my clothes away when a wolf knocked on my open door.

He stood at the threshold, arms crossed over the magnificent expanse of his chest. "I hope you were planning on saying goodbye this time."

"What?" I couldn't think while his biceps drew my attention away from the fact that I needed to breathe.

"If you've made up your mind to leave..." He stalked toward me, each step full of purpose, his powerful stare raking over every inch of me. "I'm going to fight tooth and nail to change it."

He didn't stop until he had me in his arms. He bent his head and kissed me but didn't close his eyes. He kept them locked on mine, his olive-green irises like cut glass. He was so perfect. A perfect fit. A perfect face. A perfect body. If he weren't mentally unstable, he'd be 100 percent. But how else could one explain his attraction to me? The man clearly needed to be medicated.

I pulled back when he pulled back. "That was fighting dirty."

"We wolves do that." His smirk cut straight to my nethers and rested there awhile. "We like to get dirty." He ran a large hand over my ass and pulled me against his erection as his other hand sought out one of the girls. Brushing a thumb over my nipple, he deepened the kiss, exploring my mouth with his tongue.

Sadly, after a moment, he stopped. "Is it working?"

At that point, everything was definitely working, and I was certain he could give me an orgasm just by talking to me, his voice smooth and rich and succulent like nectar. And he smoldered. For the first time in my life, I had a man who actually smoldered. All those romance novels made so much more sense now.

He slid a hand around to the front of my jeans, but I stopped him. "No way. My turn."

I ran my hand over the front of his kilt. The kilt. The glorious kilt. And the glorious what was underneath the kilt. The thin leather allowed my hand to mold to his erection. And mold it did.

He sucked in a soft breath and backed me against the bed.

Just as I was really getting into it—nope, that was a lie, I was already soooo very into it—a screech came from out in the hall.

What in the seventh level of hell?

A massive black bird flew into the room. It dive-bombed me three times. And if I didn't know better, I'd say it was trying to peck my eyes out.

Shouting, I swatted at it. "Friends don't peck friends' eyes out. It's a cardinal rule. As old as time itself." Even if it was a crow and not a cardinal.

I swatted again when it had another go, ripping a few strands of my hair out.

Meanwhile, Roane stood back, watching it gouge me to death, not concerned in the least.

It circled my high ceiling with its prize—my hair—before swooping in for a landing and parking its ass on my dresser.

And here it came. The moment I'd been dreading. I eased closer. "I know what you're thinking."

It cawed again.

"Listen, I just—"

Ca-caw!

"If you'll just let me explain."

It glared at me with the glare of a thousand needles. I never knew a bird could be so expressive. Or contemptuous. Or—

It pecked my hand.

"Ouch." I raised my hands and patted the air. "Okay—"

Caw.

"I just—"

Caw.

"If you'll—"

Ca-caw.

"Stop it."

Caw! Caw! Caw! It flapped its wings to add a visual component to the soundtrack of its bellyaching.

I folded my arms across my chest. "Now you're just being obstinate."

It glared again, its stormy gray eyes burning a hole into me as though I were an ant under a magnifying glass.

In the sunlight, I could see smoke wafting off its singed feathers, which were oddly curly. "On the bright side, you're literally smoking hot."

It lowered its beak, its eyes at half-mast, as it continued to regard me with a special, seething kind of hatred.

"At least you're alive, though, right?"

It didn't move.

"Annette, you're going to have to forgive me eventually."

Nothing. Nada. Zip.

"You can talk, you know. I mean... I think you can talk." I looked at Roane, suddenly worried.

He stood there grinning and shrugged. No help whatsoever.

I chewed on my lower lip. "You can talk, right?"

"Of course, I can talk." She had no lips. It was like watching a ventriloquist. She flapped her wings, her high-pitched voice a bit like nails on a chalkboard. "But I sound ridiculous!"

She wasn't wrong. I hid a snicker in fear of losing an eye. Or the rest of my hair. "This is amazing." I eased closer. "Can I pet you?"

"I dare you to try."

"Your after-feathers are curly! Just like your hair!" They were a lighter color too. Much like the color her hair had been, a soft chestnut. Against the raven black, she made a beautiful crow. Not that I was about to tell her that. I put a hand over my heart, dying from all the cuteness. Which was better than dying by beak.

"I will peck you to death in your sleep."

"I don't think I'd sleep through something like that."

"Change me back, or else."

I straightened. "What?"

"Change me back."

"What do you mean?" My gaze shot to Roane, then returned to her. "I can't change you back. You're supposed to shift back to human form on your own. You know, like a bona fide shapeshifter. Roane can do it."

She blinked at me, her beady eyes narrowing in for the kill. "Just how am I supposed to do that?"

"Well, I-I'm not sure exactly." It wasn't like the spell had come with directions.

Her wings flapped again, and I suddenly understood the meaning of the word unflappable. Annette being its antitheses. "Why would you do this to me?"

"Because you were about to be crushed by a building. I needed to shift you so you could get out of your bindings into something small so you could fit through tight spaces like the missing floorboard above you, and fast, so you could go airborne and fly away before the building crushed you."

She blinked again, unimpressed, her lower lids sliding up to meet her upper ones. It was fascinating.

"And crows are really smart," I continued.

"Smart?"

I nodded.

"My brain is the size of a pea, and I'm very attracted to shiny things."

"See? Nothing has changed. Wait," I said. She was missing the most important part of this entire conversation. "You're alive." I jumped into Roane's arms and kissed him. "She's alive."

He stared down at me. Pulled me closer. Brushed a thumb across my lower lip.

Just as his head descended, Annette squawked again. "Crows before bros, buddy! Out."

I stood back and smoothed my sweater down. "Maybe I should go see Ruthie."

SIXTEEN

I think I seized the wrong day.
—True Fact

"But I keep screwing up," I said to Ruthie. Roane and I had found her hanging with my dads and Minerva in the kitchen, which was a big step up from the basement. "Now I don't know how to change her back."

"Hmm," she hmmed, handing me a cup of tea, even though I needed a shot of something stronger. Like coffee. Or tequila. Or electroshock therapy.

When Ruthie turned her back to dish out some of Papi's beef stroganoff, Roane switched my tea for coffee. That's when I knew. Really knew.

He completed me.

I gazed up at him as he raked an ink-covered hand through his hair and winked, which somehow caused my nether regions to flood with warmth.

"I just keep almost getting people killed," I continued,

turning back to Ruthie. Annette had refused to come down-stairs, she was so embarrassed. And Roane... the memory of him taking my injuries into his own body clenched my stomach. "I keep hurting people."

Ruthie handed me a plate. My dads sat on barstools while we took over the table. Minerva ate like she hadn't eaten in weeks—Papi's beef stroganoff did that to the best of us—but she paid rapt attention.

"How did you know what that spell would do?" I asked Ruthie.

"Which one?"

Which one? She knew full well which one.

"The one you drew after the witch hunter knocked me into oblivion. The one where I transferred my injuries and pain to someone else. How would you know something like that?"

She took a delicate bite and swallowed before answer-ing. "Defiance, that's hardly important."

The hairs on the back of my neck stood on end as they'd recently started doing when people tried to hide something from me. "It is, actually."

She pursed her lips. She didn't want to tell me, but I figured she knew me well enough by now to realize I wasn't going to drop it. After filling her lungs, she said, "Because you used it once when you were a child."

"That doesn't sound good."

"You broke your arm on the monkey bars at the playground."

"Weren't you watching me?" I teased.

"You were in so much pain." Her smile was sad. "You didn't do it on purpose."

I stilled.

"Your magics took over. Self-preservation, I suppose. You grabbed another child's arm and drew that spell."

"Oh, no."

"I didn't know what it meant until after he screamed. His arm had splintered. And you'd given him all of your pain."

"I-I broke his arm?"

"Yes. With that spell, anything that happens to you is transferred to whoever you touch, and you are healed. But you stopped yourself with Roane."

"Why would I do that?"

"Because you didn't want to kill him. You knew how much he could—"

"No, why would I do that to a child?"

"Defiance, you were only three. You had no idea what that spell would do."

"Clearly, I did."

"All right, then you had no idea what the ramifications would be."

I scrubbed my face. "I can't do this anymore. Up to this point, I've lived the most boring, mundane life imaginable. The most exciting thing I've ever done was open a restaurant, and then I had that stolen out from under me. I don't know if you've noticed, Ruthie"—I clued her in—"but sometimes I'm about as sharp as a marble."

"Cariña," Dad admonished.

"It's true. I'm unlucky and jinxed and accident-prone to a ridiculous degree. And someone was delusional enough to entrust me with all of this power? Me? The same girl who once flashed a hottie in a Porsche because all the cool kids were doing it, only my hottie turned out to be an undercover cop?" I flattened my palms against the table and leaned closer. "I was arrested, Ruthie.

That's the kind of girl I am. Other girls could flash guys. I could not."

Roane cleared his throat and hid a grin behind his fist.

"And that pertains to the conversation because...?" Ruthie asked.

"Because I'm cursed!"

"Ah."

"I don't have the talent for this gig. Everything I do is wrong. It always has been. Everything I touch spoils."

"Defiance." Her tone stayed even. Placating. "Did you ever think that maybe all those things happened to you because you were an insanely powerful witch whose powers were suppressed?"

"How is that even relevant?"

She laughed. "You're a charmling."

"And?"

"Have you ever touched a toaster only to have it catch on fire?"

Dad nodded, and Papi held up two fingers. Dad lifted the third for him.

"That's my point exactly! Everything I touch breaks. Or catches on fire. Or explodes. Well, that only happened once."

"Sweetheart, just because your powers were suppressed, doesn't mean they weren't there. It's not like with a regular witch. Even one from a long line like mine."

"So, all of my bad luck was just really my powers trying to break free?"

"Something like that."

"Then explain... wait." Some of what happened while I'd been writhing in pain on this very kitchen table came back to me. Astonishment rocketed through my body. "You tried to take it."

"Take what, sweetheart?" She took another bite.

"The pain. The injuries from that asshole on the balcony. That's what you and Roane were arguing about."

She put her cup down. "He cheated. He got to you first." She offered him an insincere glare. "I didn't want him to have to go through that."

"And you felt like you should?"

"Defiance, all of this is my fault. If I'd found another way, if I'd let you keep your powers, or knowledge of your powers, or trained you your whole life, none of this would be happening."

"So, you have to martyr yourself as punishment?" Her self-banishment suddenly made sense. "Is that why you locked yourself in the basement? Why you stopped seeing the chief?"

"No." She shook her head. A pink hue rose in her cheeks. She was never the kind to air her dirty laundry, but if ever there were a time to display a dirty thong or two, it was now. "I can assure you, sweetheart, that has nothing to do with any of this."

"Then why? He's devastated, Ruthie."

She winced and set her jaw. "Talking about my issues is not getting us any closer to solving yours."

"I have issues?"

"You've overtaken my copies of *Good Housekeeping*. But none of your issues are your fault."

Annette flew into the kitchen like a tiny hurricane and landed on the counter next to my dads. "You are getting completely off subject," she said in her strange voice. "We need to get back to the real issue at hand."

Dad's jaw fell open, as did Minerva's. Papi dropped his fork.

"We will," I said, "but I just want to know what's going on with my grandmother."

"I would like to know that too." The chief stood in the hall, looking into the kitchen.

"I'm a bird." Annette ruffled her feathers. "My problem should take precedence." She lifted a wing to scratch under it with her pointy beak as Minerva slowly raised her phone.

The chief gawked at Annette and swayed, and I worried he would pass out. It was one thing to see a talking bird. It was quite another to see one that could provide intelligent conversation.

"Chief." I jumped up to help him.

Roane joined me, and we led the chief to a chair at the table next to Minerva.

He pointed at the bird. "Is that... Did she...?"

"Yes. Remember when I told you there was more to the story?" I gestured to Annette with a furtive nod.

"Vogel abducted me," she squawked. "And I'm certain my glasses are at the bottom of a pile of rubble." Then she turned a murderous glare on me. "Not that they would fit on my beak anyway."

My dads were still staring.

"Ruthie?" I circled back to my earlier point. "Why have you suddenly become a hermit?"

She brushed an invisible crumb off her dress. "I can't do magic."

"What?" I asked, stunned.

"I can no longer practice. My magic is gone."

That wasn't possible. "Ruthie, most witches don't have inherent magic. They are simply sensitive to the unseen. Maybe you just need to start practicing again. It could come back to you."

"Why? So I can make a love potion that does absolutely nothing?"

"Of course not. Wait, does that mean there are love potions that absolutely do something?"

I couldn't help but glance at my intended target. He folded his arms over his chest.

"Oooo." Annette's awe was more *caw*, but the sentiment was there. She was just as interested as I was.

"You don't understand," Ruthie said. "I haven't figured out how to live without my magic. I'm having a hard time adjusting. I'll get over it. It'll just take a while."

And here I was complaining about having so much power when Ruthie had none. "Gigi, I had no idea what you were going through."

"My dear, you have had more than your share of things to worry about. My paltry problems are—"

"Paltry?" I scooted closer to her. "You think this is paltry?"

"I do. I didn't want to burden you with it."

"You've really lost your powers?"

"I have. I've done everything. Scoured ancient texts. Consulted witches older and far wiser than myself."

"I doubt that." That came out wrong. "I meant the wiser part."

"I tried every spell in the book. Literally." She speared me with a hapless gaze. "Do you know how hard it is to find eye of newt?"

"You went old school. I'm impressed."

"I did. I even asked the Great Mother for a favor. My powers are simply gone."

"They can't just vanish. I'm sure they're around here somewhere. Have you checked your pockets? Looked in your bra? Tried the crisper drawer in the fridge?" I listed off all the places I'd ever lost my keys. "Or what about the oven—"

"I don't think it works like that, sweetheart."

"Did you check in the sofa? I've lost things in sofas."

"We aren't talking about your virginity, cariña," Dad said.

I gasped. "How did you know that?"

Ruthie shook her head. "I'm fairly certain my powers are not in the sofa." When I opened my mouth, she said, "Or under my bed."

I deflated.

The thing was, once I knew the problem, once she had the desire to tell me like those people who'd pounded on the door, I knew exactly where to find her lost object. She was right. It was not under the sofa.

The chief tapped me on the shoulder. "Did you know there's a talking bird in your house?"

I grinned and leaned closer to my grandmother. "When you died, your power, your energy, didn't go anywhere."

A vertical line formed between her brows. "I don't understand."

"Now, here's a twist for you," I teased. "They're still right where you left them."

She shook her head before her curiosity got the better of her. She looked at me, her expression full of a careful hope. "Defiance?"

I nodded.

"You mean they're—"

"They are. I can feel them." A soft energy hummed nearby. I just couldn't quite pinpoint the location.

She covered her mouth with a hand. After a moment, she stood and walked to the butler's pantry.

"You died in the butler's pantry?" I asked.

"The butler did it!" Annette shouted, stealing my thunder.

We looked at each other and giggled. Well, I did. Her laugh was more like the cackle of an evil crone. We needed to work on that.

"I rarely come in here," Ruthie said. "This is where I keep a few old appliances and my canning supplies. I hadn't canned in years, but I decided to can some apricots a friend brought over." She stepped to the middle of the room, and a soft glow floated up and over her.

The energy was so strong, a mundane might think the spot was haunted. From where I stood, it felt like Ruthie's powers had been hanging out, doing their hair and nails, just waiting for her to return.

She whirled around to me. "How did you know?"

"I think things are revealed to me when the person is ready to know."

The chief, who'd finally found and collected his faculties, walked up to her. "You put me through six months of hell because you lost your magic?"

"When you put it like that..."

He glared.

She explained. "I didn't want you to be stuck with me. I was giving you an out."

"An out? Ruthie Goode, why in the world would you think I'd want or need an out?"

"Houston, I'm dead." She crossed her arms.

He crossed his arms right back and loomed over her. "So?"

"I can't leave this house. We'll never have a life. We'll never get to go anywhere."

"When did we go anywhere anyway?" He stepped

closer. "I just want to be with you, woman. Why is that so hard for you to understand?"

I had a theory. "Your sudden and inexplicable inability to leave the house?"

She caved. "Contrived."

"What?" he asked, flabbergasted.

"I can't go out into the world if I'm supposed to be dead. How would I explain my existence?"

I rolled my eyes and looked at Annette, who rolled her head in solidarity. I turned back to Ruthie. "Ye of little soap opera trivia. You're... Rachael. Ruthie's twin sister, mysteriously just arrived in Salem, lurking around to steal a piece of her fortune. But instead, you fall in love with her adopted brother, only to find out he's really her son, which makes your love child—"

"Two-headed?" Ruthie asked.

"Okay, fine. But you have to admit, Rachael could work. It's worked on every soap I've ever watched."

"That does not instill confidence, Defiance."

"Sorry, Gigi," I said.

"We've been through the wringer and back," the chief said. "Have I ever left you? Did I leave when you were possessed by that lizard?"

"You were possessed by a lizard?"

Ruthie shook her head.

"Or when Percy was infested with toads?" the chief asked. "Or when you took out that female serial killer with that strange witch fire? Did I run? No. And that shit scared the hell out of me."

"Wait, what serial killer?"

He looked at me. "A member of your grandmother's coven turned out to be a serial killer. Only her victims were exclusively witches. She joined the coven, then killed two of your grandmother's best friends."

Ruthie lowered her head, the memory obviously painful.

"When she came after Ruthie, we were ready. Her entire coven lay in wait to ambush the woman. Took her out with some kind of blue fire." He looked at her. "But I stayed, Ruthie. All the hocus-pocus. All the bizarre incidents. All the secrecy. I stayed."

I rubbed my forehead. "You killed her?" I asked Ruthie.

"I had no choice. No jail could've held her, and she would've gone on killing until she got what she wanted."

My natural instinct was to ask what she'd wanted, but I already knew. She'd wanted me. Or someone like me. She'd wanted a charmling. What else would a powerful witch want but more power?

But that wasn't the most pertinent question.

"I never left," he continued. "Through all of that, I never left you. But the first time you die and come back to life without your powers, I'm history."

"I'm sorry, Houston. I just... I didn't handle things very well, did I?"

"No." He put his hands on her shoulders. "Marry me, or I'm never coming back."

She blinked up at him, her mouth forming a pretty O. "Houston."

"I mean it, Ruthie. I think we've dated long enough. It's time to take our relationship to the next level."

"You don't know what you're asking."

"I know exactly what I'm asking. If we've learned anything, it's that life is too short to live in fear." He took her hands in his. "Marry me or lose me forever."

The corners of Ruthie's eyes crinkled. "Since you put it that way."

My heart melted. They kissed, and it wasn't as icky as I thought it might be.

Everyone congratulated them, and my dads took out a bottle of wine to celebrate. But once Ruthie and the chief got settled at the table, I planned to pounce. To catch her off guard. That was the plan, anyway.

Before I could bring up her lie, she said, "Defiance, there's something I need to ask you, but I want you to feel free to say no."

"I have something to ask you too."

"You first," she said, ever the diplomat.

"No, you go ahead." I'd lost my window of surprise either way.

"I insist," she countered.

"Okay. Why did you tell me you killed my mother?"

The room quieted around us.

"What?"

"You told me you'd killed three men and one woman in your lifetime. Is that true?"

Her lids drifted shut as she realized her mistake. "I-I wasn't counting the witch. She was an unusual case."

"Gigi." I leaned closer. "Who killed my mother? Because it wasn't you."

The chief took her hand in his and squeezed. "She deserves to know, Ruthie."

Ruthie shook her head.

"Gigi." I kept my voice soft and even. "Who killed her?"

She swallowed hard and whispered, her voice so soft I almost didn't hear her. "You."

I reared back, the thought so absurd. "I was three. How could I even manage something like that?"

"You were a three-year-old with the power of an atomic bomb inside you. When I got home that night, your mother was trying to siphon those powers, like I said."

"And?"

"And I tried to stop her. You were hovering in midair, and she had one hand above your chest. She'd performed a transference ritual. Black magic. By that point, though she had only a fraction of your power, she was far too strong for me. I knew there was no stopping her, but I had to try. I recited a binding spell. She laughed at me." Ruthie's face showed the agony she felt. Her own daughter. "She sent out what power she did have to... to break my neck."

A hand shot up to cover my mouth.

Her tear-filled gaze drifted to mine. "You knew. Somewhere deep inside, you knew what she was doing. While she was focused on me, you reached up and touched her face. There was such love in your expression when you..." She sniffed. "We both collapsed. You ran to her and threw yourself over her, sobbing and apologizing."

"But in your Book of Shadows you wrote, *She's gone. I had no choice. May the great Goddess embrace her soul.*" I shook my head. "I don't understand."

"That was about you, sweetheart. When your fathers took you. You were gone from my life, and I didn't know if I could live after that. I didn't know if I wanted to."

I stood and walked to the sink to look out into the backyard, and she followed me. "Gigi, why didn't..." My voice cracked. "Why didn't you tell me?"

"I didn't want you to have to live with that, sweetheart. What would that have done to you growing up? What good could've come of my telling you now? I just thought... I wanted to keep the memory you had of your mother safe. But Houston is right."

"I usually am," he said.

We laughed softly.

Roane was at my other side. Not crowding. Just there.

I took his hand. I would deal with the emotional turmoil of Ruthie's bombshell later. I pretended to shake it off. "You had a question too?" I asked her.

"It can wait."

"No." I straightened my shoulders. "I'm okay."

She played with the sleeve of her dress. "I was wondering when you and Annette are going to get this business going."

I looked at Annette. "Are you ready?"

"I was born ready." She fluffed her feathers.

Ruthie nodded. "Then I would like to be your first paying customer, if you'll have me."

"You had me at *paying*," Annette said.

"I didn't want to tell you this too soon, but I think it's time." She glanced at the chief, seeming nervous all of a sudden. "And I didn't know how to tell you either, Houston."

He stood and walked over to her. "Tell me what, love?"

"I didn't die of natural causes. Someone killed me."

The chief and I exchanged glances.

Ruthie lifted her chin. "I want you to find out who."

"Ruthie," I said, the room closing in on me, "are you saying someone murdered you?"

She nodded. "If I had to guess, I'd say it was a combination of belladonna and a deadly mushroom called death cap."

That was specific. "How..." I swallowed, trying to keep my act together. "How did you figure that out?"

"The taste." When I shook my head in question, she explained. "Let's just say my lunch ended up in the toilet. I didn't realize it was anything more than just an upset stomach until I got to the pantry. The world started spinning, and I had severe abdominal cramping. That's when I recognized the taste." She thought back. "Definitely belladonna, but there was something more. Something to give it an extra kick." A soft shiver ran through her fragile body. "All I know is someone wanted me dead."

"I'm sorry, Ruthie," Annette said from her perch.

"It's okay, sweetheart." She glanced at me. "It brought you two into my life."

"Ruthie," the chief said, "why didn't you tell me this before? We would have performed an autopsy."

"Why didn't you?" Annette asked him, genuinely curious.

"We thought it was natural causes. There was no evidence of foul play. Otherwise, we would've requested an autopsy."

"Which is why I didn't tell you," Ruthie said to him.

"I don't understand," he said.

She brushed an invisible piece of lint off a sleeve. "Lying naked on a slab while someone cuts out my brain does not appeal to me in the least."

"Ruthie Ambrosia Goode," he said, both frustrated and hopelessly stricken with love.

Part of me wanted to remind her that she wouldn't have felt a thing, but I did understand. I wasn't sure the chief did, but we women seemed to take a different view of these things.

By the time we finished our conversation, I knew three things about Ruthie's death. She had been poisoned. She had not left the house in a few days, so whoever had done it had to have gotten inside. And whoever had poisoned her knew more than a modicum of witchcraft, because no one could've gotten past Percy without using some kind of concealment spell.

Of course, they had also had to get past Roane. He stood completely quiet, as usual, but I could sense the anger and tension coming off him in waves.

"We'll look into it," I said, glancing at Annette.

She nodded in agreement.

"As will I," the chief said, his expression grim.

"Can we circle back to me, now?" Annette pecked at Papi's hand when he tried to pet her, and I was right there with him. "I think I'm getting lice."

He jerked back his hand.

"You know," I said, taking the opportunity to tease her, "Roane figured all of this out on his own. How to change back to a wolf. Maybe you need to put some thought into it. Pull up your bootstraps and, I don't know, put your back into it." So many cliches. So little time.

She hit me with a low, grating *coo*. An evil sound that incorporated the rattles and clicks of a hell spawn fresh from the underworld. My dads backed away from the island warily. Minerva raised her phone again.

"See?" I said. "You're already getting the hang of being a crow." When she lowered her beak and gave me the thousand-needle glare again, I turned to Roane. "Any thoughts?" I asked, hopefully shifting her ire.

He grinned at her. "You'll shift back when you want to."

"But I want to now," she said, spreading the feathers on her wings and ruffling them.

"Are you sure?" I asked. "Think of the money we could make off you. We could go on tour. Do talk shows."

"You're hilarious," she said, a microsecond before Ink pounced.

We'd been so preoccupied with Ruthie's murder and

Annette's avian quandary, we didn't notice the scruffy, battle-scarred cat stalking its prey until after it leaped forward.

Annette screamed—a human scream, not a bird one— and fell backward off the island while Roane, with his own catlike reflexes, caught the stealthy creature in midair, its claws a millimeter from sinking into Annette's exposed belly.

She landed on the other side with a loud thud. Much louder than a bird would have.

We scrambled around the island and gaped at a short, curly-haired goddess in all her unclothed glory, trying to catch her breath. She lay stunned, staring at the ceiling, taking in tiny gulps of air.

"You did it!" I shouted to her just as I noticed Samuel, who'd been chasing Ink around, standing there with his hands over his eyes. I laughed and knelt next to him before looking back at Nette. "And you're naked."

Percy rose from the ground and covered her most vulnerable assets while Roane pitched in as well. He turned away, lifted his shirt over his head, and handed it back to her.

"Thank you," she said, a soft pink blossoming over her exposed skin. She sat up, and Percy shrank back as she pulled the shirt over her head. "Thank you, Percy. If only I had a kilt too."

Roane laughed softly and helped her stand. Thankfully, his shirt was plenty long enough to cover her best parts.

Samuel refused to remove his hands from his eyes. Until Ink slid past him, and he took off.

I got the feeling Ink was beginning to enjoy their game of cat and mouse, even though he was now the mouse. I turned to Minerva. "Please tell me you got all of that."

She raised a thumb from behind her phone, her jaw hanging slack on her pretty face. I knew exactly how she felt.

After coming up with a game plan as far as Ruthie's murder was concerned, I showered and got ready for bed. Showering before bed was not something I normally did. I was a morning girl. But I needed the soothing heat to detangle my muscles and my nerves and my thoughts.

I put on a T-shirt and lay on the bed, thinking about the crazy turns my life had taken. Not the least of which being the fact that I'd killed two people. Not only had I killed a man by freezing him to death, I'd also killed my own mother. I mentally carved two notches in my belt to remind myself of how quickly things could go south. Of how fast my magics could take control and do the unthinkable. Before I came to Salem, the thought of taking a life was unfathomable. Now...

It was a lot to digest.

That, combined with Annette and Minerva and Samuel and the witch hunter and Ruthie's revelation... it was all so much. Yet there was a part of it all that felt right somehow. Like I was exactly where I needed to be.

I wondered if that had anything to do with a certain sexy someone. A kilted wolf with eyes the color of the forest on a cloudy day and a mouth blessed by the gods. I also wondered what other parts of him were equally as blessed.

With a grin created from the flavorful pairing of mischief and lust, I whispered, "Just how well do you hear, Mr. Wildes?"

Thirty seconds later, I heard footsteps coming up the stairs.

ACKNOWLEDGMENTS

Thank you to everyone who helped with this endeavor and to my Grimlets for all your input. Of special note are many Grimlets who helped me with the business names that Annette throws out there for Defiance's consideration, including but not limited to Jennifer Barnes Kephart, Sonya K. Eith, Heather Chapman, and Elizabeth Cottam for the AWESOME Breadcrumbs, Inc!

Love you all!

ABOUT THE AUTHOR

NYTimes and USA Today Bestselling Author Darynda Jones has won numerous awards for her work, including a prestigious RITA, a Golden Heart, and a Daphne du Maurier, and her books have been translated into 17 languages. As a born storyteller, Darynda grew up spinning tales of dashing damsels and heroes in distress for any unfortunate soul who happened by, certain they went away the better for it. She penned the international bestselling Charley Davidson series and is currently working on several beloved projects, most notably the Sunshine Vicram Mystery Series with St. Martin's Press and the Betwixt and Between Series of paranormal women's fiction. She lives in the Land of Enchantment, also known as New Mexico, with her husband and two beautiful sons, the Mighty, Mighty Jones Boys.

ALSO BY DARYNDA JONES

Thank you for reading **BEWITCHED: A PARANORMAL WOMEN'S FICTION NOVEL (BETWIXT & BETWEEN BOOK 2)**. We hope you enjoyed it! If you liked this book – or any of Darynda's other releases – please consider rating the book at the online retailer of your choice. Your ratings and reviews help other readers find new favorites, and of course there is no better or more appreciated support for an author than word of mouth recommendations from happy readers. Thanks again for your interest in Darynda's books!

Darynda Jones

www.daryndajones.com

Never miss a new book

from Darynda!

Sign up for Darynda's newsletter!

Be the first to get notified of new releases and be eligible for special subscribers-only exclusive content and giveaways. Sign up today!

Also from DARYNDA JONES

PARANORMAL

BEWTIXT & BETWEEN

MYSTERY

SUNSHINE VICRAM SERIES

A Bad Day for Sunshine

A Good Day for Chardonnay

A Hard Day for a Hangover

YOUNG ADULT

DARKLIGHT SERIES

Death and the Girl Next Door

Death, Doom, and Detention

Death and the Girl he Loves

SHORT STORIES

Nancy: Dark Screams Volume Three

Sentry: Heroes of Phenomena: audiomachine

Apprentice

More Short Stories!

Connect with Darynda online:

www.DaryndaJones.com

Facebook

Instragram

Goodreads

Twitter